"I lost the wipes somewhere between the ice cream stand and First Street," Drew confessed.

Molly noted a series of new dark stains on Hazel's onesie that were like a dotted line connecting her to Drew. Accidents happened. Her urge to hold his hand and strengthen their connection wouldn't be an accident. It'd be a mistake.

Molly firmed her grip on the penny bag and lifted it, forcing herself to look away from Drew. "Looks like you two haven't made too many wishes."

"We detoured to touch the grass and sniff several flowers." Drew showed Hazel a penny and tossed it into the fountain. Hazel clapped her hands together.

Molly opened the bag and scooped out a handful of pennies. She blocked her heart from stepping forward with a hard hit of logic. Wishing wells were a distraction, wishes forgotten and readily replaced. As for her attraction, she had to replace that, too.

Dear Reader,

I've often heard that it is not the quantity of friends you have but the quality that matters. One or two true friends can be more fulfilling and rewarding than hundreds of casual friendships. A core theme in my City by the Bay Stories has been friendship. In my personal life, my friends make my life better in every way, and I'm so grateful for each and every one.

Three Makes a Family celebrates the power of having a friend who accepts you for who you really are, flaws and all. Molly McKinney and Drew Harrington discover that their friendship can be the foundation for a lasting and love-filled relationship neither one thought possible, if only they can trust and believe in love.

Call a friend today. Share a laugh, a secret or a shoulder and remember the joy is in the bond. In the sharing. In the being there for each other. Celebrate your friends and the richness they add to your world. I plan to do the very same right now.

Check out my website to learn more about my upcoming books, sign up for email book announcements or chat with me on Facebook (carilynnwebb) or Twitter (@carilynnwebb).

Cari

HEARTWARMING

Three Makes a Family

Cari Lynn Webb

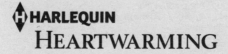

HARLEQUIN
HEARTWARMING

H HARLEQUIN®
HEARTWARMING™

Recycling programs
for this product may
not exist in your area.

ISBN-13: 978-1-335-17984-5

Three Makes a Family

Copyright © 2021 by Cari Lynn Webb

All rights reserved. No part of this book may be used or reproduced in
any manner whatsoever without written permission except in the case of
brief quotations embodied in critical articles and reviews.

This is a work of fiction. Names, characters, places and incidents
are either the product of the author's imagination or are used fictitiously.
Any resemblance to actual persons, living or dead, businesses,
companies, events or locales is entirely coincidental.

This edition published by arrangement with Harlequin Books S.A.

For questions and comments about the quality of this book,
please contact us at CustomerService@Harlequin.com.

Harlequin Enterprises ULC
22 Adelaide St. West, 40th Floor
Toronto, Ontario M5H 4E3, Canada
www.Harlequin.com

Printed in U.S.A.

Cari Lynn Webb lives in South Carolina with her husband, daughters and assorted four-legged family members. She's been blessed to see the power of true love in her grandparents' seventy-year marriage and her parents' marriage of over fifty years. She knows love isn't always sweet and perfect—it can be challenging, complicated and risky. But she believes happily-ever-afters are worth fighting for. She loves to connect with readers.

Books by Cari Lynn Webb

Harlequin Heartwarming

City by the Bay Stories

The Charm Offensive
The Doctor's Recovery
Ava's Prize
Single Dad to the Rescue
In Love by Christmas
Her Surprise Engagement

Return of the Blackwell Brothers

The Rancher's Rescue

The Backwell Sisters

Montana Wedding

Visit the Author Profile page
at Harlequin.com for more titles.

To my husband. Because love really does win.

Special thanks to my friends and my writing tribe. This book could not have been written without your constant support and reassurance. I'm truly blessed to have such friends in my life. To my family—I don't have enough words to express my love and gratitude. Family truly is everything.

CHAPTER ONE

"DENIED."

If Drew Harrington had a fairy godmother, it was time for her to make an appearance, wave her magic wand and make all the injustices against him disappear.

Drew crumpled Judge Bartlett's formal written denial of Drew's motion to dismiss the charges against him. As if the judge's verbal announcement just now inside her courtroom wasn't clear enough.

Too bad that Drew didn't believe in fairy godmothers and magic. He knew life was won by reason, sound arguments and facts.

A late afternoon on a Thursday and the hallways of the courthouse were more crowded than the sidewalks of the San Francisco financial district where the civic building was located. Clerks, court reporters, paralegals all hurried around him. Faces he recognized and others he didn't. Although it didn't matter. No one made direct eye contact with him.

Gazes slipped away before anyone acknowledged they even knew him.

No one wanted to listen to his side now. One week ago, he'd been welcomed and sought out inside the hallowed courthouse halls as a fair-minded but tough prosecutor. Now he was a pariah in the one place where he'd fought so hard to belong. In the one place where he'd fought so hard to uphold justice. In two weeks' time, at the opening of his hearing, Judge Bartlett would listen to his arguments and his presentation of the facts.

Drew straightened and crammed his dismissal paperwork into his briefcase. Slowing his steps, he kept his chin raised and his expression neutral, refusing to let the speculation and presumption chase him out of the courthouse. He had a hearing date set and then he would formally establish his innocence, following the same process of the law the entire judicial system was founded on.

Now he just had to find the evidence that would exonerate him.

Drew paused at the top of the massive grand marble staircase and stared down into the even more impressive rotunda that greeted visitors and those who worked at the courthouse. A woman, her red hair a shade too familiar, shook hands with a paralegal he recognized from the Peregrine Law Group.

Drew shifted, took in the redhead's profile. Recognition jolted through him.

Molly McKinney.

Molly McKinney was his...friend. Enemy. Ally. Adversary. They'd been all those things through undergrad and graduate school. They'd shared leftover pizza, class study guides and their dreams. He wasn't one to look back. Yet watching Molly laugh in the rotunda, he wanted to step back to a different time.

He had no clear idea of how to define Molly. Always she had challenged him. Always he'd accepted. Molly had pushed him to be a better lawyer. And in many ways, to just be better.

But that had been a decade ago. Drew and Molly had accepted their hard-won degrees and built the legal careers they had always talked about. His in the public sector in San Francisco. Hers in private practice in Los Angeles.

If he'd ever thought of encountering Molly McKinney again, he always assumed it would be inside a courtroom as opposing counsel.

Two more paralegals and a junior attorney

from the same firm gathered around Molly. Awe and reverence on their faces as they officially met top-notch criminal defense attorney, Molly McKinney. Her reputation clearly had transcended the Los Angeles county lines.

A reputation Molly had more than earned.

As for Drew's reputation, his was more than dented.

We can assure the public that we will be pursuing charges against Drew Harrington to the full extent of the law. We considered Mr. Harrington one of our own and his actions are a betrayal to everything the district attorney's office stands for.

The district attorney's quote had been printed minutes after the accusations against Drew had been announced a week ago. Every news outlet in the state had been more than eager to post, print and repeat Cory Vinson's words in its coverage.

Unease pricked at the back of Drew's neck.

If he was a scapegoat, as he'd begun to believe he was, he wanted to go down completely alone and keep his coworkers and friends, and especially his family, from becoming potential targets too. That included Molly McKinney.

Drew started down the stairs, veering away from the side of the rotunda where Molly continued to capture the attention of her admirers.

"Drew." Molly's no-nonsense voice extended like a drawn-out echo around the rotunda. "Drew Harrington!"

Drew slowed, but considered the closest exit. Twenty feet. He'd charged longer distances inside a maul on the rugby field to score for his team in college. But he refused to retreat now. He had nothing to hide from. Drew turned around to face her.

Molly excused herself from the group and walked over to him, clearly confident in her expensive heels and matching silver-gray business jacket and skirt. Her hair fell straight past her shoulders, not one strand disobeying the sleek styling. Molly looked polished, professional and put together. She'd always worn the look of success well. *It's important to always look like the person you want to become, Drew.* He'd lost count how many times she'd repeated that mantra to him over the years.

He touched the wide precise knot on his new tie. He always preferred the formal knot and a dark colored suit in the courtroom.

Today was no different. He knew who he was and had to remember that no false accusation defined him. "Molly. It's been a while. I heard you were moving to the city to expand the law offices of Loft and Concord. I didn't know you were already in town."

"I know I used to warn you about the danger of believing every rumor you hear." Molly adjusted her briefcase on her shoulder.

"If that's only a rumor, what's the truth then?" Drew walked beside her toward the exit.

"I needed a fresh start and relocated to your city."

Drew sensed there was so much more in her suitable though not quite believable answer. But he pulled back from asking for more details. Definitely not his business. This was not a reunion. Merely a chance encounter at the courthouse. One he'd anticipated, but under different circumstances. He held the door open for her. "How's that fresh start working out?"

"A bit more bumpy than I'd anticipated." She brushed at a brown stain on the sleeve of her tailored jacket.

The stain, small but still noticeable, surprised him. She'd always been meticulous about her appearance. Yet the waver in her voice drew him closer. He opened his mouth, ready to offer his help.

But he was poised to lose his career, he reminded himself. What could *he* offer one of the best attorneys in the state? Besides, she hadn't asked for his aid. He motioned toward the coffee shop across the street from the courthouse. "It's been good to see you, Molly, but I have a standing appointment that I can't miss."

Molly twisted slightly and glanced over her shoulder. "Is this appointment at Roasted Vibes Café by chance?"

"It is."

"I could use a decent cup of coffee." She smoothed her hand over her hair as if acknowledging she wasn't 100 percent her usual self. "Mind if I walk with you?"

Throughout law school, they'd walked miles together back and forth across campus, arguing, discussing, debating and laughing. The details of their conversations had faded. Yet the remnants of the connection they'd once shared tugged at him. Drew shook his head, moved toward the crosswalk and away from his past.

At the intersection, Molly paused. Her deep

brown eyes settled fully on him. "Drew, how are you?" she asked, a note of concern evident in her voice.

Her gaze had always been clear, clever and fearless. But it was the warmth in her eyes now that pinned Drew to the sidewalk and made him consider Molly as more than a peer. More than simply an old classmate.

Her plea softened her words. "And please tell me the truth."

The truth. That required a certain level of trust. Drew had trusted his former boss, the district attorney, no less, and now Drew could lose everything, including the fine reputation he'd spent the last decade building. Now, his entire future was at stake and he could not risk trusting the wrong person again. "It's been bumpier than I ever expected."

"I'm serious, Drew." She crossed her arms over her chest and frowned. "How are you?"

Alone. He stood alone on his own proverbial island. Isolated. That justice he'd worked so tirelessly to uphold every day was now someone else's job. Someone else's purpose. Drew clenched the handle of his briefcase and nudged aside the loneliness that threatened to surround him like a cold embrace. "I've got everything handled."

"It's okay if you don't. You know that, right?" She tipped her head to the side, kept her too-warm gaze on his. "It's okay to ask for help."

"Thanks, but I've been arguing myself out of trouble my entire life." Drew touched his tie again as if he'd suddenly forgotten who he was. As if he believed Molly was the solution to his problems. Except Drew refused to put her in the sightline of his enemies and risk ruining her reputation too. "It's what I do best."

"Drew, I could—"

Car horns blared. A bus's brakes squealed. The city noise disrupted Molly's words. Drew crossed the street, but Molly's unfinished statement trailed after him.

She could be the exact kind of person I need.

But at what cost to Molly? He'd reached out to his former paralegal, Elena Harper, at the district attorney's office after the charges against him had been announced. Within hours, his paralegal had been reassigned within the department, her work number disconnected and her email address locked.

Molly admitted her transition to the city hadn't been smooth. What if Drew invited Molly into his problems and caused her and her practice serious damage? He couldn't risk her future to save his own.

He was a good attorney. That would have to be enough to get his life back.

He stepped in front of Molly and swung open the door to the Roasted Vibes Café. Brandie Perkins, the owner of the café, greeted him from behind the counter. Four patrons waited near the far corner table Brandie always reserved for Drew, every second and fourth Thursday of the month.

Drew acknowledged the four women waiting for him, wished Molly a good evening and navigated through the crowd toward his table.

Yet one question lingered like the last threads of morning fog above the bay. *Could Molly really help me?*

Maybe. Doubt lodged next to his heart and he didn't think he could move it.

And it didn't seem to be leaving.

But Drew couldn't stake his entire career or Molly's on a maybe.

CHAPTER TWO

BOOKS FROM EVERY decade filled the shelves extending from the floor to the ceiling on one wall of the Roasted Vibes Café. Vinyl records lined the shelves on the opposite wall. A stage, large enough for a microphone and stool only, was tucked in a far corner. Cozy booths and mismatched tables elevated the café into eclectic and cool.

Molly stood in line behind several customers. Drew had seemed genuinely surprised to see her. She couldn't say the same. In college she'd often run into Drew on campus to invite him to lunch, join him for coffee or simply to hang out. Those run-ins hadn't been accidental, much like today at the courthouse. She'd known Drew was going to be there and she wanted to see him.

Still, she was normally straightforward. Upfront and to the point. Yet she'd acquired Drew as a client in a roundabout way. How would he react when she told him?

She stepped up to the counter covered in more vinyl records and searched the inspirational graffiti for encouragement. Drew and Molly had been school friends for a fair amount of time. Surely, that had to count for something now. She wasn't any attorney offering to represent him. She was an old chum with his best interests in mind. Yet something like unsettled nerves twitched through her. She ordered an extra tall cold brew coffee, certain it was her caffeine craving making her fidgety, and opened her purse.

"It's on the house. Courtesy of Drew Harrington." The woman behind the counter smiled and picked up a clear plastic container with a hole on top. *Donations for Lawtté Talk* had been written in marker across the front. "If you'd like to contribute a buck or two to the Lawtté Talk fund, we won't say no."

"Thank you for the coffee." Molly slipped her five-dollar bill into the donation box.

"It's Drew's idea. Lawtté Talk, that is." The woman shifted her thick braids back over her shoulder, revealing her name Brandie embroidered in glitter thread on her bright purple button-down shirt.

"What exactly is Lawtté Talk?" Molly asked.

"Sorry. You came in with Drew. I assumed you'd already heard about it." Brandie wiped a cloth over the counter. "Drew offers basic information and guidance about legal issues that customers might be facing."

"That's sounds very informal." And very problematic. Molly glanced at Drew's table, looking for a disclaimer sign that he wasn't offering legal advice or engaging in a client–attorney relationship. Lawyers were supposed to steer clear of giving legal advice to random strangers to avoid the potential risks of it backfiring on them and doing more harm than good for the "client."

Drew picked up a box of tissues from the chair beside him and handed it to the woman whom he was speaking with. Her shoulders drooped. She tugged a handful of tissues free and bunched them in her fist. Drew covered the woman's hand with his. Compassion and understanding were reflected in his eyes and the simple gesture. The woman might be a stranger to Drew, but he'd just told her without words that she wasn't alone. Molly's chest tightened. Drew had done that very same thing for her all those years ago.

"Your order is ready." Brandie set Molly's

large cup of coffee on the counter. "How do you know Drew then?"

"We went to law school together." Molly unwrapped a straw. She hadn't expected that seeing Drew again would unwrap so many memories and feelings this quickly.

Brandie lifted her head and considered Molly. "You're a lawyer too?"

Molly nodded. "Criminal defense."

Brandie's smile shimmered in her eyes like the silver jewelry sparkling in her hair. "Then perhaps you can do for Drew what he's doing for those women."

"What is that exactly?" Molly asked.

"He's giving them back their hope," Brandie said.

Molly wrapped her fingers around her coffee cup. She'd lectured Drew about studying harder. Introduced him to the power of colored notecards to cram for final exams. And discovered his tolerance for spicy foods wasn't as high as hers.

In exchange, Drew had given Molly balance. Always he'd reminded her to laugh. To pause. To breath. Skills she admitted she'd forgotten in the day-to-day stress and focus of building her career. Though thanks to her rambunctious nine-month-old daughter, those skills had recently been brought back into her life.

But Molly wasn't in the business of hope. She was in the business of setting things to rights. It made her wish that she could set her own life in balance with as solid steps as she defended her clients.

She stared at Drew. She wanted to set things right for him too. The woman shook his hand, stood and headed toward the order counter.

"What kind of tears are those, Avis?" Brandie greeted the woman.

These four women seeking Drew's help were not strangers. Not simply café customers either. Not to Brandie. And, Molly suspected, not to Drew.

"Drew says I can protect my child and place her up for a closed adoption without my ex's consent." Avis dabbed her fistful of tissues against her red-rimmed eyes. "Drew told me I have rights. I can choose what's best for me and the baby. My rotten ex doesn't get to choose for us."

Molly noted the fading bruises on the woman's arms and her barely-there baby bump beneath her yoga pants. The tightening in Molly's chest expanded around her heart.

She ached for the woman and her struggle. Becoming a new mom should be exciting, not terrifying. Molly wanted to embrace the woman too—one mother to another.

She also wanted to prove to Drew that he wasn't alone either.

"Yes. You have a voice, Avis." Brandie edged around the counter and wrapped Avis in an all-encompassing embrace. "And you have the support of your friends."

Molly walked to the condiment station, which was wrapped in blue twinkle lights, allowing the pair some privacy to discuss Avis's custody options. Molly's gaze shifted around the café, skipping from the vinyl records and book titles to the women waiting at the nearby booths. Two ladies, both well into their pregnancies, sat side by side, their shoulders touching as if supporting each other. Another woman rocked an infant to sleep, her own eyes half-closed. A fifth woman that Molly hadn't noticed earlier sat huddled inside her oversized hoodie and slipped on a pair of dark sunglasses.

Brandie pressed a tall to-go coffee cup and a paper bag into Avis's hands, held the door open for the younger woman and then joined Molly. "I thought with all Drew had going on, he'd have canceled tonight." The café owner shook her head, her voice pensive. "The newspapers sure have not been kind to him."

And yet there Drew was, offering kindness and support to a group of people in need. Molly hadn't believed him guilty. Hadn't even been searching for proof of innocence. But it was here inside the café. Good people like Drew were good to their very cores. She cleared the catch from her voice. "How often is Drew here?"

"Twice a month. Every month." Brandie checked the honey level in a bear-shaped bottle. "Over the past five years, he hasn't missed one day."

She wasn't surprised. Drew hadn't missed a day of work in college or missed helping Molly when she'd needed it. "How do people know he's here?"

"It started with the women living at Penny's Place." Brandie opened the cabinet beneath the counter. "Penny runs a home for abused and homeless women. Word seemed to spread from there."

The door to the café swung open. Another woman stepped inside. She nodded to Brandie, stuffed her hands in her pockets and slid into an empty booth. Her bleak gaze fixed on Drew. Molly asked, "When will he finish this evening?"

Brandie refilled the napkin holder from a box inside the cabinet. "He stays until closing at nine. But most nights it's later than that."

Molly checked her watch. She wanted to speak to Drew again, but she had to pick Hazel up from day care. Even more, she wanted to help Drew help himself. She wanted him to have hope.

But she'd seen his wounded pride earlier outside the café. He hadn't even let her finish her offer. His parents had already reached out to her, already paid her retainer fee. Surely, he wouldn't refuse his parents' help. Surely, together with the Harringtons, she could convince Drew to let her handle his case.

Molly thanked Brandie again, promised to return and slipped away to wait for her ride-share car. Inside the car, she dialed her ex and prepared what she would say in her voice-mail message.

An incoming video call interrupted her.

Her ex's face filled the screen. Derrick Donovan, the man responsible for breaking her heart. And the reason she'd ended her tenure at Loft and Concord and relocated to San Francisco.

She inhaled and accepted the video call. "Derrick, I was about to leave you a voicemail message."

Her ex peered into the screen. "Well, Molly, I have to say it would've been a surprise to hear from you."

"There is something else that needs to be said." Weeks into her pregnancy, Molly had taken the initiative and walked away from Derrick, convinced there was nothing left between them in terms of a relationship.

"Are you regretting your move to the Bay Area?"

"Actually, I only regret not moving sooner." Then perhaps she'd have reached out to Drew as a colleague and reestablished their friendship quicker. Meaning he might've turned to her for help now.

Her ex frowned.

"I'm filing for full custody of Hazel," Molly continued. Inside the Roasted Vibes Café, she'd been reminded of the importance of legally closing loose ends. She had to remember to thank Drew. "I'll let you know when you can expect the paperwork to arrive."

"I see." Derrick steepled his fingers under his chin as if he were searching for clarity.

Molly narrowed her gaze, trying to scrutinize her ex's expression. She'd been the one to misunderstand everything during their two-year relationship. To misread Derrick's vows of love. His promises to put her first. She'd failed to see the truth about him until it was too late. Not a mistake she'd make again. "I'll have the documents couriered to your office."

He nodded, but something about his behavior seemed off to her.

"Goodbye, Derrick." Molly disconnected the call, blanked her phone screen and pushed Derrick out of her thoughts. Molly's driver pulled the car to the curb outside her daughter's day care, and she thanked him and got out.

A rainbow and fluffy white clouds had been painted on the windows of the Tiny Sweet Giggles Day Care. A cheerful heart-shaped welcome sign hung on the door. Inside the entrance, more bright colors covered the walls and the kind staff chatted and laughed. Molly held on to her hope that this pickup would be different than those of the past week.

One of the aides carried Hazel from Lullaby Lane, the under-one room. Tears soaked her daughter's cheeks and dampened her hair.

Molly's stomach sank.

Every prior pickup, Hazel had come home in tears. Molly wanted the giggles promised in the day care's name. She wanted to believe the director's assurances that Hazel needed more time to adjust.

She wanted to believe she was doing the right thing, leaving Hazel in someone else's care while she went to work and tried to re-establish her career.

The aide handed Molly the baby carrier that Molly had left at drop-off. Molly attached the baby carrier around her shoulders and waist, then slipped Hazel into the front. With the tears wiped from Hazel's cheeks and her daughter secure, she thanked the aide and exited.

A series of cable car bells clanged loudly only a block away at the intersection. Molly smiled and kissed the top of Hazel's head. "I know exactly how to improve our moods."

Molly headed straight for the cable car. The bells clanged again. Hazel kicked her legs and babbled happily at the world in her front-facing carrier. The cable car had fascinated Hazel from their first day in the city. And now served as a perfect pick-me-up for the pair.

Molly climbed aboard, greeted the conductor and eased onto a bench in the enclosed middle section. Tourists crowded on the benches facing the street and seasoned locals gripped the poles and stood on the running board at the front.

The conductor offered Hazel a spirited greeting and checked Molly's monthly unlimited ride pass—the one she'd purchased upon arrival in the city. "Where are you two ladies heading this evening?"

Molly tucked her pass into her purse and grinned at the conductor, his wide smile infectious. "Back to our hotel." And their temporary living quarters.

"You couldn't have chosen a better way to get there." The conductor tipped his hat. "Sit back, relax and enjoy the ride."

Relax. Molly shifted on the smooth wooden bench. She hadn't had much spare time for that. Her relocation to-do list remained quite full. Even moving into their rental apartment had been delayed due to unforeseen plumbing repairs. Once they were settled though, Molly would relax.

The bells clanged announcing the next stop. Hazel clapped her hand against Molly's open palm. Joy filled her daughter and her squeal of laughter exploded inside the cable car. The other passengers smiled.

Molly hugged Hazel, wanting to absorb her daughter's delight. Wanting to enjoy the ride too.

It wasn't supposed to be like this, Molly thought. Molly, a single parent, alone in a new city. She'd mapped out her life. Created vision boards for every stage of her plan. Implemented it step-by-step like a road map to success. She hadn't ever pictured birth control failure and a positive pregnancy test.

Or Derrick not loving her like she'd loved him.

Molly should have anticipated something like this happening. Molly should have had a contingency in place. In a courtroom, she strategized every possible outcome and always had contingencies at the ready, just in case.

She had to apply the same tactics to her private life. Hazel was depending on her. Only a viable legal business of her own would give Molly and Hazel the much-needed stability Molly wanted. And finally their very own home like she always imagined for her family.

The cable car crested a steep hill. The bells clanged. Hazel laughed.

Molly's stomach tilted as the cable car descended the other side of the hill and changed her perspective.

She had to build her practice quickly. Drew Harrington, as her client, would assist her in doing that.

She may have acquired Drew as a client in a roundabout way. But now that Drew was her client, she intended to keep him.

The cable car picked up speed. The rush filled Molly.

And when she won Drew's case…both Drew and Molly would find their joy again.

CHAPTER THREE

"Drew, would you answer the door?" his mother called down from the upstairs master suite. "I'm almost ready."

Drew opened the door of his parents' house and gaped. Molly stood under the awning, an open umbrella in one hand. A blond curly haired baby girl in the other.

"Drew." Molly thrust the baby girl into Drew's arms.

Drew adjusted the baby, propping her up against his chest. Her eyes widened, revealing her bold blue gaze. Her grin widened, revealing her lack of teeth. She reached forward and smashed the tie of his tuxedo in her tiny fist, tugging it away from his neck. Even that couldn't quite open his airways or dislodge the surprise stuck in his throat.

Molly McKinney had a child. An adorable baby girl.

"I can't believe it started raining right when we got here." Molly closed the umbrella, shook the excess water onto the front porch and faced Drew. "But then it's been that kind of day."

Drew cleared his throat and stepped back to allow Molly inside. "What kind of day is that?"

"The kind where the babysitter cancels last minute. The kind where the landlord calls to cancel our lease, citing unrepairable plumbing issues." Molly unzipped her jacket and slipped it off, revealing a stunning black-and-white evening gown. She added, "You know. The kind of day where nothing goes as expected."

Drew knew that exact kind of day. He was having it right now. Molly McKinney was a mom, standing in his parents' foyer, looking ready for her red-carpet debut. He had known Molly as an aspiring wannabe lawyer. Followed her legal career over the years. But now he found himself intrigued by the woman Molly had become. Thinking of what had become of his own life meant he couldn't afford any distractions though, like the one Molly was presenting.

Suddenly Molly chuckled. The soft sound added warmth to the bare marble foyer and flowed over Drew like a balm. Molly grinned.

"And this definitely isn't how I planned this introduction. Drew, you're holding my nine-month-old daughter, Hazel."

Drew peered down at Hazel. "Nice to meet you, baby blue."

Hazel's happy babble released a trail of drool down her chin.

Molly wiped a bright pink burp cloth across Hazel's mouth, mopping up the drool. "Sorry. It's a teething hazard."

Drew's sudden interest in Molly and her daughter could prove a hazard too if he weren't careful. He eyed Molly over Hazel's head. "Not that it isn't nice to see you again or to meet Hazel, but what are you doing here?"

"I invited Molly to join us for the gala. It's a good place for her to network." His mother swept into the foyer and touched Hazel under her damp chin. "How is my sweet baby girl?"

His mother acted as if she already knew Hazel. Wariness tapped between Drew's shoulders. He eased away, closer to Molly. "How did you know Molly was in town?"

"You know I've been a fan of hers and followed her career the same as you have over the years." His mother waved a hand and a trio of silver and diamond bracelets slid toward her elbow. "You finished top of your class thanks to Molly."

His mom wasn't wrong. Molly had pushed Drew to achieve more in school than he'd ever thought possible. He'd always wanted to impress Molly. And get her attention. He felt Molly's gaze on him now. Now, he wanted...

"Molly was such a good influence on you in law school. I contacted her when the district attorney accused you of witness tampering." His mom played a quick round of peekaboo, earning a squeal from Hazel. "With Molly as your legal counsel, I know she will have an even better influence on you now."

Legal counsel? Drew's mouth dropped open. Now his mother had his full attention. "What are you talking about?"

"We can discuss it all later. First, we must get Hazel settled." His mom spoke to Hazel, lifting her voice into the high-pitched levels of baby-cute. The peekaboo continued.

But his mother had never played baby games; Nancy Harrington played in the political arena, taking down opponents and gathering the support of as many constituents as possible. They were sort of like chess pieces to her. Except, after his brother had gotten married to Sophie Callahan three years ago, and Mayor Nancy had gotten Ella Callahan as a step-granddaughter, his mom had softened considerably. With Sophie expecting twins soon, his mom seemed more determined than ever to embrace her inner grandmother.

At least, that's what he'd thought up until a moment ago. Turns out his mom had intervened in his case, which meant he had to stop her at all costs.

He'd vowed to protect his family from his own legal trouble. He pushed aside the frustration rolling through him. His voice was dry and flat in comparison to his mother's. "I think we need to discuss this now."

"We're running late for the gala I'm being honored at." His mother linked her arm with Molly's and walked down the hallway toward the state-of-the-art kitchen and the newly constructed playroom right next to it. "Hazel has not yet met her babysitter, Evie. And babies always take precedence."

Hazel reached again for Drew's tie and crumpled it in her fingers. Drew dipped his chin. Hazel giggled, ruining his attempt at a stern face and scrambling his irritation. He whispered, "Okay, baby blue, you've got five minutes to settle in with Ms. Evie. Then the adults have some serious talking to do."

His mother and Molly glanced back at him. His mom said, "That's nonsense, Drew. Hazel gets all the time she needs. We will review things when it's an appropriate time."

Drew lifted Hazel until they were eye to eye. Drool had covered her chin again and her too-long lashes framed her big searching eyes. "It's never too early for lessons, baby blue. Here's the first one. It's important to always let your mom have the last word."

"It's equally important to follow your mom's advice." His mom tilted her chin at Drew. "Mothers tend to know best."

Perhaps. But the stakes were too high, and Drew had to trust his own counsel. He shifted his gaze to Molly. "You're a mom. Do you always know best?"

"I know when it's best not to argue." Molly arched her eyebrows and angled her head toward his mom.

Molly would have to argue on his behalf if she remained his attorney. And if she remained his attorney, she could become a target too. And in that, Drew knew what was for the best. Relieving Molly of her responsibility as his attorney. Now he just needed to find the appropriate moment to do that.

Drew followed his mom and Molly into the brand-new playroom. The walls were color-blocked in lavender and yellow. Wide windows filled one wall, and would bathe the entire space with natural light during the day. An oversized couch, fluffy pillows and toys in every shape and size filled the vibrant space. A kitchen set complete with a shopping cart waited patiently for a young chef. A castle-themed jungle gym claimed the far corner. Electrical outlets had been covered. The room had been made entirely childproofed and ready thanks to his mom and her best friend, Evelyn "Evie" Davenport.

Evie set a plastic green bucket on a mat spread on the floor and walked over to them. She kissed Drew's cheeks and squeezed his shoulders with the same affection she'd shown him since he'd been a toddler. "This must be Hazel."

"Hazel, meet the best baker in the city." Drew tipped his head toward Hazel and whispered, "Blink at her with those irresistible blue eyes and you'll get anything you want."

The older woman's laughter illuminated her sharp gaze behind a pair of trendy horn-rimmed black glasses. Rather than a hand-shake, Evie introduced herself and embraced Molly in one of her all-encompassing hugs. "Pleasure to meet you, Molly, and your precious daughter."

"I'm sorry for the last-minute ask," Molly said. "I hope we didn't intrude on your Saturday night plans."

"I can't think of a better way to spend the evening." Evie leaned into Hazel's view and let Hazel take her glasses off. "Now, can I hold this darling baby girl? We need to get acquainted."

Molly lifted her arms as if preparing to snatch Hazel back. Then she quickly dropped her arms to her sides. Drew considered Molly, noted how her bottom lip disappeared and her eyebrows creased together. Hazel wasn't the only one who needed to settle in. He smoothed his tone to guarantee it would be reassuring. "Evie is like my second mom."

Molly's smile wobbled. Her words tumbled out. "I won't be too late. I don't plan to be late, that is."

Drew was stunned. He'd never known Molly to be flustered. Or insecure. Over anything.

"You take all the time you need, dear. Have

fun." Evie swapped Hazel a squishy ball for her glasses, then produced a stuffed unicorn. "Hazel and I have a full evening ahead. We have treasure baskets to explore, bubbles to blow, a sing-along and reading books to get to."

"That sounds more entertaining than a ballroom full of tuxedos and artificial small talk." His mother smoothed her hands over the neckline of her floor-length emerald green dress. "Save me some of those bubbles."

Hazel dropped the ball, babbled and stretched both arms toward Evie as if ready to begin her fun-filled evening. As if she had no reservations about Evie at all.

Molly clenched her hands together as if her uncertainty had multiplied.

Uncertain about Evie or simply leaving, Drew wasn't sure. He could try again to alleviate some of Molly's concerns. "Between Evie and my niece, Ella, they are our resident authorities on all things baby."

Evie knelt on the large blanket stretched across the carpet. Hazel scooted into Evie's side, her babble continuing at a rapid rate. The pair busied themselves pulling plastic shapes from a bucket. Evie grinned. "I'm more the co-captain. Ella is the leader of the baby knowledge brigade."

"My brother and his wife are expecting twins in a few weeks," Drew said. "Their daughter, Ella, has been instructing us all in proper baby care from infant to toddler and every stage along the way."

"With Evie—" his mother touched Molly's arm, her gaze soft, her voice soothing "—Hazel couldn't be in better hands tonight."

"I'm sorry. It's not Evelyn, it's me." Molly pressed her palms to her cheeks. "Our day-care experience hasn't been overly positive. I'm just really anxious about leaving her."

Drew stuffed his hands into the pockets of his dress pants to keep from taking Molly's hand in his. Then he pressed his lips together. She wasn't his to reassure. Or to soothe. Or to hold hands with. She was his legal counsel that he needed to fire. "To avoid the messy leaving thing, when I was a kid, my parents used to sneak out of the room when my brother and I weren't looking."

"We coordinated every exit with the baby-sitter beforehand." Drew's dad stepped into the playroom, kissed his mom's cheek and turned to greet Molly.

Evie set a purple plastic cube in the bucket.

Hazel followed her lead. The bucket was soon refilled and Hazel set out emptying it again. Squealing and babbling with every new discovery she made. With each bounce and cheer Hazel released, Molly's smile slowly returned. "Did sneaking out work?"

"Every time." His mom grabbed his dad's hand and backed toward the French doors.

Evie shifted Hazel, keeping Hazel's back to them and her attention on the array of toys spread out around her.

His mom continued but in a pensive voice. "Of course, the guilt from leaving tiptoes right out of the room with you."

Molly blinked and whispered. "What am I supposed to do with the guilt?"

"Accept it." Empathy tinged his father's words. "It's part of being a parent."

"Along with the constant worry." His mother squeezed Drew's arm as she passed. "A parent always worries about their child, no matter how old they get."

Drew nodded, acknowledging his mom's words. His parents were worried about his situation. That worry had pushed them to seek out Molly. He understood. Would they understand he wanted to protect them? And that to do so, he had to represent himself and keep his enemy's focus only on him. Would Molly understand when he refused her counsel later tonight?

Molly glanced at Drew. Her voice low. "I know I need to network. To make connections. I have to build up my practice."

And he knew having him as a client would certainly help her do just that. But he had to refuse her counsel. Still, he could help her in other ways. Drew kept his hands inside his pocket and angled an elbow for Molly to grip if she chose to. If she chose to accept his assistance, at least in this instance. "I can bring you back here in an hour or whenever you want to leave the gala. Promise."

Molly hesitated. Looking to Hazel, then back to Drew. Finally she curved her fingers around the sleeve of his tuxedo jacket. Together, they eased out of the room. Hazel's giggles trailed after them.

And the sense that his world would never be the same trailed after Drew.

CHAPTER FOUR

THE LIMOUSINE PULLED up outside the Silver Monarch Hotel in less than twenty minutes. Molly walked beside Drew as they entered the lobby of the luxury hotel. The kid-sized table and chairs, rainbow colors and baby-proofed playroom at the Harrington home had been replaced by the surroundings of a five-star hotel, its impeccable but no doubt discreet staff and multiple crystal chandeliers. An elevator ride to the fortieth floor granted Nancy Harrington the opportunity to introduce Molly to the CEO of the Bay Water Health System and her husband.

And so began Molly's evening of networking.

The elevator bounced to a stop. Molly never swayed.

She had on her favorite black heels, the same ones she'd worn to win one of her largest cases against a popular Fortune 500 corporation. She'd accepted an award for being named one of the top thirty up-and-coming lawyers in California in the same pair of heels, and when she'd mingled at her former firm's holiday gala. And she hadn't lost her balance one time.

She didn't intend to lose her footing tonight either.

If she had to trade time with her daughter to rebuild her career outside of normal business hours, she would make sure their time apart was spent productively. As for that whisper of guilt over leaving Hazel, she followed William's advice and accepted it. Tonight was about starting a new life for Hazel and herself.

The elevator opened into an opulent ballroom. The atmosphere was intimate and inviting and at odds with the formality of such a grand space. The fancy-dressed guests were anything but standoffish and reserved.

Nancy linked her arm around Molly's and guided her expertly through the crowd. Molly quickly learned Mayor Harrington's rhythm. A quick exchange of names only was a courtesy introduction. Disclosing full names, job titles and place of business was an invitation to further network later. And lastly, there was a handful of special guests. The ones the mayor presented to Molly as her dear friends who stepped in and promptly continued Molly's introductions to even more attendees.

Sometime between her introduction to the organizer of a prominent charity group and a large business owner, Drew disappeared. Later, as Molly spoke to the mayor's dear friends, Jaqueline Landry and Lewis Malone, Molly spotted Drew slipping outside to the extensive patio. Between one conversation and the next, Molly scanned the ballroom for Drew. He never returned.

An hour passed and Drew's dad, William, excused himself to find drinks for Nancy and himself. Two of the gala event planners captured Nancy for last-minute instructions regarding her award acceptance speech. And Molly decided it was past time to find Drew. There was a conversation they'd put off long enough.

Molly wiggled her toes inside her lucky black heels and pinched her shoulder blades together, drawing everything inside her straighter, allowing no room for doubt or uncertainty. The same as she did before every court appearance. Every interaction with a judge. And every conversation with the opposing prosecution team.

Drew wasn't the opposing counsel. And

the outdoor patio wasn't a courtroom, she reminded herself.

Yet Drew was her client who hadn't officially accepted her services.

He was the key to establishing her legal prowess in the city and growing her practice as fast as possible.

He was also her friend.

Lawyers tended to reject representing family and friends. Too often the lines blurred, and emotions often lessened a lawyer's impartiality and clear mindedness.

But Drew and Molly had not discussed the law, their past cases or the weather in years. Their friendship was more former than current. And Molly knew all too well the fallout from crossing boundaries.

She had been at Loft and Concord Law Group since she'd graduated from law school. Had worked tirelessly to become one of the top producing attorneys for the firm. There she'd built her reputation and staked her future: both professional and personal.

That had been her mistake—blending the two. Derrick, her ex, had been her peer and her colleague at the law firm. She'd believed in love and discovered too late it had only ever been one-sided. Derrick had confessed he'd only ever loved the image of the powerful attorney couple they'd presented, not Molly herself. She'd vowed never to fall for someone she worked with. Or let love blind her again.

Besides, falling in love would only give her a broken heart, not a practice for herself or a home for Hazel. Work had to be her focus.

She could represent Drew and remain objective and neutral about his case. He would remain simply her client.

Now, she just had to convince Drew to let her be his legal counsel.

She plucked two champagne flutes from the tray of a passing waiter and walked out onto the rooftop balcony. She located Drew in the farthest corner, stretched out on a plump sofa, surrounded by darkness and solitude. His feet rested on a coffee table, his tuxedo jacket was draped over the armrest and his phone was propped against a tasseled throw pillow.

The tap of her heels on the tiled patio gave her away.

Drew stacked his hands behind his head and watched her approach. The shadows concealed his gaze, but not the indifference in his voice. "Shouldn't you be inside meeting folks and making connections?"

"I needed a moment." *In fact, I wanted to check on you.* She lifted one shoulder in a small shrug, knocking against Drew's reticence. And her own rebellious thoughts. Drew was strictly a client to her. He didn't need her looking after him. "Your mom wanted me to tell you that only the guilty hide."

"I'm not guilty." He sat up. His feet thudded against the floor. "I'm also not hiding."

The raw frustration in his gaze made her breath catch. "Then what are you doing?"

"Same as you." The irritation eased from his face, tempering his words. He stretched his arm over the back of the couch, slow and casual. "Taking a moment."

Molly set the champagne glasses on the table and sat beside him. "You've been out here since we arrived."

"What can I say? Some moments take longer than others." He brushed his hand behind his head as if resetting himself. Then he tipped his chin and his one-sided grin toward his phone. "And it's the seventh inning of the Bay Area Angels' game. Tied at six. Bases loaded. Nobody out."

"You've been out here watching a baseball game?" Molly adjusted her gown around her heels. Drew's ability to swiftly and seamlessly shield his true emotions knocked her off-balance.

"I've been a fan since I was a kid." He drummed his fingers on the back of the sofa. "Don't you remember always asking me if I had anything else to wear besides sports T-shirts and baseball caps?"

His fingers tapped a silent tune on the cushion inches from her bare shoulder. Distracting her. If she leaned in, the smallest of moves, she could draw from his warmth. Molly straightened. "You wore a T-shirt to an interview for a competitive internship. Then ruined your only debate dress shirt with grease from a loaded cheeseburger."

"I still miss those hamburgers from The Pickled Burger." He leaned forward as if ready to impart a secret. "I haven't found sweet potato fries like theirs anywhere. It's not for lack of trying either. I've been sampling them at every restaurant with sweet potato fries on the menu."

"That's dedication to a cause," she said.

"I learned that from you," he said. "It's entirely your fault."

The sudden amusement glinting in his gaze

trapped her. A different sort of awareness spread through her. "My fault?"

"I was a perfectly content below-average student in undergrad." Drew picked up the other champagne flute and tipped it toward her. His voice tipped from teasing to an exaggerated tragic tone. "Until you offered to proofread one of my history papers. Then Dr. Reynolds accused me of paying for the paper to get a passing grade."

One history paper. One chance to show her appreciation. And nothing had worked out as she'd intended. Molly stared at the champagne in her glass as if her memory surfaced inside the bubbles. "Dr. Reynolds called me into his office too. I was so nervous. I'm surprised I even spoke coherently to your professor."

Molly had always studied late until the library closed. Drew had always worked out at the gym at night. And he'd always managed to be outside the library to walk her home. She'd wanted to thank him for looking out for her. She'd wanted to pour her gratitude into a kiss. Instead she'd proofread his history paper. Offering tips and feedback enough that his professor mistakenly thought someone else had written it.

"I was terrified. Scared I was going to be expelled and sent home to face my parents' wrath. Then you came to my defense." Drew lifted his glass to her in a toast. "I vowed to never let you down again and dedicated myself to my education."

He hadn't wanted to let her down? She skimmed over that revelation, opting to focus on the playful and light. "Dedicating yourself to your schoolwork is not the same thing as dedicating yourself to finding the ultimate sweet potato fries."

"That's just it." He laughed. "I learned the rewards of perseverance and focus from you. The reward of biting into the best-tasting sweet potato fry is out there somewhere, waiting on me to find it."

"I get the rewards of concentrating on your education. And I suppose fries too." Molly sipped her champagne and stared at Drew. "But I don't get the connection to me."

"That was simple." Drew set his glass on the table and centered his full focus on her. "The real reward was spending more time with you."

Her heartbeat tripped into rapid, pulsing speed in the silence.

"To be around you, I had to step up my game." Drew relaxed into the couch.

All that time, Drew had only wanted to spend more time with her. "You never said anything."

"I never wanted to be a distraction," he said. "Or to keep you from your goals. I remember you wrote your goals on little pieces of paper and stuck them everywhere as reminders to stay focused."

She'd had big goals and even bigger dreams back then. Some dreams she hadn't made public. Or posted around her college suite. But her time spent with Drew, she remembered all of it. And now she was beginning to recall how much she'd missed him. None of that was relevant. "I remember I had to order my own fries at The Pickled Burger because you refused to share yours."

"I always got the ones you couldn't finish." He chuckled. "It was a win-win."

Would he consider it a win-win if she were his legal counsel? Would he turn away if she confessed that she wanted to spend more time with him after tonight? She took another deep sip of her champagne and centered herself. She needed a client more than a friend. "Drew. When can we talk about your case?"

He blinked and shook his head as if she'd suddenly dropped a roadblock on their memory lane. "I have a possible lead on an apartment for you and Hazel."

He eased his arm off the back of the sofa, shifting away from her and closing himself off.

The tiniest twinge of hurt twisted inside her. "What kind of a place is it?"

"It's not the Los Angeles dream house you always described." He crossed his arms over his chest and eyed her. "The one with the glass doors that would fold into the wall to allow the ocean breeze inside and the infinity edge pool that was designed to reflect the sunset."

"And don't forget every room would have ocean views and there would be chaise lounges on the rooftop for star gazing." She pictured her dream home—the one she'd imagined and perfected in her childhood daydreams.

Molly had spent her entire childhood moving from one apartment to another. One city to the next. Never staying longer than six months in any one place. Then her father had walked out. Molly's mother had simply packed up their meager belongings, relocated to a new town and continued their nomadic lifestyle. Molly had always wanted a house. A permanent place to call home.

Now, she intended to give Hazel the home she herself had never had growing up.

"Did you ever buy your dream house on the beach?" he asked.

The hint of curiosity in Drew's words pulled her back to the conversation.

"It never quite worked out like I had envisioned." She shook her head and shifted her gaze toward the city skyline. "My ex, Hazel's father, had a different plan."

A plan that had included reconciling with his first wife and not building a life with Molly and Hazel.

"San Francisco has every type of house you can imagine," Drew offered. "Ocean, city skyline or Golden Gate Bridge views. Your choice. Your dream."

Could San Francisco be the home she'd always wanted? Perhaps. But she had a defense to present first. "I'll have to start with a reasonable rental unit and move up from there."

"My friends have a detached one-bedroom unit at their house. It has recently been renovated." Drew's voice dropped away as if he were reluctant to disclose any more details.

Molly homed in on his hesitation. "Why do I sense a but coming?"

"Not a but exactly. And it has nothing to do

with the apartment." Drew shifted on the sofa and faced her. "But I want to request that you refund my parents your retainer fee."

"Why?" She studied him. His expression was calm and composed. His crossed arms were more casual than tense. She added, "Are you going to pay my retainer fee yourself?"

He never winced. Never flinched. "I believe I mentioned the other day that I have everything handled."

"Yet you never mentioned that Judge Bartlett denied your request for a dismissal of charges earlier this week," she countered.

Only his eyebrows flexed into his forehead. "Word travels fast."

"The legal community is small." She picked up her champagne flute and swirled the last of the bubbly liquid around the glass. "You're a part of the community. We look after our own."

"Really? Because that hasn't been my experience so far. But is that what you're doing?" Disapproval thinned his mouth. "Looking after me."

"Is that so wrong?"

"It's all rather convenient." He shrugged. "Too convenient."

She tilted her head, letting the censure in his

words barely brush against her. Keeping her cool in the moment, she admitted, "Perhaps it is convenient. I won't deny it's a good opportunity for me and I never liked to let those slip by."

"I can't be your opportunity." His face was set, his tone unyielding. "You can't be my counsel, Molly."

"Why not?" she pressed.

"Remember when Dr. Reynolds accused me of plagiarism over that history paper." Drew straightened. His posture, his face and his voice serious. "Dr. Reynolds also warned you that if it was true, getting involved would reflect badly on you too."

"I accepted that risk," she argued. "I knew you'd written that paper. Someone needed to have your back." That's what they did. Had each other's back.

"This isn't a call to go to the dean's office this time, Molly." His deep voice dropped into the stilted space between them.

No, it wasn't college, and this wasn't some disputed paper. They were no longer students with lots of ambition and plenty of bravado. "I know exactly what this is, Drew."

"My case…my case is serious, Molly. Everything I have, everything I've worked for is at risk." Drew set his elbows on his knees and gripped his hands together. "And if I can't produce the evidence, it could very well lead to your downfall. That's something I won't risk."

She folded her arms over her chest, absorbed his refusal to let her represent him. Quickly and efficiently, she swept the hurt aside. Then she spoke unrushed. Unaffected. "I'm very good at what I do, Drew. Exceptionally good. And I can help you, but you have to get out of your own way first. Don't let this be about your ego, Drew."

He scratched his cheek as if her words had stung him. "Refund the retainer, Molly. I won't be your client."

She launched one more offer. "Why don't you think about it?"

"I already have." His words were succinct and sounded final.

Molly set her crystal champagne flute on the table and rose. At the open glass doors leading into the ballroom, she stopped and turned around.

Drew sat, his arms still at his sides. The baseball game played out on his phone beside him. Still, his gaze remained fixed on the city skyline. Car headlights streamed over the bridge spanning across the bay. Squares of light sprinkled across the high-rises looming around them. There was always activity in the city. Always life. Always movement.

Except for Drew. He was completely still aside from his jaw shifting. The barest of movements as if he were fighting back words.

This wasn't the man she'd known. Her Drew always had words and opinions and counter arguments. Molly shook her head. "Drew."

He looked at her.

The loneliness in his gaze spoke to her. How she could relate.

She took a step toward him and paused. He'd accuse her of playing on his emotions to get what she wanted. He might be right if she wanted him. Not as a client. Not as the next step on her path to success. But instead wanted him as a man.

He didn't want her, she told herself. Not as a lawyer. Possibly not as a friend. If only she'd known this just as clearly where she'd once stood with her ex, she would've avoided the tears, the turmoil and the heartache. She should thank Drew for his candor.

She didn't though.

She tipped her chin and settled her gaze on his. "Good luck. You're going to need it."

CHAPTER FIVE

"Milo, you don't seem to be finding anything useful either." Drew picked up the silver tabby from the coffee table and the large senior cat released a rumbling purr. Milo's brother, Felix, launched himself onto the coffee table and picked up where his brother had left off. The smoky-gray cat knocked several pages of the investigation file from the State Bar to the hardwood floor. Then he pounced proudly on the remaining papers, proving even senior cats had moves.

The State Bar had provided the investigation file to Drew after the charges of witness tampering against him had been released to the public. Drew had read and reread every page enough times to have the information memorized. Unfortunately the paperwork and his memory failed to provide the evidence he required to prove his innocence.

Milo nuzzled his head against Drew's neck and his loud rumbling purr revved up as if the cat was offering Drew his personal brand of encouragement. Drew paced around his loft, stopped at the floor-to-ceiling windows, then moved into the kitchen. Examining the contents of the refrigerator, he considered last night's cold pizza and the assortment of takeout containers from a variety of restaurants. He'd failed to discover the needed answers for his case. But he had determined he seriously needed to start cooking again, if not for his arteries, then for the enjoyment it gave him.

For now, he was stuck when it came to his own case. And the solution he'd always relied on over the years was to find a different perspective. Approaching the situation from another direction.

Molly could offer a new viewpoint and an alternate approach. Drew held up Milo and looked into the cat's clear blue eyes. "You'd like her. I like her. That's why she can't be involved."

Milo yawned as if unimpressed by Drew's argument.

"Molly has a daughter. A reputation she needs to rely on to grow her practice. She can't afford to have an enemy, especially like mine, whoever that may be." He returned to the living room and set Milo on the fluffy charcoal throw draped over the back of the sofa. "I have to do this alone."

That meant he had to leave his flat. Go and search out a new perspective.

But he had no destination in mind. No specific place to go. It was Monday. A workday. His typical workday used to include jury selection, requests for evidentiary hearings, negotiating pleas and rendering decisions on charges.

It wasn't a typical Monday. He checked his to-do list for inspiration. Only one item was listed: buy cat food.

Thanks to his sister-in-law, Drew was the proud owner of the two senior cats. Sophie owned a popular pet store and never could turn away any animal in need. Brad simply shook his head and called for reinforcements when Sophie's pet store got too crowded with rescues. Drew was happy to oblige and volunteered at the pet store as often as he could.

He had a destination.

Felix scurried across the coffee table, swiping the last of the paperwork onto the floor. One long stretch and he rolled onto his back, covering the newly cleared table. Drew gathered the paperwork, offered Felix an approving rub under his chin and went into his bedroom for his running shoes.

He'd always lived alone until Milo and Felix had moved in. Now he couldn't imagine not having the cats in his loft.

Twenty minutes later, Drew opened the front door of The Pampered Pooch. Chimes announced his arrival.

Evie appeared around an end cap in the center aisle and grinned. "Drew! What a nice surprise."

"Just came for a quick visit. Running low on cat chow." Drew hugged Evie and walked with her to the checkout counter.

"You look like you could use something sweet." Evie leaned over and pushed a plastic container toward him. "Peanut butter. Just made this morning."

Drew adored Evie, always had, ever since he'd been a kid. She was like Drew's other mom. The mom that baked homemade cookies, remembered important dates and only offered advice when asked. Also, she always encouraged. However Evie's real gift was listening.

Evie had the ability to pull a confession from Drew like no one else. Once, she'd needed no more than a warm-out-of-the-oven peanut butter cookie and a soft smile for Drew to admit he'd trampled her lilies to claim his baseball from her garden. Three cookies and he'd acknowledged he might have been the one who'd hit the baseball into her garage window and broke it in the first place.

Drew reached inside the container and grabbed a cookie. Sugar rushes might have loosened his tongue as a kid and had him revealing things to Evie he'd never intended to, but he had better control now. "You're still my favorite lady."

"Speaking of ladies, Molly McKinney is certainly a lovely woman." Evie snapped the lid closed and tucked the container away.

He swallowed the bite of his cookie. The amusement in Evie's gaze evaporated any happy cookie rush inside him. Uncertainty, not the peanut butter, made his words stick together. "Why are you talking about Molly?"

"Why not?" Evie rearranged the quick-sale items on the counter, sorting the plastic balls with bells inside by color. "I'd like to know more about her."

Drew only knew the Molly from his past. But the Molly he'd run into at the courthouse, the one he'd been with at the gala and the mom he hadn't known she was, intrigued him. He could want to get to know the woman Molly was now.

Learn why she still tucked her hair behind her left ear only. Why she always looked Hazel in the eyes when she spoke to her daughter. And how she always captured his full focus. As if she were—and had always been—the center of his world.

He blinked, cursed fate and bad timing, then stammered, "You should go to lunch with her. She likes spicy nachos the same as you." At least he assumed Molly still liked spicy foods.

He knew what college student Molly had liked and disliked. Knew he had enjoyed being with Molly back then. And being with Molly now was both familiar and disorienting. Perhaps if he stopped reminiscing, he'd see Molly for who she had become. Then he'd realize his past, including his former feelings for a classmate, had no place in the present.

"Maybe I will ask Molly to lunch." Evie chuckled. "What about you?"

Drew located Evie's small thermos of her specially blended Irish cream coffee under the counter. "I'm off to spend time in the cat room."

And not spend time with Molly. Nor getting to know Molly. Because spending time with Molly and getting to know her would not win him his freedom. Or help her build her new practice.

"People come into our lives for all different reasons, Drew. Some folks stay. Some leave." Evie wiped off the counter. Her voice was knowing. "It's when those people return that we need to pay attention."

"Because they are up to no good." Drew picked up a cup from the stack Evie always kept available.

"Don't be so flippant." Evie tapped him affectionately on the shoulder. "Sometimes people come back to change our worlds."

Drew gripped the thermos and refused to admit the same sentiment had already whispered through him after his first run-in with Molly. But the charges against him were life-changing. World flipping. That was more than enough to make him keep his distance.

"I'm not about to confess that Molly is a long-lost love. A soul mate. Or even a potential permanent part of my life." He eyed Evie. "Molly is simply a part of my past," he stated with conviction. Or what he hoped sounded like conviction.

"What about your future?" Evie's eyebrows

lifted over her glasses. Her gaze sparked. "What about love?"

Only a distracted, irrational fool fell in love when his entire life was on the line. Love would not save him. After all, there was no room for emotion in the court of law, only facts and reason. "Love can go find another unsuspecting victim."

"Mark my words, Drew." Evie's voice lifted to follow him into the backroom. "Love will find you and you won't be able to reason it away."

But he could ignore it.

Drew walked through the kennel area reserved for the dogs and opened the door to the cat room. He released a litter of six kittens onto the floor, gathered the kitten toys around him and leaned back against the soft big pillows Sophie had decorated the room with. Ten minutes later, two pure white kittens with silver-tipped ears pounced on the laser beam light he swirled over the floor. A calico curled on his lap and slept. A tabby stretched out on its back against his leg. The two black-and-white tuxedos wrestled beside him. The kittens offered a quiet, calm sanctuary. And yet his mind wouldn't stop searching for that new perspective. That missing piece in his case.

Sophie opened the door and peered at him. "Evie claims you stole her entire thermos of Irish cream coffee."

Drew pointed to the thermos beside him. "I did. And I'm not even sorry."

"Want to talk about it?" Sophie pressed her back against the wall and lowered herself to the floor next to Drew. Her hands cradled her stomach and the twins growing inside. "I will regret this later, so you have to promise to help get me off the floor."

"I can't give you any coffee." Drew set the thermos of whiskey-spiked coffee away from his very pregnant sister-in-law.

Sophie sighed. "Go figure. Today I really need it too."

"It helps if you talk about it." Drew considered Sophie a sister and even more, a good friend. Sophie and his brother had built a family and a home that swelled with love. Guests were family as soon as they walked inside. Strangers became instant friends inside their house.

Drew had never considered a home and a family for himself. He'd dedicated his life to his career. Hadn't regretted it. Now he wondered...

He blamed Molly. Seeing her again had stirred up too many old wishes. He brushed his hand across his face, trying to push the past aside.

"You talk first." Sophie nudged her shoulder against his. "You're sitting in my cat room alone and drinking spiked coffee on a Monday afternoon."

"It's a good place to think." Drew stroked his fingers over the calico's back. "And the kittens don't judge. They just keep purring."

"Bad day working on your case?" Sophie asked and quickly added, "You're wearing mismatched socks, an Angels T-shirt and Pioneer jogging pants. I've never seen you wear your workout clothes out of the house."

"It's nothing I can't handle." How many times had he repeated that tired line? Drew tugged his pants over his mismatched socks. "What about you?"

"It's good to hear you've got things under control. Wish I could say the same." Sophie picked up the tabby and cuddled the kitten against her chest. "I was asked to step down as the president of Paws and Bark. Auditors from the attorney general's office are investigating my foundation."

Drew scratched the back of his neck and the unease skimming over his skin. "For what?"

"Complaints have been filed against the foundation." Sophie pressed her cheek against the kitten's fur. Her voice wavered. "I don't know why this is happening. We've always had professional independent audits. Filed all our paperwork to the state on time. No discrepancies or issues ever."

Drew wiped his hand over his mouth, wanting to catch his sudden alarm. The attorney general had released a statement to the press about the charges against Drew. On the same day the district attorney had insinuated in a press conference that Drew was guilty. Cory Vinson, the current district attorney, had lied. Now, suddenly the attorney general's office was looking into Sophie's nonprofit. Drew never subscribed to coincidence. "Why were you asked to step down Sophie?"

She refused to look at him. A quiver worked across her chin before she buried her face in the kitten's fur.

Apprehension bit into his skin, spreading more and more with every moment of

Sophie's silence. "You were asked to step down because of me, weren't you?"

Sophie simply cuddled the kitten closer and imitated the animal's soft purr.

"Sophie," Drew pressed.

Finally she nodded.

That dread sank through Drew's chest. He was being unjustly accused of witness tampering on a murder trial he had led and won two years prior, his paralegal who'd been with him from his first day at the district attorney's office had been randomly reassigned within the department and now this.

He switched off the laser beam pointer, faced Sophie and did his best to bury his frustration. "But I'm not associated with the Paw and Bark foundation. Other than attending its fundraising gala, I'm not connected."

"We're associated." Sophie flicked her wrist between them.

"We're family." His family was supposed to be off-limits. In fact, they should have been protected. The charges against him should not have impacted them. But his enemies seemed to be playing according to their own rules. All of this was because of him.

It was worse than he'd suspected.

He no longer wondered if he was being

framed. He knew it and he had to find the evidence to prove it before it wasn't only his potential downfall on the line. He inhaled once. Slow and steady. Then again. Outbursts and temper flares solved nothing. No one had ever won in a courtroom that way.

One more inhale and he tested his voice, pushing resolve into each word. "I'm going to fix this, Sophie. Get you back as the chair of your foundation."

She reached over and grabbed his hand. "You're going to concentrate on your case and forget my foundation."

"I can't do that." He wasn't guilty. Neither was Sophie. Yet he'd started to fear that might not matter. Still, Sophie didn't deserve this.

"You have to." She squeezed his hand until his gaze met hers. "And you have to let us help you. Let Brad help you. He's your brother. You guys would do anything for each other."

The brothers never had to ask each other for help. It had always been freely given. Drew hesitated, then nodded. The same way he had as a kid after Brad had described one of his latest stunt-inspired ideas. Somehow Drew had always ended up involved in Brad's ploys no matter the ploy.

He acknowledged Sophie's words. Yet he refused to entangle his brother or his family any further. "You guys have enough to worry about. The twins are going to be here any day."

"That doesn't mean we can't be there for you too," Sophie challenged.

"If I told you that I had outside help, would that make you feel better?" Would it make him feel better? He twisted the cap back on the coffee thermos. The Irish cream suddenly curdling in his stomach.

"Is this good help?" she countered.

"She's one of the best attorneys in the state," Drew admitted.

She was also the one Drew had refused as his counsel, insisting he wanted to protect her reputation and livelihood. Still, Molly had been convinced she could defend him. But he hadn't told Molly what he suspected was really going on. Would Molly even want to help him once she understood the real risks to her own career? Having his back in a professor's office was a far cry from going into court against an enemy like the current district attorney.

He glanced at Sophie and saw the tears she refused to release. Anger and anguish twisted around his spine. He had no choice. He had to try before more of his family suffered.

"Why am I sensing a but coming?" Sophie's smile was fragile. A flicker of hope flashed in her tear-soaked eyes. "She's one of the best attorneys in the state, but…"

Drew scrubbed his hand over his face. "But I might have already dismissed her as my legal counsel." Turned away her intelligence and experience. And hurt her feelings.

"Might have." Sophie frowned. One of her eyebrows arched up. "Or did."

No, that hadn't happened. It wasn't my fault. That was what he wanted to say to Sophie. It was Molly McKinney after all. Molly had gone through law school with an unyielding composure. One she hadn't lost. But he'd seen Molly flinch on the balcony the other evening. The smallest of tells, there and gone on her face. But even in the shadows of the night sky, he'd noticed his refusal had gotten to her. Guilt knocked through him.

"I need to make this right," Drew vowed. For his family. "I need to apologize to Molly too."

He gathered the tuxedo kitten twins and slipped the pair back inside the oversized kennel. Scooped up the tabby and calico, easing the pair into the same kennel. All the kittens returned to their temporary home, the toys returned to the toy bin and the cat room returned to normal, Drew faced Sophie.

Now he had to return their lives to normal.

"Apologies always go better with gifts." Sophie held out her hands and let Drew pull her to her feet. "And not just any generic gift either. Make it thoughtful."

"How hard can that be." Drew hugged his sister-in-law, silently vowing all would be fine. He would make sure of it.

One hour and a wardrobe change later, Drew strode through the lobby of the Fog City hotel, a shopping bag from Peapod Toy Parade in his right hand. A bag from Bouquets by Baylee in the other. With luck, he had captured *thoughtful*. But would his gifts and apology be enough?

To find out, he just needed Molly to open her hotel room door.

CHAPTER SIX

THE KNOCK ON the hotel room door interrupted Molly's latest attempt to sooth an unhappy Hazel. Molly opened the door, eyed Drew and tried not to be too envious of his wrinkle-free, no-spit-up-embellished attire. Across the hall, another suite door opened, and the older woman in the doorway aimed a put-upon grimace in Molly's direction before stuffing earplugs back in her ears.

Molly shifted a crying Hazel to her other hip and scowled at the older woman. She focused again on Drew. "This is definitely not a good time. I'm trying to get Hazel to sleep."

"I only need five minutes." His shopping bags transferred to one hand, he lifted his arm and spread out his fingers. "Just five minutes."

That was enough time to drop off takeout. Or, in Drew's case, give Molly an apology for firing her the other night. But she suspected he wasn't there to give her the job back. Molly stroked Hazel's flushed cheek and her daughter grabbed a hold of her finger. She opened her mouth to speak.

But a foursome of twentysomethings spilled out of the elevator, each one struggling to prove their mastery of the luggage cart. Loud voices and laughter bounced along the hallway. The clunking of ice from the machine into a bucket and the knocking of the luggage cart into the wall startled Hazel back into her tears and the start of a full-blown wail.

Drew lunged forward, set the two shopping bags he carried on the floor inside Molly's hotel room and reached for Hazel. The little girl dropped into his arms willingly and eagerly. Molly welcomed Drew as if he were her personal baby whisperer. Turning him away was no longer an option.

She pushed him inside and quickly shut the hotel room door. He plucked one of the folded clean burp clothes from the side table, draped it over his shoulder and adjusted Hazel in his arms. Hazel buried her tear-stained face in his shoulder and quieted.

Molly added a silent thank-you. Without the piercing stab of Hazel's cries, she could finally hear her own thoughts again. For one brief, impractical breath, Molly considered asking Drew to stay longer than five minutes. His baby-whisperer ways aside, she remembered he'd let her go. That had to matter.

"You know my friends, Dan and Brooke Sawyer, with the in-law apartment." Drew moved around the suite, his body swaying from side to side, his hand rubbing Hazel's back. "It's available now."

"That's convenient." She mimicked his tone from their rooftop conversation at the gala.

Slowly, with each step-sway, Hazel calmed. As for Drew, he remained in constant motion as if afraid to stop and possibly recharge Hazel's crankiness.

"I need to apologize. I will apologize properly and sincerely for not keeping you as my counsel." Drew's voice lowered into a soothing murmur. Hazel sighed and pressed her cheek against his shoulder. "But please consider the apartment. It gets you out of this hotel room. Gives you some space."

She needed space from Drew and his amazing baby-whispering ways. He wasn't doing anything she hadn't already done with Hazel. The same sway. Similar circles over Hazel's back. He even added the occasional encouragement of, "Shhh. It's all right." And a, "There. There. I got you."

Even Molly's tension eased out of her. But Molly was used to doing everything for herself. She'd approached the role of single motherhood with the identical strategy and determination. She'd assumed only she could settle her daughter. Here Drew was, proving her wrong. And she felt...not anger, but relief.

And it scared her. Drew was not her partner. He wasn't there to hold her and promise her everything would be okay. That Molly wanted to set her head on his shoulder had her retreating, one step, then two. "You could have texted to tell me that your friends' perfect apartment is suddenly available."

"But then I couldn't have given you the teddy bear and amethyst air plant." Drew pointed toward the bags at the door.

"An amethyst air plant." Molly's mouth dropped open.

"Baylee at the flower shop told me amethyst brings positive energy and balance." He paused and cleared his throat as if reconsidering his explanation. "And the air plant needs very little care like those cactus plants you had all around your apartment at school."

Her frustration dimmed as if she'd pressed

mute. He remembered her apartment from college. Remembered she liked cactus plants. Hadn't wanted to put her reputation at risk by letting her represent him. He was considerate and protective like a good friend should be.

But who was protecting Drew?

Molly stepped closer to Drew and peered at Hazel. Her blue eyes were open. No more tears dampened her former red cheeks. Finally. The poor thing had been crying since Molly had picked Hazel up from the Tiny Sweet Giggles Day Care. Not even their daily cable car ride had improved Hazel's bad mood.

Nothing had worked until Drew had arrived.

A deep sigh escaped from Hazel. Molly picked up Hazel's favorite llama blanket and arranged it around her daughter. Hazel was completely content. Drew's manner had always reassured and bolstered Molly. If she stepped into his arms, would she discover her own kind of contentment too?

Wait. Contentment had never been a goal. The collapse of Molly's relationship with her ex had taught her the consequences of complacency. Not a mistake she'd ever make twice. Molly retreated. "What's really going on? You just show up unannounced with gifts and an apartment for no reason as if you've become Santa."

"You make Santa sound bad." The tease in his voice tipped one corner of his mouth up.

"You haven't believed in Santa ever." The same as Molly. She sorted the small pile of Hazel's clothes she'd washed earlier at the laundromat, rather than lose herself in Drew's half smile. The one that used to hook inside her and urge her closer and closer to him. Back then, she'd been a silly college student with a crush. "Remember that Thanksgiving we spent together on campus in undergrad when we shared our holiday horror stories growing up." She sat in front of the coffee table and finished folding Hazel's tops.

Drew's grin expanded in stages as if the memory was coming back to him in pieces. "Your mom never signed any Christmas presents from Santa and she forbid you from taking a picture on Santa's lap as a child."

Molly's smile widened from the inside out as more of their shared memory surfaced. "We went to the mall that Saturday after Thanksgiving. We stood in line with all those little kids for over an hour and took our own picture with Santa."

Drew's shoulders shook, but his laughter remained muffled. "My parents had decided to spend Thanksgiving on the open seas that year. A cruise without port stops."

"And you told them you had to work over the holiday anyway" Molly added. "And had to miss the cruise."

"Best decision ever and I did take on extra shifts." More silent laughter escaped.

"You took on those extra shifts at the student center because of your guilt," Molly said. "You never could lie well."

"It was lucky for me, not so lucky for my family, remember?" Drew shifted Hazel carefully in his arms. "My parents ended up with some kind of food poisoning. I ended up with overtime pay, free meals from work and Santa pictures. And I haven't been to a mall since."

Last Christmas, Molly had patiently stood in line with Hazel at the shopping mall for the first time since her own Santa photo with Drew. Several weeks ago, Hazel had taken a picture with the Easter bunny too. Hazel would have a collection of these fun photos from her childhood to look back on. And her daughter could believe in Santa, the tooth fairy and the Easter bunny for as long as she wanted. Molly was desperate that

Hazel should be a kid and not grow up too fast. That meant having a house to decorate and celebrate in every holiday from Easter to Christmas to New Years. Giving Hazel a home mattered.

Concentrating on memories and revisiting her onetime attraction to Drew put her no closer to her goals. After all, Molly was a single mom now, not a single-minded college student. "Are you going to tell me what this is all about?"

Drew rearranged Hazel's blanket as if he needed a moment to arrange his own thoughts. "I'll take you to see the apartment if you'll reconsider representing me."

We've exhausted all your options. That had been her real-estate agent's text to Molly on her way back from the laundromat this afternoon. Her realtor had canceled tomorrow morning's meet-up unless Molly was willing to put in an offer on a place they'd already visited. Those places were overpriced in not-so-good neighborhoods. She wanted the perfect home and refused to settle. Now Drew had an available apartment. But at what cost?

She dropped Hazel's flower power onesie on the table. "Why have you reconsidered hiring me? At the gala, you claimed you didn't need more time. Your decision was final." What was she doing? She should be shouting, *I accept!*

"There are things about this case I haven't told anyone." He continued his slow side-to-side sway, yet his gaze remained fixed on Molly.

"But you've decided to tell *me.*" She failed to keep the sarcasm from her words.

"I don't trust anyone outside my own family and friends." He stilled for a beat and stared at her. "I can't trust anyone else. I also can't do this alone either."

The fear in his voice made Molly pull back and really consider him. Not the excuses he'd given her earlier. But the man before her. The one unable to mask the distress thinning his mouth or the unease reflected in his gaze. "Are you guilty?"

"I will enter a plea of not guilty, Counselor." His voice was firm. Certain. "I also know I wasn't the initial person working on the Van Solis murder case."

The Van Solis murder trial was the very one that had instigated the charges against Drew. After the key witness in the murder trial recanted his testimony two weeks ago. "Who was the first one working on the trial?"

"Cory Vinson." He watched her as if waiting for her recognition to flare and ignite the room.

Molly frowned, nothing more. Despite the quick race of her pulse and her whirling mind. "You're talking about Cory Vinson, the city's current district attorney."

Drew nodded. "The same one who is up for reelection this fall."

Molly stood, clasped her hands behind her back and paced around the suite. She'd trained herself to remain neutral, unaffected no matter what her clients disclosed to her. She leaned into that side of herself now. For her sake and for Drew's. "Then you're suggesting Cory Vinson is setting you up as the fall guy."

He never hesitated. Never disputed her claim. Never retreated. "I just can't prove it. I haven't found the evidence yet."

"Why are you telling me this?" She set her hands on her hips, fighting to remain impassive.

"If you're going to be my counsel, you need to know everything."

"I never agreed to be your lawyer." She watched him. "More importantly, we haven't signed an attorney–client contract." Which meant whatever Drew said to her before that could be used against him later, if she ever chose to reveal it.

"You also haven't kicked me out and it's been way more than five minutes." A small grin lifted the corners of his mouth. Drew tucked Hazel's tiny hand under the blanket, then tipped his head at Molly. "You always were fearless. I don't believe you've lost that," he whispered.

Ten years had passed since she'd last seen him. Yet he looked at her as if he knew her even better now. Impossible.

Still, she felt compelled to prove herself. Taking on Drew as a client would allow her to do just that. She asked, "Are you still cautious and overprotective?"

"Whoever wants to ruin my career has pivoted to include hurting my family." His voice was grim. "You're going to be in their line of sight too, if you represent me. You need to understand that."

She stiffened and pushed her shoulders back. Her gaze fell on her daughter. "I understand the stakes. I've taken cases before with higher risks."

"But you didn't have Hazel then." He set

his hand on Hazel's back as if shielding her. "You didn't have a daughter to look out for."

The intensity in his gaze, the honesty in his tone made her heart flutter. Drew held Hazel like a father would, looking out for his little girl. It was all Molly had ever wanted from her ex. Instead, Derrick had told Molly he'd never wanted children with her when Molly had revealed her pregnancy. After Molly had ended things, Derrick had promptly returned to his ex-wife and his former life as if Molly and their relationship hadn't ever existed. Hadn't ever mattered. She'd been wondering if she'd expected too much of Derrick. Now she knew. She hadn't expected enough from Derrick or their relationship.

Now she had to fill the role of two parents for Hazel. She couldn't and wouldn't fail her daughter.

Drew Harrington's case would get her noticed in the San Francisco legal community. Clearing Drew of the charges against him would establish her credibility among her peers and her skill in the courtroom. Winning created a solid foundation to build her new practice on.

And that solid foundation ensured she had the stability she wanted to provide for her daughter. "It's because of Hazel I have to do this. I will clear your name."

"I know it's a lot to ask." He motioned toward the shopping bags near the door. "An air plant and a stuffed animal aren't enough to negate the risks."

"We took an oath as lawyers, Drew." She stepped closer to him. "Now one of our own has broken that oath. I cannot turn my back on that." *Or you.*

Drew closed his eyes and exhaled. "Thank you."

"Save the gratitude for after the plea hearing." Molly rubbed her hands together rather than reach for Drew to reassure him. He was a client, nothing more. "Tomorrow morning we can discuss your charges and the Van Solis case in detail."

"Or we could start now." His eyebrows lifted. "You always were the most curious person I've ever known. The first to get to work and the last to leave."

He wasn't wrong. But tonight she needed Drew out of her hotel room before she forgot their working arrangement and let her curiosity extend to the man Drew had become. "Tomorrow at nine am we begin. Meet me here."

Surely, by tomorrow she would have focused her curiosity on the case only.

She eased Hazel from Drew's arms without disturbing her sleep. "Do you have information on your friend's in-law unit?"

"I left the phone number of my friends, Brooke and Dan Sawyer in the bag with the air plant." Drew walked to the hotel room door, opened it and turned back. "I'm sorry this is our reunion."

Molly nodded and pressed a kiss to the top of Hazel's head. Drew left and eased the door shut behind him with a soft click.

Molly was sorry too.

Sorry she hadn't met Drew in another time. One where she still believed in love and listened to her heart. Now she had to concentrate on her career and Hazel instead.

Being a good mom and lawyer would take all her resolve and energy.

There simply wasn't room for anything or anyone else.

CHAPTER SEVEN

"WE'VE BEEN IN this hotel too long." Molly stared at the collection of Hazel's things that were missing their partners. From the purple polka dot bootie to the green stacking cup to four stray socks. The whale and shark water squirters had escaped from the mesh bath bag and two rings were not on the red stacking base.

Hazel, strapped into a baby carrier on Molly's chest, kicked out her legs and babbled as if supplying the location for each missing item.

"Hide-and-seek is your favorite game." Molly sighed and kissed the top of Hazel's head. "Time to seek."

A knock on the door disrupted Molly's search. It wasn't housekeeping, who usually announced their arrival. Molly stood sideways and peered through the peephole. She jerked back. Drew, not housekeeping, waited on the other side. Molly pressed her palms against her temples, speared her fingers into her hair and glanced at the bedside clock. The red digital lights flashed like a silent alarm. Mortification rattled through her.

She forgot. Forgot a business meeting. Forgot about her client.

Her client: Drew Harrington.

She had not forgotten a client meeting. Until today.

Hazel giggled and chewed on her frozen washcloth.

Molly had indulged in extra mommy–daughter time earlier, extending their morning walk another mile to continue their one-sided game of I spy. Then she'd returned to their hotel room to pack. She hadn't even showered yet. Hadn't even fully prepared for her day.

And her client waited out in the hallway. Ready to discuss his case.

Molly looked like she was ready for a play-date.

She gripped the door handle and paused. The facts remained the same whether she wore a power suit or yoga pants. She was a fine lawyer and a fine mom. She could do both well. She would ensure Drew knew that.

Hazel giggled before chomping on a corner of the washcloth she held in her tiny fist. Molly's inner battle between mom and lawyer was over.

She unlocked the door and opted for a cheerful but professional tone of voice. "Drew. You're early."

Hazel squealed, her body wiggling, at the sight of Drew.

"Hey, baby blue." Drew greeted Hazel with a quick tickle under her chin and tender smile. "You look rested and ready for adventure."

Molly wasn't ready for Drew. Her bare feet and the baby attached to her chest all but shouted that Molly was in full mommy mode. And definitely not ready to fend off Drew's soft side and the sudden sigh coming directly from her heart.

She touched her messy bun, but then dropped her arm. He could keep his sweet smiles and endearing qualities for Hazel. Drew was both a client and a peer, so two red flags. Not to mention, the statistics proved that the majority of work romances were doomed to fail. She knew that from bitter experience. She was part of those statistics. And the fallout from crossing a line with Drew would only be more heartache.

Winning Drew's case boosted her reputation. As for a boost to her heart, Molly would leave that to her daughter. She motioned Drew inside, silenced her sighs and her heart. "Good timing. We're just about to begin our toy hunt."

"Toy hunt." Drew gripped a black leather briefcase and glanced around the suite.

Molly pointed at her display on the bed. "You're looking for items that go with those ones."

"We need to discuss my case." Drew aimed a frown, not his charm, at Molly. The easy affection he'd shown Hazel dispersed.

Score one for Molly. She had to transition out of mommy mode and quickly. The tough attorney inside her could fend off her misplaced attraction to Drew in a heartbeat. Molly squashed one of the lone socks between her hands. *Flexibility.* That had been the critical advice in a parenting book Molly had read. Now she had to get Drew on board for a slight schedule change. "First, we're collecting toys. Then we're finishing packing. And finally, we're moving."

"Moving?" Drew shifted his briefcase to his other hand. "Right now?"

"Yes. Brooke and I spoke on the phone last night after you left, and we worked out the rental terms." Molly lifted the cushion off the couch, discovered a pale green sock and earned a giggle from Hazel. However, nothing about her increasing interest in Drew made her want to cheer. "Brooke babyproofed the apartment this morning. It's ready for us now."

"That was fast," Drew said.

"I don't like to waste time." And she hated that she forgot something as important as a client meeting. Now her heart wanted to join the chaos too. But distractions like emotions could ruin her goals. She would not let that happen again. "Brooke was more than willing to do the babyproofing for us."

"Fair enough, but we have work to discuss." Drew tapped his briefcase.

"We also have toys to find and a move to complete." And her work armor to put on. Molly waved the sock and picked up her partly packed suitcase.

Drew's eyebrows pulled together. "How are you planning on getting to Brooke and Dan's house with all this?"

"I'm really hoping you drove here" He wasn't dressed for moving in his button-down shirt and navy dress pants. She wasn't dressed for business yet, but everyone had to adjust sometimes. "You did drive, right?"

He nodded, a slow up-and-down motion of his chin. "My life is on the line. All of our futures are on the line."

"I'm fully aware of the stakes." Molly stepped into his space, settling into her stand-off stance. Toe to toe. Briefcase to suitcase. Mom to lawyer. "We do this. Hazel naps. We get to work uninterrupted. You're still new to this, I'm not."

Certainly, by then Molly would remember the boundaries of their relationship. Certainly, by then she'd stop noticing the silver shards in his light blue eyes. Stop considering the fatigue framing him like a shadow. Stop the concern building inside her for him. As if he meant something more to her than a client.

Drew's gaze shifted to Hazel. A large yawn traveled through the little girl, sighing into the small space between Drew and Molly. Drew's chin lowered. "Look, baby blue. You only get to win once. This is it, understand?"

Hazel reached toward Drew, handing him her frozen washcloth as if to thank him.

Molly stiffened, refusing to surrender to his charm.

Drew shook his head, a soft smile curving

over his face. His piercing all-too-perceptive gaze locked on Molly.

Something inside her chest unlocked. But that was only the mom inside her responding. The nurturing side she hadn't known existed until Hazel had arrived. Work Molly would remember the risks. Recall Drew's faults and secure her heart from them.

"I'll find the toys," he said. "You find the missing clothes."

Thirty minutes later, with the last of the three large suitcases zipped closed and stacked on the luggage cart, Hazel and Drew traded a blue plastic ring and green stacking cup back and forth on the couch. Hazel's delighted babble bounced around the room. Drew revealed what seemed like endless patience. And the twinge in her chest—the one that had her forgetting Drew was a peer and off-limits—grew.

She concentrated on the lost items inventory and tucked the last of the matched sock pairs into a suitcase pocket. "I think that's everything."

Drew picked up Hazel and helped Molly secure her into the baby carrier. He tapped Hazel on the nose. "Time to get our move on, baby blue."

"I'm not sad about leaving our hotel suite." Molly followed Drew out into the hall. He pushed the full luggage cart toward the elevators. She added, "But I will miss the daily housekeeping."

Drew laughed. "Don't tell Brooke. She'll arrange something to make your stay more comfortable."

"She's already done enough to ensure we are comfortable." Molly had yet to meet her new landlord. But she'd liked Brooke immediately on their phone call. Molly pressed the elevator call button. "I appreciate the introduction."

"Brooke and Dan Sawyer are good people." Drew maneuvered the luggage cart into the waiting elevator. "You'll be safe there."

Molly pressed the lobby button, distracted Hazel from touching every button on the panel and glanced at Drew. "Do I need protection?" she asked warily.

Drew gripped the luggage cart. His gaze remained fixed on the descending numbers flashing on the elevator screen. "Let's get you and Hazel moved in and then we can talk without distraction, like you said."

Hazel gripped Molly's thumbs. One in each of her small fists. Molly curved her fingers around her daughter's and drew their arms together for a hug. As if that would shield them from Drew's somber attitude. The day she'd heard Hazel's heartbeat for the first time, she had vowed to protect her child with everything she had. That had not changed.

She would represent Drew and defend herself and Hazel from external threats and invisible ones that could be even more dangerous. If she had to lock down her heart too, so be it. She was committed to her career and Hazel. That was more than enough to fulfill her.

Drew rolled the luggage cart off the elevator and through the lobby. Molly walked over to the valet's station.

"No wait time." Drew grinned at Molly and tipped his head toward a silver truck. "In the city, large trucks don't usually get parked in the garages."

It took only a few minutes and the luggage was stored in the truck bed. Molly muttered and for the fourth time unsuccessfully yanked Hazel's car seat into place.

"Are you sure I can't help?" Drew stood behind her, entertaining Hazel. His voice cheerful.

"I got it." Molly scooted farther into the truck and tugged on the seat belt.

"Maybe if you…"

The seat belt snapped back against the frame and frustration snapped through Molly. She jumped out of the truck and faced Drew. "How many car seats have you ever installed in your truck?"

Drew lifted Hazel until they were eye to eye. His voice lowered into a not-so-quiet whisper. "Here's another lesson, baby blue. Your mom is a take charge sort of person, which is perfectly fine, except when I can lend a hand when she seems to need it."

"Hey, I just like to get things done." Molly tipped her chin up, but she'd already lost the edge of her irritation thanks to Drew and his spontaneous life lesson. "I've installed this car seat in a lot of cars without any problems. It's your too-big truck that's the issue."

"It's not too big and it's not the truck," Drew said.

"Now who's acting like an expert?" Molly set her hands on her hips and stared at him.

"Watch and learn." Drew handed Hazel to Molly and scooted into the truck.

Seconds later, Drew clicked the seat belt into the buckle and stepped away from the truck. He raised both arms over his head. "Done. In less than a minute, too."

"I need to make sure it's right." Molly inspected his installation.

Drew leaned his arm against the open door and laughed. "In school, we lobbied against each other for climate change reform, argued over the death penalty, challenged animal testing as well as drug legalization. I never thought we'd debate a car seat."

Molly grinned and shook her head. "Really, how did you know how to do this correctly?"

"I've been given lessons, then ordered to practice often," Drew said. "Don't forget the twins are arriving soon. My niece has been doing baby research ever since Sophie announced her pregnancy."

"How old is your niece again?" Molly secured Hazel into the car seat and spread the favorite soft llama-print blanket over her.

"Ella is twelve." Drew opened the front passenger door for Molly.

"I could have used someone like Ella when I first brought Hazel home." Molly climbed into the truck and buckled her seat belt. One long deep exhale had her easing into the soft leather captain's chair. She hadn't sat all morning. Not since she'd climbed out of bed at sunrise to answer Hazel's early morning wake-up call. The drive to Brooke and Dan's offered her the perfect opportunity to restore and recharge.

Drew settled into the driver's seat, fired up the engine and pulled out of the hotel's drop-off area. "Ella believes the more prepared we are, the better we will handle potential problems."

His niece's lessons explained why Drew knew how to handle Hazel's crying jags and needed little convincing to help Molly that morning.

The moment she'd told Derrick about her pregnancy, he had warned her not to expect his assistance. Not for a diaper change, late-night feeding or even a pick-me-up embrace. Then he'd dropped his big reveal: he'd never wanted kids with Molly. That he'd never really loved her. Thanks to her pregnancy news, Molly had learned exactly what she could expect from Derrick: nothing. She'd ended their relationship that night, walked out of Derrick's life, determined to rebuild a better life without him. She pinched the bridge of her nose.

Molly had wanted her baby. Accepted she would be a single parent. Now she had to accept every part of that decision, including the exhaustion. And the occasional twinge of loneliness.

"You okay?" A pair of sunglasses blocked Drew's gaze, but not the concern in his voice.

Molly straightened in the seat. She'd never been weak. She wasn't about to start now. Besides, she knew how to be alone and thrive. One morning with Drew acting like a co-parent changed nothing. "Do you have one thing that would make you happy? Completely satisfied. Totally fulfilled."

"Besides clearing my name?" Drew turned onto a busy one-way street.

"That's a given."

"I've worked one case after another for so long, that's all I know. Work has been my focus. I assumed I might find someone..." His voice trailed off as if he doubted his own claim. Stopping at a red light, he glanced at her. "What about you?"

"It's all I've been thinking about recently." Molly ran her palms over her yoga pants. "I keep wondering if I'm not meant to be fulfilled or satisfied, and whether I will spend my life on an endless, futile quest to try to find it."

"You don't really believe that do you?" he asked.

"I've always had a plan. Detailed and specific." Molly looked out the truck window at the street crowded with cars and the sidewalk swarming with a crowd. People rushed in every direction, in constant motion, determined to reach their destination. Everyone knew exactly where they were going and how to get there. She wanted to be like them again. "I've pursued my goals so relentlessly and so doggedly. Now I'm wondering what I might have missed during the pursuit."

"Regret was never your style."

"It's not regret exactly," she said. "It's hard to explain."

"It's about considering if you'd taken a left turn instead of a right after graduation or at some turning point in your life…where would you be now?"

"Yeah." She studied Drew's profile. He'd been able to read her all those years ago and always understood what she'd been trying to say even while she'd often lacked the right words. All except for the most important thing she had to say: her true feelings for him. Those she'd kept well hidden. She disliked the what-if rolling through her now. Refused to let it haunt her. Her feelings for Drew were part of her past. Nothing real. Nothing to reconsider. "It's exactly like that."

"Is here so bad?" he asked.

"I'm a single mom without a steady source of income or a home." She glanced over her seat at Hazel. The hum of the truck had put Hazel to sleep quickly. "It's not exactly ideal."

"It doesn't have to be perfect to still be good."

"I never knew you to be so philosophical." *Or to be so very comfortable with a baby.*

"There's quite a bit you don't know about me," he said.

And quite a bit Molly was learning about herself. Like the fact that she very much wanted to know more about Drew and the man he was now.

She had to stick to the truth though. Drew was a client.

Once his case was resolved, their relationship would be resolved too.

CHAPTER EIGHT

SUITCASES STORED IN the bedroom closet. Hazel sleeping soundly in her pack and play, temporarily positioned next to Molly's four-poster bed. Molly quietly closed the bedroom door behind her and checked the time. "I can't believe we did all that in less than an hour."

"You had excellent help." Drew moved a large magnetic whiteboard on a stand in front of the corner fireplace and gave Brooke Sawyer, Molly's new landlord, a silent high five.

"I can't thank you enough for all you've done for us. We hadn't even met before today." Molly smiled at Brooke and set a cloth shopping bag on the kitchen counter.

"I was a complete stranger to the Sawyers when I moved in here, looking for a temporary place to live." Brooke placed several markers on top of the dry-erase whiteboard. "I'm still grateful that Dan's father offered the place and brought me here. Rick claims he's never met a stranger, only a future friend."

"Future friend. I really like that." How long had it been since Molly had a friend? A friend not from her firm. Someone to share more than the last cup of coffee from the break room with.

"You're going to really like the entire Sawyer family." Drew sounded positive.

"I'm sure I will." Molly set several jars of baby food in one of the kitchen cabinets.

"You should know our son, Ben, plays soccer and basketball in the backyard all the time." Brooke opened the shutters covering the front windows, allowing the afternoon sun to illuminate the space. "And we have two dogs and two cats as permanent residents at the main house."

"Do you have temporary pets too?" Molly asked.

"Always. I've gone back to work as a mediator, but I haven't stopped rescuing animals either." Brooke lifted her hands. "I'll try to keep them contained, but we do venture into the backyard quite often."

"Hazel will like that, I think." And Molly too. She'd never had a pet growing up. Only a memorable run-in with a dog. Her parents had claimed their apartments were too small. Pets were forbidden. Pets were too much work. Molly had simply craved a companion to grow up with. To fill the solitude. Things would be different for Hazel.

"What I would like to know is what we're doing with this dry-erase board?" Brooke grinned and rubbed her hands together. Excitement streamed across her face. "This board is like the ones they use for solving murders on those TV crime shows."

Drew laughed. "It's nothing like TV."

Molly wasn't so sure. After Brooke had called to let Molly know the babyproofing had been completed, Molly had asked her if she would mind accepting a delivery. The delivery was the oversized whiteboard from the nearest office supply store that Molly planned to use for her discovery and research on Drew's case. She tipped her head. "I suppose it is sort of like something on TV."

Drew frowned at Molly.

She shrugged back. "I intend to make very good use of this board."

"I know this isn't like TV." Brooke held out her hands "Dan says the same thing about the paramedics on the TV shows. Although, there's a certain energy to your work as lawyers and to Dan's being an EMT. Can't you feel it?"

"That's because there's also an incredible pressure to get it right." Drew crossed his arms over his chest.

"That's the adrenaline rush. It's what drives you." Brooke touched her stomach. "Now what's driving me is hunger pains. I must eat before going to The Pampered Pooch and my afternoon session to mediate for an extremely uncooperative couple. I'm picking up lunch from The Boot Pizza. Want anything?"

"We'll take a pizza with olive oil sauce, extra tomatoes and fresh basil." Drew looked at Molly. "Still your favorite?"

Surprise shifted through Molly. Good with babies and at recalling insignificant details about her. Molly swallowed her sigh. "Yes, it is."

"Got it. I'll be back." Brooke walked out, but leaned in again. "By the way, if you need a mediator's advice or assistance on this case or any others, look no further."

Molly uncapped a dry-erase pen and pointed it at Brooke. "You're already on my list."

"Now I'm even more excited." Brooke's eyes sparkled. "You should know, Molly, I looked you up online after we talked last night. You seriously downplayed your success and your talent. You're one of the best criminal defense attorneys in the state and you're living here? With us?"

The apartment door clicked shut on Brooke's cheer. Molly clicked into attorney mode and faced Drew. "It's time to earn my reputation. You might as well get comfortable. I have a lot of questions."

"Let's get going." Drew set his briefcase on the table and unzipped it. "Where do you want to start?"

"At the beginning of the Van Solis trial." Molly wrote the name of the defendant at the top corner of the dry-erase board. "Walk me through the details of the charges and the DA's case against him."

Drew nodded and closed his eyes as if preparing to step back in time to two years prior. Then he began to relay to Molly the details of the shooting at the small grocery store, the death of the owner who was a pillar in the community, the arrest of Van Solis and explained every step of his trial preparation after Cory Vinson's involvement. The soon-to-be district attorney at the time had asked Drew to take the lead on the case.

Molly listened, wrote notes on a legal pad and on the dry-erase board.

Drew finished with a description of Van Solis's sentencing hearing that came ten months after the trial had concluded and the man's reaction to the life sentence without parole. "Van kept claiming his innocence in the courtroom over and over." Drew paused and cleared his throat. His voice remained distant. "Van never cried. Not one tear. Never shouted or cursed fate. Just kept his composure and repeated in a whisper, *But I'm innocent*."

Anguish cut across Drew's face. His voice drifted off into the silence as if he could hear Van's words all over again. Molly set her pen on the legal pad. "Drew?"

"Van was tried as an adult. And I went on to get that innocent boy-almost-man convicted." Torment tracked through his cloudy gaze.

"You secured a conviction on a man you believed was guilty. All the evidence pointed that Van Solis was guilty of murder." Molly walked to Drew and grabbed his hands. "You did your job."

"No. I ruined a man's life." Drew's fingers curved around hers as if he sought her touch. Sought her strength.

Like so many of her clients before him. Yet Drew's touch was different. Never before had she considered how right someone's hands felt in hers. Molly tightened her focus. "We're going to get Van's life back and yours."

"Now that the key eyewitness has recanted his testimony given at the trial, we know witness tampering did occur. I'm sure it was the original prosecutor on the case who pressured the man. Cory Vinson needs to answer some serious questions." Drew squeezed his eyes closed. "But I have no evidence, only suspicion that the district attorney is guilty."

Molly tugged on his hands and pulled his gaze back to hers. "Trust me to find the evidence we need."

Drew released her to run a hand through his hair and paced away. "I don't know where to look for the proof."

"You're too close to it." Molly picked up her legal pad and studied her notes. "There were no rumors about Cory before or after he was elected district attorney. After all, he won after Van Solis's conviction."

"I was deep into Van's trial during most of the campaign. If it was related to the case, I listened. If not, I tuned the chatter out." Drew strode from the kitchen to the couch and back. "After that trial, I moved into a robbery and forgery case."

"But before Van Solis's trial, no rumors of anything unusual circled around the offices about Cory," Molly pressed. "What about your paralegal?"

"Elena." Drew shook his head. "She made a point not to gossip or to feed those who did. One of the reasons I hired her."

"Still, she had to have heard something around the ol' watercooler." Molly tapped her legal pad. "I want to talk to her."

"It has to be offline," Drew said. "As far as I know, Elena hasn't left the DA's office. She hasn't returned one of my calls or emails."

"I'll work it out." Molly dropped the legal pad on the table, set her hands on her hips and looked at the dry-erase board. No office was without gossip. And the assistants always knew more than anyone. "If Cory Vinson isn't as perfect as the outside world believes, somebody in that office building knows it. People share the scandals. Always. As if the juicier the gossip, the more they are compelled to pass it along."

"Cory is likeable and friendly. A seemingly good guy. I never had an issue with him." Drew dropped onto the couch and leaned his head back into the cushion. "But Cory was originally the lead on the Van Solis case."

"Was there anything out of the ordinary that happened in the office when you stepped into the lead on Van's trial?" Molly asked.

"Nothing really. Employee turnover, but that was fairly common."

"Employee turnovers or firings?" Molly stared at Drew.

Drew rubbed his forehead. "One paralegal was reassigned from Van's case to another assistant DA. He was one of the more experienced paralegals, so I noticed his absence during the trial preparation."

"Were there others who'd gone, as well?"

"There were several who'd been hired as temporary staff and were reassigned." Drew scratched his jaw. "Also, Elena was upset when Gina, that's Cory's administrative assistant, left suddenly."

"How suddenly?" The back of Molly's neck tingled. And that feeling Brooke had referred to earlier skimmed over her. That rush of energy Molly never ignored. Never dismissed.

"Overnight, according to Elena." Drew waved his hand as if skipping to the next slide in the deck. "But Cory shuffled through administrative assistants regularly, ever since he started in the DA's office. It wasn't unusual."

"You know there is no detail too trivial or

too insignificant in any case." Molly sat on the couch and shifted to face Drew. "Why was Gina's leaving different?"

"Elena liked Gina. According to Elena, Gina was more focused on her schoolwork then finding a boyfriend. The same as Elena was. They were walking buddies during their breaks at work." He was silent for a moment. His fingers restless, tapping on the couch. "Elena even helped Gina with her homework. Gina was getting her degree in paralegal studies from Bay College."

"Did Gina get another job?" Molly reached for her legal pad and flipped to a new page.

"No idea." Drew stared at the ceiling. His eyebrows pulled together. "Elena was upset Gina never mentioned anything about leaving to her."

"Gina wasn't part of the temporary staff?"

"No. She was full-time and putting herself through school."

"Then Gina needed her job."

"Or a job." Drew sat up and rested his elbows on his knees. "She could've simply gotten a better offer that paid more at a private firm."

Molly set her pen on top of her notepad and frowned, searching for that rush of a lead.

"I have to talk to her and Elena. What was Gina's last name?"

"Her first name was Gina…" He rubbed his chin. His voice was thoughtful. "Her last name was Vaughn? Or maybe Hern. That doesn't sound right. Maybe Gina Horn."

"Horn," Molly repeated.

"A face and a first name I don't forget. I could even draw you a picture of Gina if I had the skill." Drew pushed himself off the couch and walked into the kitchen. He took a bottle of water from the refrigerator. "But last names have always escaped me."

Molly tracked his movements. His gaze never fixed on one point, simply skipped around the room as if he translated something she couldn't see. No doubt he'd worn a path in his office carpet. He'd always processed facts the best when in motion during college. And she'd bet anything he paced and planned his opening statements, rebuttals and closing arguments for each and every case in the same meandering, circular pattern.

Finally he slowed, sipped his water before glancing at her. "Knowing first names matters. People like to be greeted by their first names. It's a well-known fact."

"It shows you care enough to remember

them." It showed Drew cared. And that made another one of those sighs attempt to surface inside her.

"Exactly." The plastic water bottle crinkled in his grip. "But I'm still at a loss for Gina's last name."

"We'll figure it out." Molly went over to him and touched his arm to reassure him. "It's good to know you haven't lost who you are because of this."

He set his hand over hers. His intense gaze searched her face. "What keeps you from losing who you are?"

The warmth from his hand instantly soothed her. The vulnerability in his open gaze caught her completely. One tiny shift, one half step and she'd be against his chest. If he curved his arms around her. If he held her close. Then she'd remember. Remember the power of an embrace.

And, in his embrace, she could give in return. Help him remember too.

She tugged her hands free and retreated. There was only one reminder of good she needed in her life. "Hazel. She's my reason for everything."

CHAPTER NINE

THE NEXT MORNING, Drew pulled into the Sawyers' driveway, dropped the visor on his windshield to block the sun and waited for Molly to close the garden gate to Dan and Brooke's backyard and her new apartment.

Molly gripped Hazel's baby-seat carrier in one hand and a sleek leather briefcase in the other. Her crisp black pants, white blouse and pink heels belonged on the thirtieth floor of a high-rise in the financial district. The unicorn-print diaper bag hanging on her shoulder belonged in a lively baby playgroup.

She combined both roles effortlessly. Then again Molly had always been more than capable of handling everything seamlessly. He appreciated her business attire, although he preferred her with her hair twisted in a confused sort of bun, no makeup and looking very approachable like she'd been yesterday.

But yesterday's moment was a onetime event and the woman approaching his truck now was the one he'd hired to prove his innocence. The relaxed, dedicated mother might have fit into his world before. He might have welcomed her there. But that was then. Now he acknowledged that only facts, not emotions, could restore his life and his future as an attorney.

Molly secured Hazel's baby carrier, got in the front seat and tugged her phone from her briefcase pocket. "One call and we'll have the legal assistant's full name and a place to start our morning."

Drew played a quick round of peekaboo with Hazel, continuing the game until he earned the little girl's delightful squeal.

"Gina Hahn." Molly tapped on her phone screen to end the call and beamed at Drew. "Cory's former administrative assistant and Elena's friend is Gina Hahn."

"I can't believe you found that out so quickly." Drew rubbed his eyes and started the truck.

"Connections, Drew. As your dear sweet mama said, it's all about connections. Having friends in every corner." Molly nudged his shoulder. "You were close when you suggested Horn yesterday."

"I won't forget her name anytime soon." He

reached forward to press the phone button on the truck's touchscreen and called his brother.

Brad answered on the first ring. "Bad time. Can't talk."

A scratching sound grated across the speaker.

Drew leaned forward and listened. In the background a woman shouted, "Over there." Another voice yelled, "Dad."

Drew backed his truck out of the driveway. "Where are you?"

More static interfered with Brad's voice. "Alley behind Tally's Corner Market on Bay-view Street at Vine Avenue."

"On my way." Drew quit the call and made a quick right turn.

"Isn't your brother a private investigator?" Molly scrolled through her emails. "Should we be disrupting his work in an alley?"

"Brad owns and manages a private inves-tigation and security company. He locates cyber criminals, corporate embezzlers and money launderers within the US and glob-ally. If he's working, he could be doing any-thing from a recon operation to sitting in on a debriefing from a high-level govern-ment official. And he wouldn't answer his phone." Drew slowed to a stop at a red light and glanced at her. "Right now, Brad is rescuing either a dog or a cat. He'll welcome our help."

Molly's mouth dropped open. "You know this how?"

"I heard Ella yell *dad*." Drew grinned at Molly. "Then Sophie, his wife, yelled at him too. Sophie owns The Pampered Pooch pet store and doggy day care. And she rescues every animal she gets a call about, day or night, rain or shine. Fog or no fog."

"I haven't even owned a goldfish. Let alone rescued a dog." Molly frowned and put her phone away. Uncertainty was obvious from her expression. Her fingers smoothed a nonexistent wrinkle from her pants. "And you're telling me that we're really going to rescue some animal right now."

"There's a first time for everything." Like it was the first time he'd ever noticed Molly fidget. She never hesitated. Never appeared unsure. Something about a pet rescue unsettled her. And something about that realization made him want to calm her. To be there for her. "You can wait in the car while I help Brad."

"I'm not afraid." Resolve bracketed her stiff shoulders.

"I didn't think you were," Drew lied and reached over to hold her hand. All part of being a good buddy. A friend. From a romantic standpoint, the gesture was insignificant— it meant nothing. "Do you want to talk about what happened?"

"It's nothing." She laced her fingers around his and exhaled. "I was a kid. I was outside drawing on the sidewalk with chalk. The neighbor's dog got out of their yard and joined me."

"Joined you," Drew repeated. Her grip on his hand tightened.

"It just wanted to play." She waved her other hand around in the air. "That's what the owners told me. My parents told me to stay off the sidewalk."

"But the dog scared you."

"It was twice my size, knocked me off my feet and nipped at my hands to eat the chalk." Molly shuddered. "I thought it wanted to eat me. I was five years old. What was I supposed to think?"

"I'm really sorry that happened to you." Drew pulled into the alley and parked behind his brother's SUV. "You can wait here."

Molly pointed at the open passenger door

on Brad's SUV. "Do you think that's Sophie in the front seat?"

The only part of Sophie that was visible were her legs and her all-too-familiar purple running shoes resting on the running board. "Yes. I'm sure Brad asked her to wait in the car. Otherwise, she'd be climbing into the dumpster herself, pregnant or not. She's that determined when it comes to saving animals."

"Hazel and I can wait with Sophie." Molly got out of the truck, removed Hazel from her car seat and tucked her daughter on her right hip.

Drew joined the pair at the front of his truck and set a burp cloth over Molly's shoulder. "There's something you should know about my niece, Ella."

"She's blind," Molly said softly. She tipped her head toward Brad's SUV.

Drew followed Molly's gaze and smiled. A young girl, blond braids tracking down either side of her head and a wide smile pressing her dimples deep into her cheeks, walked toward them. She relied on an extended white cane to navigate the short distance between the cars.

Drew called out, "Ella Bella."

"Uncle Drew!" The joy in Ella's voice was unmistakable. "Now you can help Dad. He won't let Mom help. Even though she's pregnant, Mom could still get the dog faster than anyone else."

Sophie slipped from the passenger seat of the SUV, put a hand on her stomach and joined them. She set her other hand on Ella's shoulder. "Thanks for the vote of confidence, Ella. But I'm not sure how fast I could be with these two babies weighing me down."

"Still faster than Dad," Ella whispered.

Sophie laughed, then introduced herself and Ella to Molly.

Ella folded her walking stick and reached for her mom's hand. "Can I meet baby Hazel?"

"I think Hazel would like that." Molly moved closer to Ella and Sophie.

"Hazel hasn't been able to stop watching you, Ella." Wonder eased into Drew's words. "Each time you talk, Hazel's smile grows bigger."

Ella beamed. "Hazel's like the baby sister I never had."

"What about the twins?" Sophie rubbed her lower back.

"They might be boys and then I won't get a sister." Ella's eyebrows lowered, then lifted. "So, I need to claim Hazel right now."

Hazel giggled and waved her arms.

"Did you hear that?" Ella clapped. "Hazel agrees too."

"From what I've heard, Ella, you are quite an expert on all things baby." Molly shifted Hazel so her daughter's back was against Molly's chest and stood in front of Ella.

"Evie and I have been researching and teaching everyone." Wisdom coated Ella's musical voice. She added a sage nod to reinforce her words. "Babies are a lot of work."

"I wish I'd had you with me when Hazel was born," Molly said.

"Well, you have me now." Ella clasped her hands together. "Can I meet the sister of my heart now?"

"You sure can." There was a catch in Molly's voice.

Drew edged beside Molly and Hazel.

Sophie guided Ella closer. Ella reached out both arms, but paused. Indecision shifted across her kind face. She chewed her bottom lip. Drew stepped forward to intervene. Ella always asked permission to touch someone's face to learn who they were. But Hazel was only a baby.

Molly's sweet child reached out and grabbed Ella's hand first. Her tiny fingers curled tightly around Ella's, as if Hazel were claiming Ella. Sisters of the heart indeed.

No further permission was required.

Drew cleared his throat.

Molly dabbed at her eyes.

Ella, refusing to release Hazel's hold on her hand, patted Hazel's cheek with her free hand. The young girl touched Hazel's cotton headband and her grin blossomed into recognition. "I wear these too, Hazel. We're going to get along perfectly. I already have so much to tell you."

"Ella, you'll have to talk to the baby later." Brad walked up, hands on his hips. The tenderness in his gaze ruined his attempt at a serious frown. "I need some help before the puppies decide the sewage drain looks like a fun place to play."

"Puppies?" Molly glanced at Drew.

Drew shrugged, then introduced Hazel and Molly to his older brother.

"That's right. There are five sad puppies and their mom looks sick," Brad said. Concern suddenly washed over Ella's face. "We have to save them as soon as possible."

"And we're going to." Drew leaned over and kissed Ella's forehead. "Right now."

Ella's eyebrows bunched together. "Uncle

Drew, do you know what you're doing? This is a dog rescue, not a courtroom."

"I have your dad to explain it all to me." Drew slapped his hand on Brad's shoulder. "He likes to tell me what to do all the time. He's been doing it since we were kids."

Brad elbowed Drew in the ribs. "You better listen a lot more than you did back then."

Sophie sucked in a breath and touched her stomach.

Brad scowled. "Please, Soph, you need to sit down."

"I can't tell you what you need to do from inside the car," Sophie argued. "You can't hear me."

Drew opened his mouth. Molly cut him off. "I have an idea."

Everyone turned to look at her. Molly continued, "If Sophie doesn't mind holding Hazel, I can stand with Ella near the car. We can pass on Sophie's instructions and relay to Sophie what you two are doing wrong."

"I should take offense at that." Brad chuckled. "But it's a good plan."

"We'll collect the puppies." Ella beamed.

"We have a laundry basket for them." Sophie took Hazel and cradled the little girl against her chest. "Aren't you precious?"

Ella placed her hand on the back of Molly's arm and ran through a quick recitation on how to guide a visually impaired person. Drew waited for the pair to get into position in front of the SUV, which was close enough to hear Sophie in the front seat and within calling distance of the dumpsters.

Molly kept her head tilted toward Ella. His niece had launched into a running commentary, but Drew wasn't close enough to hear the topic. Only saw Molly's quick smile, Ella's animated expressions and their shared laughter. Molly had taken to Ella as quickly and easily as Hazel had. He wanted to tell himself it wasn't anything unusual. But he'd witnessed the discomfort of strangers around Ella and understood Molly's reaction was special. She'd never blinked, never hesitated. Never treated the sweet little girl unlike the sweet little girl that she was.

And that made Drew even more captivated by her.

Brad slugged Drew on the shoulder. "You going to help or just stand there staring at Molly?"

"I was watching out for Ella," Drew argued.

"You were staring." Brad's laughter bounced around the alleyway. "Don't deny it."

Drew closed his mouth and conceded. Molly intrigued him. It was nothing he couldn't manage. He followed his brother farther into the alley toward the twin dumpsters behind Tally's Corner Market.

"Here's the situation." Brad knelt and pointed at the two dumpsters. It turned out a black-and-white dog was squeezed against the back wall between the dumpsters. Five tiny dirty puppies huddled near her. "The dumpster that we need to move is too rusted to roll more than an inch."

"So, we lure the mother out." Drew watched the mother dog panting. Her intelligent eyes remained fixed on him and his brother. "And the puppies will follow."

"I think we scoop the puppies out and come back later for the mother." Brad picked up a long pole with a net on the end.

"Sophie says you can't leave the mom here," Molly called out. "Absolutely no dog can be left behind."

Brad shook his head. "I swear my wife has supersonic hearing."

Drew glanced over at Molly and Ella. Molly arched an eyebrow at him as if challenging him to argue. She'd lost her earlier apprehension. Determination was etched on her face now.

"On second thought, if we get the puppies out, maybe the mother will come forward to find them." Drew dropped to his hands and knees on the pavement to look underneath the dumpster. The puppies squirmed. The mother dog, obviously exhausted, laid her head on the ground. Even her panting sounded frail. Only her gaze tracked the brothers' movements. Drew agreed no dog would be left behind. No matter if he had to crawl between the dumpsters himself.

Drew and Brad worked in tandem to separate the closest puppy from its siblings.

"Using the right tone of voice, make sure you tell the mom that you mean no harm," Molly suggested. "She should understand."

Drew peered up at the duo by the car. Ella held on to Molly's hand, while Molly's focus was fixed on the dumpsters. They both chewed on their bottom lips.

Drew offered more assurances to the mother dog and wanted to do the same for Molly and Ella. Finally he and Brad scooted the first puppy close enough for Brad to scoop it up. The second puppy proved larger, sturdier on its feet and required less scooping.

Ella and Molly cheered behind them.

Brad wrapped the wriggling puppy in a towel that Sophie had given him earlier and eyed Drew. "Molly find anything yet to help your case?"

"Yes. But I need a last-known residence or location for Gina Hahn." Drew burrito-rolled the next puppy, thankfully smaller than the last, in another towel and tucked it into Brad's arms beside its sibling.

Molly intercepted the puppies, kissed each one on its head and promised they were now safe. Then she placed them carefully in the laundry basket beside her before she grinned at Drew. "Sophie wants you to stay within sight of the mother, so she doesn't get too anxious."

Drew nodded and marveled at Molly. Ella and she had launched into a puppy name discussion after Molly described each dog's coloring and personality to Ella. Molly had gone from cautiously reserved to fully invested.

He dropped into view of the mother dog and gave her more encouraging words. He worked to nudge the third puppy, all black except for one white paw, toward him. With the puppy handed off to Brad, he worked on the last two puppies, all the while talking softly to the mother. Behind him, the name debate continued.

The only hold-up in the rescue came from Brad. His brother had wiped his hands on his jeans and pulled out his cell phone. One quick call to his PI office and his request made, he looked at Drew. "Should have the information on Gina Hahn in about fifteen minutes."

"Thanks." Drew dropped back onto the pavement and considered the mother dog. "Let's finish this, okay, mama? So Molly and I can get to work on my case..." he tried.

Drew had to remind himself Molly was his legal counsel, not his dog-rescue partner, or a part of his family, no matter how seamlessly she fit in.

Fifteen minutes later, the smelly dog hadn't shifted an inch and had even ignored offered food. Since they'd made no progress on moving the mother, Drew and Brad stood shoulder to shoulder and regarded the dumpsters.

Molly stepped up beside them and pointed at the rusted bin. "Good work, guys, but you've got no choice. You have to roll the dumpster out of the way to get to the mommy dog. Sophie agrees with me."

Determination strengthened her words and she lifted her chin. She'd become the dog family's advocate. Molly was a fighter. She always had been. And Drew knew she'd fight for him too.

Brad's shoulders dropped. "Why did I know we were headed for this?"

"Because you know Molly is right." Drew peered inside the old dumpster. "At least it's empty."

The brothers managed to pull and shove the dumpster far enough away from the wall for Drew to squeeze in and reach the mother dog. He noticed her injured hind leg immediately and shouted to Brad for advice.

Molly yelled back. "All you can do is move her carefully, Drew. Don't cause her any more pain, okay?"

Unsure of how he was supposed to accomplish that, Drew only nodded, then crouched onto one knee beside the hurt dog. He set his hand on her ribs, pressing against her too thin skin and matted fur. "I've got really worried mothers out there. If we don't get you out of here, they're going to be really mad at me. Upsetting a mom is a really bad thing."

The dog tilted her head to peer at him, revealing her one pale blue eye and one brown eye. Drew kept his gaze locked on the dog's and tightened his hand under her rib cage.

Praise and prayers issued, one on top of the other, Drew finally lifted the dog into his arms. She whimpered twice, but rested her head on his bicep.

He worked his way out from behind the dumpster and barely missed bumping into Molly.

"You got her." Relief with a flash of worry creased her face. "She's so emaciated. Poor, brave mama."

Drew lifted the exhausted dog into the lowered back seat of the SUV, placing her on a thick blanket beside the puppy basket. He stroked the mother dog between her ears. "Sophie will make sure she recovers and thrives."

The dog set her paw on Drew's arm. He stilled.

Beside him, Molly gasped. "Look. It's like she's thanking you."

"That's exactly what she's doing." Sophie sniffled from the front seat. Tears tracked down her cheeks.

Brad handed a box of tissues to his wife. "It's not the pregnancy bringing on the tears either."

Ella nodded. "Mom always cries after every rescue. Always."

Molly leaned in and pulled a tissue from

the box. She dabbed at her eyes and shrugged at Drew. "I've gotten more emotional since giving birth. I've learned to just go with it."

Drew agreed. There was something very right about Molly displaying her feelings without apology. He took Hazel from Sophie, grabbed Molly's hand as if that were the most natural thing in the world for him to do and walked to his truck.

"There was something so powerful about this." Molly blew her nose. "I can't explain it."

"A mother's bond translates across cultures and to the animal kingdom. That's what Ella tells me anyway." Drew wiped the drool from Hazel's mouth. "You understood her need to protect her babies."

Molly opened the truck door and took Hazel into her arms. "Yes. That I do understand very well."

The resolve in Molly's tone caught Drew's attention. He knew nothing about her ex or her situation. But he suddenly wanted to fight for her too. Drew waited for Molly to settle Hazel in her car seat, climb into the passenger seat and shut her door.

He walked around the front of his truck, trying to outdistance his thoughts. He wasn't Molly's champion. She'd never needed one.

Hadn't asked him to rescue her now. He'd never been anyone's hero. He'd only ever upheld justice.

But the urge to defend Molly followed him into his truck like a dust storm, clouding his vision and his mind. He started the engine, reached for his pinging phone and the immediate distraction. He read the text from his brother and grinned. "What do you want to know about Gina Hahn?"

"What do you have?" Molly unzipped her briefcase and pulled out a legal notepad. "I will work with any lead."

"We have more than a lead." Drew handed Molly his cell phone and backed out of the alley. "I'm thinking we're heading to Girasoli Ristorante for lunch."

"Your brother is good." Molly stared at the phone. "He got more information about Gina, specifically that she uses her mother's maiden name as her last name. And he included her relationship history and current status—single and never married. It's more than I would've known to ask for."

"Brad is one of the best," Drew said. "And his people are even better."

Molly set the phone in the cup holder. "I'm

going to keep him on speed dial if you don't mind."

"Not at all." What he minded was his pre-occupation with everything Molly. From her patience with Hazel to the lightness in her smile as she and Ella debated puppy names, even when she was teasing him. Her gentleness couldn't be ignored. Her kindness and thoughtfulness extended from her family, to his family and friends, to the rescued dogs.

Fortunately Molly spent the entire drive to the Italian restaurant scribbling notes on her legal pad. Hazel napped. And Drew kept his attention on minding the traffic and following the GPS directions to the eatery located north of the city across the Golden Gate Bridge.

If only he could direct his interest in Molly back to the professional and away from the personal.

CHAPTER TEN

MOLLY TOOK STOCK. A mother dog and her puppies successfully rescued—check. Gina Hahn located, thanks to Drew's brother—check. And Hazel was dozing blissfully in the back seat—check, as well. It all made Molly's mood optimistic. That was good because she was looking for a solid point of entry into Drew's case. A place to begin her investigation into the seemingly perfect district attorney. She was hopeful Gina might know something important, even if the former administrative assistant considered the information trivial. The key would be persuading Gina to help them.

The staccato voice of Drew's navigation system disrupted the silence. Molly rearranged the legal notepad on her lap and made an outline of possible questions. She paused once to take in the beautiful view from the Golden Gate Bridge and to peek at Hazel asleep.

It wasn't long before the hostess of Girasoli Ristorante led Molly and Drew onto an outdoor covered patio at the back of the restaurant. A busboy carried over a high chair for Hazel. Menus were handed out, and the hostess slipped back inside.

Molly noticed Drew's focus was fixed on the waitresses walking in and out through the swinging door to the kitchen.

Molly snapped a bib around Hazel's neck and scattered a handful of toasted cereal onto the high-chair tray. The three of them looked like any other family spending their lunch hour together. But this was work. Dog rescues and family introductions aside, Molly had a job to do and a client counting on her. "Do you recognize anyone?"

"I do." Drew straightened in his chair and tipped his chin. "Gina is coming to our table now."

Gina Hahn strode up to the table. The deep red stripes in her glossy black hair highlighted a spark of irritation in her brown eyes.

"Gina. It's good to see you." Drew offered the woman a small smile. "It's been a while."

"Ha. I worked at the DA's office for four years. I've been gone from there for almost two years. In all that time, you never came to my family's restaurant." Gina tapped her pencil against her order pad. "But now, suddenly, you're here. It's no coincidence, is it?"

Drew nodded and motioned to Molly. "Gina, this is my friend and legal counsel, Molly McKinney and Molly's daughter, Hazel."

Gina tucked her pencil behind her ear and her notepad in her apron, then shook Molly's hand. She gave an exaggerated wave to the baby and followed it with a cute drawn out, "Hey, Hazel."

Molly quietly watched as the woman's demeanor relaxed the more she interacted with Hazel. Molly unfolded her napkin, set the white fabric across her lap. She hoped she sounded casual. "Gina, I'm sure you're aware of the charges against Drew."

Gina moved beside Hazel's high chair and pulled a bright pink uninflated balloon from her apron pocket. "I keep up with the news."

"We wanted to talk to you about the DA's office." Molly stepped into the lead, kept her tone professional and her words direct. Molly and Drew had practiced mock trials and witness depositions while stealing French fries from each other's lunch plates in law school. If only a French fry swap was the objective now. "Specifically, we'd like to know about your time working as an administrative assistant for Cory Vinson."

"I was fired." Gina inflated the balloon, tied the end and began twisting it. Her face was pleasant, her movements unrushed as if she were discussing nothing more serious than the weather. Only she never made eye contact, not with Drew. Not with Molly. Gina added, "It was an immediate termination for doing my class homework on my work computer during my lunch breaks. There's a policy that states the property of the district attorney's office cannot be employed for personal use."

"That's unfortunate." Molly aligned the silverware on the table in front of her and worked to align herself with the young woman. "Usually, written warnings and measured work assignments are given before termination."

"That would be due process. It only exists at Cory Vinson's whim in his world." Gina completed three more twists on the balloon, creating what looked like the front of a poodle. "As Drew knows."

Drew's shoulders rolled back. "Do you know something about the charges against me?"

Gina lifted one shoulder. Again, nothing disturbed her pleasant expression or easygoing manner. "Only what I've read online or in the newspapers and heard on TV. The same as everyone else."

"But you were Cory's lead administrative assistant," Drew countered.

Finally Gina lifted her gaze and looked directly at Drew. "And you were Cory's favorite assistant district attorney."

Hazel patted her palms against the highchair tray and bounced in her seat. Her attention fastened on Gina's balloon animal. Gina completed her balloon dog with a poodle puff to the end of the tail and presented her creation to Drew. She added, "Curious, isn't it? We're both no longer at the DA's office, but Cory Vinson is."

"Another coincidence." Drew tapped the balloon dog's nose against Hazel's cheek. He smiled when Hazel laughed, then set the animal on the table in front of her.

Gina skipped her attention to Molly. "Drew always told his paralegals and research assistants that coincidences were messages. That they had to find the connection and it wouldn't always be obvious."

Molly glanced at Drew. "That's good advice."

Drew swirled the ice around in his water glass. "It's what I believe."

"I shared it with my professors when I was still in school." Gina stretched out another balloon. "It always stuck with me."

"Then you know it's no accident we're here." Molly added more dried cereal to Hazel's tray.

"It's no accident I'm here either." Gina's eyebrows lifted as she blew up the balloon.

Drew ran his palm over the table. "Gina, you're connected to the DA's office."

"I *was* connected to that place." Gina tied the end of the blue balloon in a quick knot as if she wanted to tie off her past too. "But that's behind me. And I want it to stay that way."

Molly shifted and thought she caught the slightest fragment of uncertainty in Gina's gaze. Whether real or a trick of the afternoon sun, she wasn't certain.

An older gentleman, his gray hair thin on top and his waistline soft, stepped beside Gina. "My daughter is the best balloon creator in the Bay Area. I taught her myself when she was young."

"Papa, you're too kind. This is my father and

owner of Girasoli, Antonio Porta." Gina expanded a second blue balloon. Hazel squealed. Gina smiled. "Papa always made balloon animals for my sister and me. Now I make them for my daughter and our patrons' kids."

"I remember when my granddaughter was this age. So precious." Affection was laced in Antonio's accent. He held his hand out to Gina, wiggled his fingers and grinned. She placed several balloons on his open palm. "My granddaughter is a princess. I believe all daughters are princesses."

Molly liked Antonio instantly. His love for his family was endearing. But this wasn't a fun family lunch. She needed real information. Something more than the fleeting thought that she'd like to return for a casual lunch with Drew and Hazel. "Antonio, how old is your granddaughter?"

Antonio made quick work of his balloon crown and revealed it to the table as if he were presenting a fine piece of jewelry. Then, with the flair of the crown jeweler, he placed the crown on Hazel's head. "My grandbaby, she turned two last month."

Molly picked up her glass of ice water and sipped. The cold water sent a shiver over Molly's skin. Or perhaps that was the rush of energy returning, the kind she'd sought yesterday in her apartment with Drew. Gina left the district attorney's office two years ago. The same exact time Drew took over the case. And now Gina's daughter was two. Brad's information had indicated Gina had never been married. Gina might have told Elena she wasn't interested in having a boyfriend, but perhaps Gina had simply wanted to keep her relationship secret. And dating her boss would definitely qualify as secret worthy. The timing could not be a coincidence. Molly tried to signal to Drew over her water glass.

His head lifted, but he kept his attention on adding Gina's balloon kitten and elephant to the collection gathering on the table. Then he busied himself organizing the animal display for Hazel.

Molly adjusted Hazel's crown and guided the conversation into informal territory, hoping to establish a connection. "I've been told two is a very busy age. Hazel already keeps me on my toes."

Antonio released a deep rumbling laugh. "My granddaughter is always on the go. Same as her mother was."

Gina finished a horse and set it on the

table beside the others. She wrapped her arm around her father's waist. "Don't let him fool you. My dad is the busiest one in the family."

"Family." Antonio's bushy eyebrows arched high onto his forehead. "If you have that, then you have everything you'll ever need."

Family mattered. So did Drew and Gina. She worked on the connection—the one that would lead to trust and eventually to information. She was intentional. Some would say cold and methodical. But she had to be. "How long have you owned Girasoli?"

"Three generations. My wife and I cook. My other daughter bakes." Antonio's chest puffed out. "It hasn't always been smooth sailing, but we've weathered every storm together. As it should be. Right, Gina?"

Gina's hands fluttered in front of her as if she'd suddenly lost her balance. But she recovered and quickly pulled out her notepad and seemingly her focus. "I should take your lunch order. It is why you're here after all."

Molly opened her menu. She scanned the contents, but her mind skimmed over the variety of choices. Too many questions about Gina and her young daughter crowded her thoughts.

Drew asked, "Do you have any chef recommendations?"

"I can recommend the pappardelle in a Bolognese, topped with aged Parmesan," Antonio offered and snapped his fingers. "Of course, the four-cheese spinach manicotti are handmade and the wild mushroom ricotta raviolis too. Both are exceptional and quite popular today."

"You had me at handmade." Molly smiled. "I'll have the raviolis."

Drew touched his stomach as if he were famished. "The same please."

"I'll prepare a delightful ricotta pancake for the princess." Antonio winked at Hazel, pressed his palm over his heart. "They are my granddaughter's favorite."

"That would be wonderful," Molly said. "And very much appreciated. Hazel will definitely enjoy more than toasted cereal."

Gina finished writing in her notepad and looked up. "I'll bring your fresh bread basket soon. Let me know if you need anything else."

Gina hurried inside the restaurant. Antonio strolled down the patio to check in on another table of guests, once again releasing his deep rumbling laugh. Hazel giggled too.

Drew picked up the horse-shaped balloon and turned it over in his hands. "I know what you're going to ask, Molly."

"Really?" Molly claimed the poodle. "What is that?"

"Can I learn to make balloon animals too? That way, we'll always have entertainment at whatever dining table we find ourselves at." Drew lifted his gaze to hers.

Laughter rushed out of Molly, before she could think better of it. He'd always made her laugh during their mock-trial practices. Or before midterm exams. Or after all-night study sessions. As if he always recognized when she'd gotten too serious and had forgotten to take a moment to relax. She smiled. "That's exactly what I wanted to know."

Drew set the horse into a make-believe gallop over the dishes to Hazel's delight. "And yes, there were rumors of a romance in the department. One that involved Cory."

"I thought you never listened to office gossip." Molly perched her dog beside her water glass as if it needed a drink too. And she held on to the laughter—the lightness inside her— that reminded her fun was allowed. And even welcomed in her life.

"I listened when Elena told me something."

Drew slowed the horse and set it next to the others. "If Elena was pausing her work to pass along gossip, it was usually interesting or entertaining. And often times true."

"Who was the other half of Cory's office romance?" Molly set her elbows on the table and leaned toward Drew.

"That's the piece no one ever figured out." Drew shook his head. "It amused Cory. He always liked to hear the guesses, which made me think he could've started the rumor."

Molly snatched one of Hazel's dry cereal pieces and popped it into her mouth. Hazel squealed and handed Molly another. Molly asked, "For what purpose?"

"It kept people talking about him," Drew said. "Kept him the main topic of discussion. But the conversation stopped during his run for DA."

"That seems odd. Because he wanted to protect his upstanding image maybe? And there was you at the same time taking over on the Van Solis case." Molly wiped a napkin across Hazel's chin. "And when did Gina leave?" she asked, although she knew the answer.

"The same time I came on board with the Van Solis case," Drew repeated.

"That was all two years ago."

Drew looked at her and nodded. "Same age as Gina's daughter."

Another waiter dropped off their meals and Hazel's ricotta pancake, grated fresh Parmesan over their plates and refilled their water glasses. Molly said, "There are no coincidences, only connections."

Drew nodded again and pierced a ravioli with his fork. "Let's eat and figure out another way to access those connections."

Gina checked on them once, then returned to drop off the bill. Molly wiped off Hazel's face and hands, then passed her to Drew. "Can you take her to look at the fountain at the front of the restaurant? She loves water."

Drew snuggled Hazel into his side. "What are you going to do?"

"Use the restroom." And find Gina one last time.

"Meet you at the front." Drew headed off and wove around the tables, in search of the fountain.

Molly walked through the swinging door and located Gina at the bar. "Our meal was excellent, and I appreciate the collection of balloon animals."

"They are always a favorite of the kids." Gina filled a glass with the soda sprayer. "I'm sorry I can't help you or offer any more information for Drew's situation."

"It was a long shot." Molly set a business card on the polished bar top. "This is my information. If you think of anything, please call me."

Gina ignored the business card. "I was just an admin assistant. There's not much to tell."

"Drew told me you would've been an outstanding paralegal. You were always astute, alert and quick on your feet." Skills Molly imagined served the former administrative assistant well in her work and life.

"That's kind." Gina filled another glass and set it on a serving tray. "Those are skills that come in handy here at our family's restaurant."

"And when raising a child alone." Molly hated that she might have to expose the hardworking single mother. She considered Drew's reaction. But she also knew she might not have a choice. She had a job to do and she had to accept the cost. "I know the struggles of single parenting. I'm living it."

"Then you also know every decision we make is for the benefit of our children." Gina picked up the tray and held it over her shoulder. "Family has to come first."

"Always," Molly said. Everything she did was for her family.

CHAPTER ELEVEN

MOLLY BLEW BUBBLES as she sat on the large blanket she'd spread out on the grass in Brooke's backyard. Hazel reached out, trying to capture the bubbles. Each one she popped brought a burst of giggles.

Brooke and her best friend, Nichole Jacobs, had arrived earlier with the five puppies and their mom that had been rescued yesterday. Brooke had agreed to foster the family. Dan had carried the mother dog into the house to keep her from putting any pressure on her broken hind leg. Brooke and Nichole had taken over puppy care.

After introductions, Molly shared the names Ella and she had come up with for the puppies. They settled on Nala for the mother. And Wish for the mostly black puppy with the one white paw and clear blue eyes. The other puppy names they agreed Ella and her friends would choose.

Nichole stepped out onto the back porch,

Brooke beside her. The two women hurried toward Molly and Hazel.

"The puppies are settled in," Brooke announced. "Nala is comfortable and resting. The family is together in the laundry room."

"I got my puppy fix. Now I've come to sweep up all this cuteness." Nichole dropped onto the blanket and scooped Hazel into her lap. "My son, Wesley, is twelve. He's a good kid and funny, but the preteen attitude is not so cute."

"Molly and I are going to decorate the alcove in her apartment tonight." Brooke sat beside Molly. "Transform it into Hazel's happy nook."

"I can help." Nichole walked Hazel through the motions of patty-cake to Hazel's obvious delight. "Please let me help. My house is boys, soccer and football. I want to see happy in the form of pink, sparkles, and sunshine."

Molly replaced the cap on the container of bubbles. She was truly grateful, but she'd been in Brooke's apartment less than a week. It didn't feel right to make too many changes to a temporary place. "It's just a small space."

"But it's Hazel's special space." Brooke touched Molly's arm, her voice sincere. "It has to be perfect."

"I don't want this to be a big deal." Molly ran her hands over her yoga pants. Changes that could quickly be reversed would be fine. Her parents had never allowed her to fully settle in anywhere as a kid. They kept their apartments sterile to ensure the return of their rental deposits. "We've been living out of suitcases for quite a few months."

"Hazel hasn't had her own nursery?" Brooke asked.

"My boyfriend and I broke up when I got pregnant. I left him the same night I told him about the pregnancy. The same night he told me not to expect him to participate in my idea for a little family." She'd returned the following day only to pack the few clothes she'd left at Derrick's condo. Then she tossed her keys on his sleek non-kid friendly kitchen counter.

"Wow. That was brave," Nichole said.

"My pregnancy wasn't easy. Neither was the delivery." Derrick and she had planned to buy a house together—modern, efficient, expensive. That had never happened. Instead she'd stuck to her rented, furnished town house. She added, "Decorating a room for Hazel kept getting put on hold."

"I had Wesley by myself. I moved across the country when I was four months pregnant." Nichole frowned, then shifted until she was eye to eye with Hazel. She sang a couple more lines of pat-a-cake in an exaggerated voice, earning Hazel's rapt attention. "But the reward is our kids," she said as she continued to clap the baby's hands. "They make it worth all the struggles."

"They certainly do." Molly's smile grew along with her daughter's. But it wasn't only Hazel's happiness that filled her with joy. She'd also felt an instant affinity to Brooke and Nichole.

"And you have us." Brooke looped her arm around Molly's shoulders and squeezed her. "And soon, the perfect happy nursery in the making."

"Then it's settled," Nichole said. "It's girls' night after we get the kids off to their Spring Dance tonight."

"I'll text Sophie and tell her the plan." Brooke pulled her cell phone from her back pocket and glanced at Molly. "Wesley, Ben and Ella are best friends and go everywhere together. They've been talking about the dance all week."

"Hazel and I have a gift Ella might like for the dance." Molly grinned and stood up. "Let me get it."

"No, wait. You can give it to her tonight." Brooke tapped her phone screen. "We'll do pictures here before the dance and let the guys drive the kids over to the school."

"Excellent plan." Nichole returned to her patty-cake lessons with Hazel. "I need to go shopping and I personally love any night the guys get carpool duty."

Another hour together in the backyard and the women dispersed. Hazel to snooze, Nichole to shop and Brooke to check on the puppies and Nala. Molly settled onto the couch in her apartment and worked through her notes on Drew's case.

Evening arrived, bringing pizza for the kids and parents, followed by a round of loud preteen groans and grumblings over back-yard pictures. Ella sparkled as much as the rhinestone star headband Molly had bought for her. Wesley and Ben, the girl's two best friends, flanked her on either side, always at the ready to assist, but never overbearing. Their friendship reminded Molly of the kind Drew and she had once shared: easygoing, honest and rewarding. Finally the trio of pre-teens piled into Brad's SUV and headed off to their school dance. Nichole ran to her car to gather her nook decorating supplies. Brooke headed up to the main house for their girls' night snacks.

Molly stood in the doorway of her apartment and watched Drew head toward her. He carried two large boxes marked Office. "These are my personal files from my old office."

Molly held the door open and pointed at her kitchen floor. "Set them there for now."

After their lunch encounter with Gina at the Italian restaurant, Molly had asked Drew if she could look through his files from his time as an assistant district attorney. It was a long shot, but Molly believed in being thorough. And there was a chance Drew had missed something important in his files. One small detail could change the entire course of a trial. But after lunch, Drew's brother had requested Drew's assistance on an important case and Hazel had required a long afternoon nap. Drew's consulting work for Brad had extended into the morning and now was the first Molly had seen of Drew or the boxes.

Anticipation swirled around her. "We're looking through these files tonight."

"I've been recruited." Drew mimicked shooting an invisible basketball into an imaginary basket. "Dan and I need to beat

Nichole's husband, Chase, and Brad on the basketball court first."

"We have our own plans tonight." Brooke squeezed around Drew to set several trays of snacks on the counter. She pulled a sunshine-colored fluffy throw rug from another bag swinging on her arm. "This is Ella's contribution to the nook. I'm going to see how it fits."

Molly grinned. The brightness matched Ella's smile.

"Are you going to talk about me and drink wine," Drew teased.

"This may come as a surprise, but it's not always about you Drew." Sophie strolled inside, cradling a wine bottle in one arm and an apple cider bottle in the other. "And they all get wine. Moms-to-be get sparkling cider."

Drew dropped his arm around Sophie's shoulders. "You can pretend it's champagne."

"And you can pretend I didn't just kick you," Sophie countered.

"Why are we kicking Drew?" Nichole stepped inside, her bun slipping off the side of her head, her hands full of shopping bags. "And do you need more help?"

"We always need your help, Nichole." Brooke laughed from the family room and grabbed several bags from Nichole. "What did you get?"

Molly twisted her hands together. The nook was becoming a bigger project than she'd expected. She'd assumed it would be a quick evening. A rug and a few twinkle lights maybe. It needed to be an early night. She and Drew had to look through his files and concentrate on the case. Decorating felt like procrastinating and that wasn't her work style ever. "I thought fixing up the nook for Hazel was going to be simple."

"This is nothing." Nichole piled the shopping bags near the coffee table. "I don't get to shop for a baby girl ever. I couldn't seem to stop myself. Besides, they grow up so fast, you have to spoil them before time runs out."

"Speaking of girls growing up." Sophie set her bottles on the kitchen counter and glanced at Drew. "Did you see Ella before the kids left?"

Drew's gaze and smile softened. "Yeah. She looks like spring."

Molly forgot her urgency to unpack Drew's office files. Suddenly, she wanted to procrastinate. In that moment, she wanted only to reveal Drew's layers. Finally learn all she could about the man he'd become. What had happened to her boundaries?

Nichole set her hands on her hips. "Did you tell Ella that she looked like spring?"

Drew backed toward the door and massaged his neck. "Maybe."

"Which spring did you tell her she looked like?" Brooke touched her throat as if alarmed. "The one that causes red blurry eyes, runny noses and sneezing from all the pollen? Or the spring that brings rain that flattens hair and washes out curls? Both are great looks, by the way and highly sought-after."

Drew's eyes widened as if he'd stepped in a pollen cloud.

Molly bit into her bottom lip to keep from laughing at Brooke's dry tone. Surely, Drew recognized the women were only teasing him.

The ladies stared at him.

"Ella's lacy dress was pale pink and the same color as her favorite cotton-candy-flavored ice cream," Drew said. "She's wearing her favorite pink lace-up canvas shoes. And she's got a glittery pink ribbon wound through her curly hair like the bottle of stardust she gave me to ensure my wishes come true." His gaze shifted to Molly and locked on her. "That's what spring is. That's what Ella is, fairy dust and joy."

Sophie dabbed at her eyes.

Nichole did the same.

Molly sighed from her heart to her toes. Drew was charming and considerate. Worse, he made Molly sigh again.

Molly wanted someone to remember her favorite things. To think of spring and automatically think of her. Or perhaps it was much more simple. She wanted someone to think of her with genuine affection.

Not Drew, of course. Drew was a client. A peer. A friend she'd started to respect more and more. Nothing wrong in admitting that. As for her sigh, it was nothing more than a glitch.

"Okay, seriously, Drew. We were just trying to mess with you. Have a little fun." Brooke stepped forward and tapped her fist against his shoulder. "And you just had to go ruin it with all your poetic words."

Drew's shoulders relaxed. "You guys are not nice."

"You know what would be nice," Nichole suggested. "If you step onto the basketball court out there and teach our significant others the importance of remembering the little things about us."

"I agree." Brooke opened the bottle of red wine. "Can you please talk to Dan?"

"Oh, and remind your brother that I love lavender-and-rose-scented bath bombs and chamomile tea." Sophie popped the cork of her sparkling cider and toasted Drew with the open bottle. "Those two things will make my entire day. Heck, my entire week."

Drew kept his back to the door and avoided direct eye contact with any of the women. "Anything else?"

"Since you asked…" Nichole's laughter burst free.

Drew gaped and used his back to prop open the door. He escaped outside before Nichole could continue.

Brooke set several wine glasses on the kitchen counter. "How is that man single?

All three women turned to stare at Molly.

"Don't look at me." Molly picked up the wine bottle to start filling the empty glasses. "I haven't seen him in years. I barely know the guy anymore."

But what she'd seen of him the last few days had her wondering the same thing about Drew. Why was he single? Perhaps if she discovered Drew's flaws, she would also discover a way to disconnect her growing interest in him too.

Nichole leaned against the kitchen counter. "But you're seeing him now."

"He's a client." Molly sipped her wine and checked on Hazel in her swing. "And an attorney."

"Same as you." Sophie carefully sat on the sofa and propped her feet on the coffee table.

"And the same as my ex." Molly drank a large sip of wine.

"Workplace romance gone wrong." Nichole slipped her arm around Molly's waist and clinked her glass against hers, "I've been there. Definitely not a good place."

Molly glanced at Nichole and saw only a strong woman who by all accounts had thrived as an entrepreneur and mom. And she saw a friend she could relate to. "I vowed not to have a work romance ever again."

"Here's to not repeating past mistakes." Nichole lifted her glass in a toast.

Brooke joined them. "But we must still have the courage to take risks."

The risk for Molly was getting to know these women better. Becoming friends with Drew's friends. Once the case was over and

Drew returned to his career, would she lose her new friends too?

Nichole settled on the floor in the family room and picked up one of her shopping bags. "You have to see what I found for Hazel's nook."

Molly watched Nichole reveal her finds, from a tie-dyed stuffed elephant, to a moon-and-star light, to a pair of fuzzy blankets. Several pillows and more toys emerged from other shopping bags. Molly picked up a framed picture of a cuddly teddy bear and a quote about the smallest things taking up the most room in a heart. "I thought we said nothing on the walls."

No big changes. Nothing that couldn't be easily dismantled. Easily removed to return the apartment to its former state.

"I'm the landlord and as such I get to overrule you." Brooke revealed a series of wall decals ranging from a princess castle to fairy friends.

Everything was adorable and wonderful. More than Molly would've picked out. It all felt somehow more permanent. Hesitation tempered Molly's words. "But the unit might be harder to rent later."

"This is your home right now." Brooke

hugged a soft heart-shaped pillow Nichole had purchased.

"And it needs to feel like a home, even if it's only temporary." Sophie touched her stomach and eyed Molly. "Everyone needs a home to come back to at the end of the day."

The four-poster queen-sized bed in her room was exactly what Molly would've chosen for her own home. And Hazel deserved more than a suitcase and a playpen. "What do you guys have in mind?"

The women jumped right in. Sophie cut tags off Nichole's purchases and opened packages. Nichole and Brooke debated the exact location for every decal.

Maybe it was the wine. Or the easy banter of the women. But Molly confessed, "I'm worried about finding a nanny. Our day-care experience has been far from what I hoped for. Hazel cries at every pick-up. The director says Hazel just needs more time to adjust." Molly hadn't adjusted and disliked her daughter's continued tears.

"Brad and Drew had a nanny." Sophie assembled the moon-and-star light and chuckled. "Look how well they turned out."

"It's not the turning out. It's more the bonding between me and Hazel. It's my career versus being a mom." Molly pinched her lips together. She'd never been one to overshare or complain. She always handled her own worries. Her own fears. Why was she airing things now?

"Why is it so hard to do it all?" Nichole moved to the end of the dresser Brooke had found in the attic. The guys had carried it in before they left for the drive to the dance. Nichole motioned for Molly to pick up the other end. Together they lifted the antique furniture piece into Hazel's tiny corner.

"It fits great." Brooke watched from the family room. "Better than I thought. As for your question, Nichole. I don't know what you're talking about. I'm doing it all perfectly."

Nichole laughed and tossed a soft plush star at Brooke. "You lie so well."

"As it happens, I have a rogue idea. One that isn't popular among the be-everything-to-everyone moms." Brooke sipped her wine and wisdom filled her gaze. "What really matters is the quality of time spent with our children over the quantity."

"I think I like that." Nichole lifted Hazel from her swing. "Someone needs a diaper change."

Sophie spread a diaper-changing mat across the couch and reached for Hazel. "I've been worried about the pet store, the twins and Ella. They all need me."

"Just be present with Ella, even if it's only ten minutes at a time," Brooke said. "If Ella has all your attention in those few minutes, that's more important. An hour spent with her in the same room with you working on your accounting for The Pampered Pooch isn't the same."

"Why does it sound so simple when you say it?" Molly asked. Brooke gave Molly hope. She wanted to believe quality over quantity. Wanted to believe Hazel wouldn't suffer if she fully pursued her career.

"We are all works-in-progress." Brooke handed Molly her glass of wine.

"Just remember you will miss things." Sophie peeked inside Hazel's diaper and twisted her face into an overblown grimace. Hazel giggled and babbled.

Brooke handed Sophie the baby wipes container.

"Then what do you do?" Molly picked up one corner of the playpen and Nichole the other. In step with each other, the women scooted Hazel's temporary crib, and final piece for her special space, into the small alcove.

"You work hard to be there for the next thing," Sophie said.

"If it's a soccer goal because you showed up late to the soccer game, you celebrate with ice cream before dinner." Nichole picked up her wine glass from the coffee table and clinked it against Brooke's.

Brooke added, "Or you just have an ice-cream sundae dinner."

The women laughed and offered their collective agreement.

"Same goes for class speeches, Christmas performances and art shows." Nichole drummed her fingers against her wine glass. "Try to be there for each one of those, but if you can't, then make arrangements to have it videoed so you watch it together later."

"Don't miss kindergarten graduation for any reason." Sophie finished the diaper change and zipped Hazel's teddy-bear-print onesie up under her chin.

"Or Halloween," Nichole said. "The costumes are a really big deal."

"The most important thing is to learn to forgive yourself." Sophie propped Hazel next to her on the couch and set her favorite floppy-eared pink bunny in her lap. "You aren't going to always get it right. After all, perfect moms are a total myth."

"I feel like I've been getting it all wrong since Hazel's birth." Molly folded a blanket to cover the numerous stains on the llama-print cotton fabric. The ones she'd failed to get out even after several washings. Worse, it was Hazel's favorite blanket and went everywhere they did. She draped the blanket over her arm and considered looking online to order a replacement. "All the books I read…"

"Stop. Right. There." Nichole held up her hand like a strict school-crossing guard, her voice firm. "Those books are wrong."

Molly glanced at Sophie and Brooke. But those books offered sensible, if not sometimes unattainable, solutions. In fact, those books had failed to offer an actual stain-removal suggestion that worked.

Sophie shrugged. "It's true."

"Besides." Brooke walked over to Molly and linked arms, then turned her to face Hazel's makeshift nursery. "You don't need books now. You have us."

"Just look at the baby nook we created tonight." Nichole turned on the moon-and-star light they'd set on a small table out of reach of the playpen. The old dresser from Brooke's attic they'd turned into a usable changing table. And the thick yellow plush throw rug Sophie had borrowed from Ella added a much-needed pop of color and a burst of sunshine in the windowless space.

"Cozy and comfortable," Sophie offered.

"I like it," Brooke said. "A lot. I want to stay here and absorb all the happy."

"It's really perfect for her first nursery." Molly hugged the blanket against her chest. "Thank you."

"No thanks are necessary." Brooke squeezed Molly's arm. "It's what friends do."

Friends. Molly soaked in that one word. Marveled at the instant welcome she'd received. How they'd readily given support. And immediate acceptance.

"Friends also finish wine together." Nichole picked up the bottle and refilled their glasses. "The school dance ends soon."

"And that means our girl time is almost up." Sophie snuggled Hazel into her side and then set her other hand on her stomach. "And I really need to discuss this whole giving-birth-to-two-little-people-at-the-same-time thing. My body isn't ever going to be the same, is it?"

The women laughed, gathered around Sophie and offered their encouragement. For the first time that Molly could remember, she readily joined in.

CHAPTER TWELVE

SHOWERED AND BACK in clean clothes after his basketball game, Drew walked from the Sawyers' house to Molly's apartment. The cold night chilled his still-damp hair. He balanced several packages on top of a large box and knocked on, then opened Molly's apartment door. "I have deliveries for you. They were left on the front porch."

"Perfect. I ordered more baby supplies." Molly grabbed the two soft-sided packages and dropped them on the kitchen counter. She touched the large box Drew held. "This is a new walker for Hazel now that she has more space than a hotel room."

"Want me to put it together now?" Drew set the box in the family room.

"It can wait until tomorrow." Molly pointed to his file boxes. "I'd like to start going through your files tonight."

"Do you really think there's some kind of smoking gun in there?" Drew eyed the office boxes that held more than office supplies and books.

Inside, too many memories lingered. His handwritten notes from every case. His law books highlighted and bookmarked for every one of those cases. Those boxes were a timeline from his first case to his last at the district attorney's office. A road map of his victories and losses. And Molly wanted to search through them. But they brought his past into sharp focus. And made him question himself. If he'd erred on the Van Solis trial, had he made a misstep on other cases too?

"I think this is all part of my job." Molly lifted the first box onto the square kitchen table. "We have to be thorough."

"I'll let you get started." He never imagined one allegation, even a false one, would have the power to shake the foundation of his core beliefs. "I'm going to check on Hazel."

"She's asleep." Molly watched him.

"What if she woke up?" And was scared. No one so little and so very innocent should be afraid. Not even for a minute. If he could protect Hazel, he wanted to.

"I'd have heard her." Molly released the tape and removed the cover from the first box. "She likes to announce herself when she wakes up."

"Still, she could be lying there awake with nothing to do." He knew that feeling all too well. He walked toward Hazel's alcove. His voice deepened into a whisper. "It's only her third night here."

Charges had been levied against him more than a week ago and he still hadn't found his balance. Except with Molly.

Drew peered at Hazel. She'd turned over onto her stomach, pressed her left cheek into the mattress and tucked her knees underneath her. The little girl had turned her pseudo-yoga pose into the most comfortable-looking sleeping position ever. Drew pressed his fingers against her neck, checking to make sure she wasn't too cold or too hot. Molly and Ella had already lectured him about the no blankets in the crib rule. Hazel looked small, fragile and entirely peaceful in the otherwise empty crib.

He watched the lamp swirl soft glowing stars across the ceiling. Shooting stars in a slow-motion arc down the wall. The background faded from pale pink to pale blue to pale lavender. Every color change quieted Drew, evening out his own pulse. Calm.

Hazel and her tiny nook gave him that. He wanted to linger.

But the rustling in the kitchen could not be ignored.

Somewhere between the kitchen and Hazel's nook, the tiniest hint of hope looped around him. Hope that Molly might uncover something. Yet he was afraid to grab on to that thread, only to have it unravel in his hand.

Back in the kitchen, the open box on the floor revealed the titles of various law books, from a law dictionary to a thick volume on courtroom etiquette. Molly sorted through the files. Restless, Drew walked into the kitchen and started to load the plates and wine glasses from earlier into the dishwasher.

"I knew it." Accusation dusted the amusement in Molly's voice.

Uncertain, Drew practically croaked, his voice was hoarse and dry, "What?"

"That you would have candy." Molly held up the apothecary-style candy jar. Empty candy wrappers filled the glass container. "You always liked those butterscotch candies."

"Still do." Drew dried his hands and reached for the candy jar, lifted off the top and sorted through the empty wrappers. He'd always had two things in his office: a full candy jar and a robust supply of pencils. "I always work more efficiently with butterscotch."

"Duly noted." Molly laughed. She peeled the tape off another item, unrolled the wrapping and revealed an oversized coffee mug.

"Best Uncle in the Universe," Drew read the inscription and grinned. Ella hadn't wanted to wait for Christmas morning to give Drew his present. He'd been the only one in the family allowed to open his gift two days early. "Christmas present from Ella. She made me promise to use it."

"So, you brought it to work." Molly tipped the mug toward him. "Have you started drinking coffee then?"

He shook his head, wanting to shake away his satisfaction that she remembered something inconsequential about him. He remembered so much about her. Too much. "I set my coffee mug on a bookshelf in my office to keep it safe. Ella also gave me skeleton-shaped flash drives that year."

"Skeleton," Molly repeated.

"Ella picked them out." Drew smiled and shrugged one shoulder. The skeletons were squat and comical. Whenever he had used one, clients and coworkers had laughed, and then he'd been given an opening to talk about his favorite niece. Bringing Ella into his workday always relieved the tension.

Much like Hazel had been doing for him recently. He backed away from that thought. Hazel wasn't his family. Or his kid. She belonged to Molly, his attorney. And he wasn't about to get attached to either one. He hadn't been cleared and there was still a substantial risk for Molly and Hazel.

Besides, once he got his life back, his career would come first. It always had. "Thanks to Ella, I always know which flash drives are mine. It was sort of genius on her part."

"I'm going to ask her for a flash drive recommendation for myself. I like the way she thinks." Molly walked into the family room and placed the candy jar and mug on the coffee table. "I'll put these back in the box after I finish sorting through your files and paperwork."

Drew fiddled with the child lock on the cabinet door. Finally he succeeded, opened the cabinet and found the dishwasher pods.

"Before you start the dishwasher, add these please." Molly picked up one of the soft-sided packages. "I ordered more baby spoons and forks in fun colors. They can go on the top rack."

She opened the soft-sided envelope and frowned. One shake and a red-and-black flash drive dropped onto the counter. Drew closed the cabinet door and stepped closer to Molly. "What is that?"

"I have no idea." Molly reached inside the envelope, pulled out a folded piece of paper and read out loud. "I kept this for insurance to protect my daughter. Drew needs it more. Please don't contact me again."

Drew reached for the paper. That hint of hope spread through him, but he cautioned himself. Hope could prove to be disappointing. "Gina?"

"No return address. And she didn't sign the note." Molly checked the envelope, then picked up the flash drive. "But it's from Gina."

Molly went into her bedroom and returned with her laptop. She sat on the couch and opened her laptop on the coffee table.

He sat beside her, close enough that his thigh connected with hers as if Molly were that thread of hope he needed.

She logged in and inserted the flash drive into her computer. Glancing at Drew, she said, "Ready to find out exactly what Gina sent us."

Drew leaned forward, propped his elbows on his knees and steepled his fingers under his chin. Anticipation roared through him, but he forced himself to breath normally. "Please let it be more than vacation photographs."

Molly double-clicked on the drive and file folders populated the screen. Her finger tracked down the screen and stopped. "Van Solis." One double click to open the folder and she read out loud, "Witness statement."

Drew leaned in and studied the screen. The disappointment felt overwhelming. His hope crushed. "These are just files from the trial."

"Maybe. Maybe not. Maybe there were files you weren't given access to." Molly opened the witness statement folder and once again used her finger to track the list of document titles.

Drew touched his stomach and convinced himself a late-night snack would relieve his sudden indigestion. What if seeing Gina Hahn yesterday had somehow put her in jeopardy too?

Molly rose, walked over to the dry-erase board, then examined something on her legal pad. She returned to the laptop, cross-checked something on the screen to the legal pad. Triumph widened her gaze. "Look at the date of the witness statement file at the bottom of the list."

Drew read the date twice, then rubbed his hand over his jaw. His pulse picked back up. A new kind of energy—the kind that claimed him when he knew he'd persuaded a jury to the side of justice—recharged him. "That's not the date of the witness interview I have on my calendar. That's ten days earlier."

"Exactly." Molly sat on the couch and clicked the relevant file open.

Her movie player window launched, and the video filled her computer screen. An older gentleman, his head covered by a Bay Area Angel's baseball cap and a matching windbreaker bunched around his lean frame, gripped a soda can in one hand. He ran his other fingers over the conference table as if tracing a scratch. Reuben Cote—the only eyewitness for the Van Solis murder trial.

Drew had spent hours with Reuben during discovery, preparing him for the witness stand. Reuben had always requested orange soda and only ever drank two sodas no matter how long their pretrial sessions had lasted. Reuben had been instantly likeable, humble and believable. His dry wit and down-to-earth manner had endeared him to everyone on the case from the paralegals to the court reporters to the entire jury.

Reuben Cote had recently recanted his testimony from the Van Solis case, so Van had hired one of the top appeals attorneys to get his verdict quashed. Reuben's claim, that he didn't see Van, was responsible for the witness-tampering charges that Drew now faced. Drew tucked away his emotions and focused on the computer screen.

Another man sat across from Reuben, but only his left arm was visible in the video frame. He gripped a pen that he pressed into a legal pad, but said nothing. Reuben went on to describe exactly what he saw on the night of March 17, detailing the crime scene and the victim's body. Yet he never provided a description or any specific information about the shooter. He offered nothing that matched the description of Van Solis. He offered no real proof that Van had shot and killed a local store owner in an apparent robbery gone wrong.

Thirty minutes into Reuben's account, Molly pressed pause on the video. She waited another beat, then spoke softly into the silence. "I very much want to assume that's not the same testimony the witness gave on the stand, under oath, during the trial."

"Not even close." Drew's own voice was hazy, as if he spoke through the smoke of that smoking gun. "Nor was it the statement Reuben gave to me."

"Your witness falsified his testimony." Molly closed the video. "You know what this means?"

Drew's head fell forward. A numbness overtook him. "I knew I was innocent."

"We have exactly what we need to win your hearing." Molly clicked open another folder on the screen. Her disbelief and curiosity framed her next words. "Look at this. There's information about other prior cases in here as well, Drew."

Drew set his hand over hers and stopped her from scrolling through the other folders. "First, let's concentrate on Van. Once the DA is exposed, then we'll determine if there were other wrongful convictions."

"We need the last known address of your witness." Molly grabbed her legal pad. "We need Reuben Cote to testify at your hearing. We need his verification that the other man in the video is Cory Vinson. As it stands, the other man could be anyone. His voice is too quiet to hear on the recording and he never reveals more than his arm."

Drew and Molly remained on the couch, hip to hip, for another two hours. They checked Reuben's statement changing his original testimony to the statement supplied by the appeals attorney who was now leading Van's attempt to overturn his conviction. Without success, they dug into Reuben's past, trying to find possible reasons for his lying under oath. Then finally they opened another bottle of wine and the container with the last of the brownies.

Molly finished her brownie, brushed her hands together and reached for Drew's Best Uncle mug that she'd set on the coffee table earlier. "There's something inside here."

"More candy wrappers most likely." Drew stuffed the last bite of his brownie into his mouth, savored the chocolate and the welcome release of so much stress from his shoulders. It felt like the weight had been lifted.

"A picture." Molly unrolled the photo and pressed a hand over her mouth. Her smile reached her eyes. "I cannot believe you kept this after all these years."

Drew snatched the photograph from Molly

and shook his head. Two college kids, each perched on one of Santa's knees, laughed into the camera. Actually, the photographer had instructed them to shout, *Candy canes rock.* They'd been young, full of dreams, wishes and absolute certainties about their futures. Two friends who'd discovered a connection and shared a moment. He'd been grateful to spend that Thanksgiving week with Molly all those years ago. He was more than grateful now to have her on his side, fighting for his innocence. Without Molly, it was unlikely he would've discovered the evidence they'd found. He owed her.

Drew leaned back against the couch and stared at their Santa photo. "This is still one of my favorite Thanksgivings ever."

"Seriously?" Molly sipped her wine.

"It's one of the few I didn't spend with my nose in a law book the entire time," Drew admitted.

Molly swirled her wine in her glass. "We were good that way, weren't we?"

"What way?"

"We balanced the school and work with the fun," she said. "Remember flag football."

"And trivia nights." He nudged her shoulder with his. "You always hated when you lost."

"I still hate to lose." She laughed and finished her wine. "I don't miss those late-night burrito runs when we left the library after a study session."

"Best burritos in town." Drew touched his stomach. "You always ate half of mine even after you complained you weren't hungry and didn't even want a burrito."

"It always looked better when you were eating it. I don't know why."

"Everything is better together." Drew wanted to swallow those words but it was too late. They were already out. In the sudden quiet, he realized a truth. Things had been better with Molly in his life. *What happened to us?*

Drew cleared his throat. They'd been friends and grown apart. He wouldn't mistake the gratitude and respect he felt for Molly now to be anything more than that. But his gaze returned to the picture and thoughts of Molly as something more rumbled inside his chest.

"I bet you never knew you were my only real friend." Molly scooted into Drew's side, set her head on his shoulder and traced her finger over the picture. "I've really missed you."

He had to admit it. "I've missed you too."

CHAPTER THIRTEEN

MOLLY ANSWERED HER PHONE, greeted the caller and pulled her gaze away from Drew. He stood on the other side of Hazel's stroller, leaning casually against the elevator wall. The elevator that was taking them to the twenty-fourth floor of a high-rise in the financial district and the location of Brad Harrington's offices. Drew had texted his brother last night, letting him know they'd be coming by in the morning.

Hazel had been Molly's sunrise wake-up call. She'd prepared for work between diaper changes, the introduction of a new food texture in the form of oatmeal and an unscheduled bath.

Now, she was supposed to be acting in an official role as Drew's counsel.

Yet Hazel was chewing on a teether in her stroller between them. And Molly had just accepted a personal phone call. Hardly professional and the entirely wrong way to run her practice. But the business and personal lines had been blurred since she'd run into Drew at the courthouse. She would reestablish boundaries after her call.

She shifted, wedging herself into a corner of the glass elevator. As if that suddenly granted her privacy. She quickly finished her phone call.

"Everything okay?" Drew asked.

Molly tucked her phone into her briefcase, not the outside pocket of the diaper bag. She was with a client, not on an adventure to the park. Time to set those boundaries. "Fine."

Drew looked at her. "Are you sure?"

She had to keep the focus on her client and his case. Her personal business was just that…personal. But the concern in Drew's voice and the warmth in his gaze loosened her resolve. The truth spilled out like wine from an overturned bottle, unstoppable. Unavoidable. As if Drew weren't simply her client. As if boundaries never existed. "That was the office of Judge Martina Reilly. I'm filing for full custody of Hazel. I don't foresee any issues, but in case of a hearing, I want to have it here, not Los Angeles. I've been granted time Monday morning to state my reasons in person."

He pushed away from the glass wall. "What do you need?"

She needed him to stop acting as if she could always lean on him and that he would expect her to. To stop being concerned. To stop making her think she could forever count on him. "I think I've got it covered."

Or she would have everything covered after the nanny interviews she'd scheduled for the afternoon at Sugar Beat Bakery. Once she hired a nanny, Hazel wouldn't have to return to the day care. And Molly could concentrate on her practice, follow up on her networking and grow her client list, locate an office space. Then she'd stop looking to Drew as if he were meant to stand by her like a partner in every sense of the word.

He was not hers.

And a picture with Santa from their past and his fondness and affection for Hazel would not change that. Hazel filled her heart and her career filled her life. Nothing more was required.

"I can help if you need me," Drew offered.

The elevator doors opened. Molly stepped behind Hazel's stroller, gripped the handles and blocked Drew from pushing. Time to re-commit to those boundaries. Right now, she had to concentrate on the case at hand and get the information that would help them prove Drew's innocence and restore his career and reputation.

Hazel launched her teething ring into the air as if testing those boundaries. Drew swooped in and caught the colorful ring before it hit the floor.

Drew acknowledged several employees and led Molly and Hazel toward a corner office. He knocked once on the closed door and strode inside without waiting for permission. Molly pushed Hazel's stroller into Brad's office and offered Drew's brother an apologetic smile.

"We need to find this man." Drew slapped a piece of paper on Brad's sleek glass-topped desk. "Now."

"Reuben Cote? Isn't he the one who recanted his testimony recently?" Brad nodded a greeting to Molly and shifted his chair, booting up his computer.

"Yes. He's also the man who will prove I had no part in manipulating a witness," Drew declared.

Brad tapped on his keyboard. "This is welcome news."

Molly wasn't surprised Drew had confided

in Brad. Or that Brad seemingly dropped everything at Drew's arrival to assist his brother. Family first seemed to be an unwritten rule with the two brothers. She'd watched them work together to rescue the puppies and mother dog. Both refusing to give up. Heard their banter and good-natured ribbing on the basketball court the previous night. Remembered Drew talking about his older brother's achievements when Drew and Molly had their reunion.

As an only child, she'd never had that same kind of relationship with anyone. The kind built on a foundation of complete trust and unconditional love. She had Drew for a short while in college. Maybe they could have had that kind of connection. But that seemed a lifetime ago.

She lowered onto one knee and unbuckled Hazel from the stroller seat. She wanted more for Hazel. Wanted her daughter to have a sibling if possible and a bond that no one could take from her. Molly coughed, dislodging her sudden disbelief. She could not be considering more children. She didn't even have full custody of Hazel yet. Or a potential future father in mind.

Her gaze tracked to Drew as if he were the

sign she'd been looking for. But Molly never relied on fate or luck or signs. She wouldn't allow her heart to offer a plea bargain now.

With Hazel propped on her hip, Molly rose and paced around Brad's office, locking down her errant thoughts and restoring her focus.

"Last night, Molly received a package we think came from Gina Hahn." Confidence filled Drew from his easy smile to optimistic tone. "We have actual proof now."

Molly leaped to insert the reality of the situation before Brad jumped on Drew's hope train. "Evidence that is not admissible without a sworn testament from the witness. Nothing is a given yet. We still have a lot of work to do."

Work. Molly had to concentrate on work too. Then she would shake the idea of Drew as her partner for life.

Drew rubbed his hands together and hovered over his brother's shoulder. "Even better would be Reuben attending my hearing."

"Let's locate Mr. Cote first." Brad kept his attention on his computer screen.

"Gina left us more than we could ever imagine." Drew shook his head from side to side as if still stunned Gina had dropped the flash drive on Brooke and Dan's front porch.

"I have more information on Gina Hahn." Brad tapped a purple folder on his desk.

"Keep it." Drew stepped around Brad's desk and scooped a squirming and slightly cranky Hazel out of Molly's arms. He flipped Hazel upside down and transformed her into giggling and content in an instant. "We don't need anything more from Gina."

Molly eyed Drew and Hazel. If only she could have a quick moment in Drew's arms to leave her so content. She squeezed her forehead. Drew's embrace was not part of their attorney–client agreement.

Brad glanced away from his computer screen and shifted his focus from Drew to Molly. "Gina Hahn sounds like a key witness too. Not that I'm a lawyer."

"She gave us the evidence that's gotten us here. There's no reason to keep Gina involved." Drew tipped Hazel upside down again and considered Molly. "You agree, don't you?"

"It's worth taking the folder Brad put together on Gina." Molly moved toward the desk and the purple folder and away from the distraction that was Drew.

Drew lifted Hazel against his chest and

stepped closer to Molly. "Gina asked us not to involve her further."

"We never promised to stay away from her completely." Molly reached for the folder on Brad's desk. "We may need her. You know that."

"We have Reuben Cote." Drew set his hand on her arm, keeping her from picking up the folder. "Gina has moved on. She has a daughter to protect. Her family has a viable business in this city. I don't want to put her or that at risk."

"Even if it means proving your innocence?" Molly set her hands on her hips. "Are you willing to give up your life, your career, to protect Gina's?"

"It's not relevant," Drew argued. "We have Reuben."

"You're too close to this," Molly countered. "You're not thinking clearly."

"For the first time in months, I am thinking very clearly." Drew held his hand up for a Hazel high five. His serious gaze returned to Molly. "I ruined one man's life. I won't do that to Gina too."

Molly straightened. "I won't ruin Gina's life either."

"That's right." Drew nodded. Hazel patted his cheek, tugged on his ear and his hair, but his focus never trailed from Molly. "Because you're going to promise me you won't involve Gina any further. You'll leave Brad's file folder alone, as well as Gina."

Molly crossed her arms over her chest. He hired her to be his counsel. He had to allow her to do her job. Her way, not his. "You have to trust me."

"Just promise me, Molly." He tickled Hazel to get the little girl to release her grip on his hair. "Please."

Please, trust me. Molly tucked the burp cloth over Drew's shoulder to protect his shirt from Hazel's drool. If only it was so easy to protect her heart from him. "Fine."

Drew smiled and looked at his brother. "How much longer?"

"The Cotes cancel phone lines faster than teenagers text." Brad tapped on his keyboard. "And they relocate even more often."

Drew strolled to the door. "I'm going to show off Hazel to the team. They keep walking by and peering inside to see her."

Molly waited for Hazel's laughter to fade in the hallway and stepped up to Brad's desk. "I'd like you to put a twenty-four-hour surveillance on Gina Hahn."

Brad paused and shifted in his chair to face her. "Why?"

"I believe the former administrative assistant is a flight risk." Molly slanted her gaze to the open doorway. She hated to defy Drew. Or break her word. But she had a client to look out for. A job to do. After all, Drew had hired her.

"But you have the information you need from Gina," Brad said.

"I also have a strange feeling in my gut." Not that she only ever relied on her instincts, but she always listened. Like right now. One more quick glance at the empty doorway. "Call it a contingency plan."

"You're thinking this is all too good to be true. That it's been too easy." Brad returned to his keyboard and computer screen. "Drew will not like this."

"Drew's life is at stake." Molly set her palms flat on the desk and leaned toward Drew's brother. Determination fueled every inch of her. "I don't have time to consider his feelings."

"Just wanted to be clear. Make sure we're both on the same page." Brad stilled and stared at Molly. "Drew will be mad about this. He'll be mad at me, but he'll blame you."

"I know the risks and accept the fallout." Molly pushed off the desk and stepped away. Just as she understood the risks of falling for Drew and why she wouldn't accept that fallout. "I will not lose this case. Or watch Drew's livelihood shatter when Gina or someone else on the sidelines might've been able to change the course of the hearing so that the right decision was made. The same applies to overturning Van's verdict."

Brad pressed a button on his keyboard. His attention never veered from Molly.

Molly crossed her arms over her chest and tipped her chin up. "If you won't do it, I'll find someone who will."

"I like you, Molly. I really like you." Brad rose. A wide smile stretched across his face. "And that twenty-four-hour surveillance is already done. Set it up while we were talking."

Molly's shoulders released. "Just like that."

"Yeah." Brad picked up the folder on Gina and set it on a shelf behind him. "You'll let me know if you want this."

Molly nodded and exhaled. In another life, she would've welcomed Brad as a friend. And an ally. But she knew his loyalty would always remain with his brother. "What about Drew?"

"My brother believes his way is the only way. He's a lot like our mother. Though he'd argue just the opposite." Brad motioned to the open doorway. "But I've learned that other ways are not always wrong. And if it comes from the heart, how can that be wrong?"

From the heart. No, Molly relied on her mind. She'd put an unbreakable wall around her heart. She followed Brad into the hallway. "You know Drew is a client. And I've built a career on leaving my heart out of the courtroom."

"But you technically aren't in the courtroom." Brad stepped around the corner and paused. He tipped his head toward a glass wall, separating a large break room from the offices and cubicles.

Inside the break room, Hazel removed Drew's baseball cap, handed it to a laughing older woman who passed it back to Drew. He settled the hat back on his head and the cycle was repeated. Hazel laughed and squealed. And Molly's heart, the one with the unbreakable wall, squeezed.

Brad opened the door to the break room for Molly to enter.

Drew turned and smiled. "Come on in and join us."

Drew thrust his free arm out to his side as if inviting Molly to step into his embrace. As if welcoming Molly into his inner circle.

As Molly passed by Brad, he murmured, "Are you sure Drew is only a client?"

CHAPTER FOURTEEN

OUTSIDE BRAD'S OFFICE building, Molly paused Hazel's stroller and shoved her sunglasses on. The polarized lenses filtered the sunlight, reduced the glare off the sidewalks and concrete buildings, but failed to do anything about her concern.

She wanted to rush back inside, take the elevator to Brad's floor and convince Drew's brother that, *Yes, Drew is definitely only a client*. She wanted to argue until she removed all doubt from Brad's mind and her own.

"Hazel and I want ice cream." Drew leaned forward and adjusted Hazel's headband.

Molly blinked and focused on Drew. More specifically the one corner of his mouth tipping into his cheek. Boyish and charming. She shouldn't be enchanted. Crossing her arms over her chest, Molly arched one eyebrow. "Hazel told you that she wants ice cream?"

"What kid doesn't want ice cream?" Drew

straightened and stretched his arms to his sides. His voice was good-natured, his smile ratcheting into captivating. "As if she needs to tell me."

"Why ice cream?" Molly asked.

"It's a little early for cocktails." Drew dropped his chin the tiniest of notches and settled his gaze on Molly. "And I really don't think we should bring Hazel into a bar. Bad form and all that. Baby blue here will have too many hearts breaking when she gets older as it is. It's better she learns to avoid bars now," he teased.

Molly adjusted her sunglasses and her surprise. "You're serious?"

"Every day I swear her blue eyes get brighter and wider." Drew grabbed the stroller and spun Hazel around to face Molly. He motioned to Hazel as if in a courtroom presenting newly discovered evidence. "Haven't you noticed that?"

No. Hazel's blue eyes had always been the most prominent feature of her face and reached right into Molly's heart. But she had noticed Drew was much more animated whenever he talked about Hazel, as if she somehow energized the world he saw. Hazel had changed Molly's view, but that was expected, since she was her daughter. "So, we should have ice cream, not cocktails, because…"

"Because I feel like I want to celebrate." He held his hands up, palms out. His tone was buoyant. "I know we have a lot of work to do. I know nothing is settled. But it's the first time I have real hope. That's worth celebrating."

She wanted to celebrate too. With Drew. As if she shared that same full hope. But she couldn't lose her professional objectivity. Attorneys and clients shook hands and retreated to their own homes once their business concluded for the day. Brad had given Drew and Molly the information they needed to contact Reuben Cote. Their time together was now officially concluded. "We can't join you for ice cream." At Drew's frown, Molly quickly added, "I have interviews with potential nannies already booked this afternoon at the Sugar Beat Bakery."

"I should join you guys then." Drew settled his hands on the stroller handles as if he intended to do just that.

Molly sputtered. "Why?"

"Second opinion." Drew turned the stroller toward the street corner. "You're a first-time mom. You need to hire a nanny. What if you miss something and hire the wrong nanny?"

"And you believe you're qualified to pick out a nanny?" Molly walked beside him, unable to think of a good way to shake off Drew. He'd outrun them for sure. Her heels were not conducive to running. And she'd already told him their destination.

"Well, growing up I had nannies, so that might qualify me to pick out a good one, but not necessarily." Drew tipped his head at her, then pressed the crosswalk button on the light pole. "Also, I'm pretty good at reading people and can spot a liar or a fraud quickly. Reuben Cote notwithstanding."

"You think my nanny candidates are going to be lying about their qualifications?" Molly asked.

"I hope not." Drew waited a beat before he pushed the stroller into the crosswalk.

Molly appreciated his caution. And his protective nature.

He added, "But who wants to hire a nanny without experience? No one, so, you'd have to embellish your résumé."

"Tell me again what you bring to the table for these interviews?" Molly lifted the front of the stroller onto the sidewalk. "You're going to know that a candidate is overselling herself."

"A second opinion is what I bring," Drew said. "You can't just leave Hazel with the first nanny you meet because she's available. You can't do that to this cutie. It'll leave an indelible mark."

Molly chewed on her bottom lip. She already worried Hazel's bad two weeks at the Tiny Sweet Giggles Day Care had left a permanent bad memory with her daughter. But Molly had to hire a nanny quickly. Though Drew offered a good point. Would urgency shadow her objectivity? Perhaps Drew could help. "Do you have a scar from an old nanny experience?"

Drew shook his head. "We had terrific nannies. Hazel deserves the same."

Molly studied him for a long moment. "You aren't going to leave, are you?"

"Took you long enough to catch on." Drew smiled. "Besides, Hazel and I can have cupcakes at the bakery and still celebrate."

Molly shook her head. He was determined to have a celebration. Would he be as relentless as a father? As committed as Molly was to being the best parent she knew how to be. She shifted the diaper bag to her other shoulder—the one closest to Drew as if she required a physical barrier between them.

She certainly required more than her imaginary boundaries. Boundaries she kept breaching. Drew's skills as a parent were not her concern. His parenting style had no bearing on his hearing or its outcome. But envisioning Drew as a dad had too much impact on Molly's heart.

She had not moved to San Francisco to add to her family, she admonished silently. She'd moved to restart her career and give Hazel and herself a better life.

Drew would make a great father. That much Molly admitted. As for her own family, it was fine the way it was. And that, Molly determined, wasn't negotiable.

To expand her family, she would demand love. But love was never simple—all too often it was painful and required more than Molly could give. She'd simply love her daughter with all she had and that would be enough.

At the next street corner, Molly tugged on Hazel's blanket and pointed out a pigeon. Then she launched into one of her favorite games of I spy with Drew.

Twelve blocks later, Molly laughed and rubbed at her eyes. "I give up. What looks like it has absorbed the last rays of the sunset, always catches people's attention and belongs to only one special person?"

"I'm not telling," Drew teased. "I might keep it for our next battle."

Molly held open the door to the Sugar Beat Bakery and stared at Drew. "You can't do that. I'm sure it's a rule."

"Oh, really." Drew pushed the stroller into the store and paused when he was beside Molly. He leaned toward her and whispered, "In that case, the answer is your hair."

Molly sputtered. *Her hair.* Drew compared her hair to the sunset? Her mother had only ever lamented Molly's hair—it wasn't red enough. Nor was it blond enough. Her mother considered Molly's hair color indecisive and set out to make sure her daughter never acted accordingly. *Never settle for the middle ground, Molly. Take a stand.*

She should take a stand now and demand that Drew retract his statement. Remind him that she wasn't special. Couldn't be special. Not to him. That disrupted those pesky boundaries.

Drew parked Hazel's stroller near a corner table and waited for Molly to join them. He took her order and walked to the service counter. Molly settled Hazel into a high chair, pulled out her stack of nanny résumés and pushed her wayward thoughts of Drew into the to-be-dealt-with-later category.

AFTER TWO HOURS of sitting in the bakery, Molly watched the fourth nanny candidate leave the Sugar Beat Bakery, then stared at the bottom of her empty coffee cup. Too many espressos consumed, and her list of potential nannies had dwindled. Thanks in part to the man beside her. And to think she'd been relieved that Drew had insisted on joining her for the interviews.

"She was definitely all wrong." Drew marked a thick line across the list on her sheet of paper.

"I liked her." Molly frowned into her cup.

"Did you like the faint smell of smoke on her?" Drew asked. "Or her wrinkled shirt and pants?"

"She could've walked through a smoker's cloud of exhale outside on the sidewalk." Molly tapped her mug as if it would automatically refill. As if more caffeine would solve her not-having-a-nanny issue. Only asking Drew and his common sense to leave would do that.

Molly was desperate for childcare that would work for Hazel. She couldn't keep disqualifying a candidate for being late or having too stern a smile or bad breath or a weak handshake. Even though Molly noticed every one of those details and others that had given her pause. On the other hand, Hazel couldn't join Molly in the courtroom, or go along to a deposition or a witness interview. A criminal defense attorney distracted by a baby and asking for a recess for a diaper change hardly instilled confidence in her potential clients.

"Hazel didn't like her." Drew leaned toward Hazel, held out a wilted piece of lettuce from his sandwich and shook his head. "We didn't like her, did we?"

Hazel scrunched up her nose and shook her head back and forth, mimicking Drew.

"She's making the face at the lettuce." Molly's voice was dry like the crumbs from their shared cupcakes.

Drew dropped the lettuce leaf back on his plate and launched more rationale at her. "Hazel refused to go to that woman. That has to count for something."

Molly wanted Hazel to like the nanny, but not prefer the nanny over her. If Hazel took time to warm up to her nanny, was that so bad? "All babies around nine months like Hazel go through separation anxiety and only want their mom. It's completely normal."

Just as Molly's feelings were normal. She still wanted to be the center of Hazel's life. Surely, that wasn't wrong.

Drew held his hands out to Hazel. The sweet girl reached for him, her smile growing. "She likes me."

Molly liked him too. Too much.

Drew set Hazel on his lap and tucked her into his side. "Who's up next? Hazel and I are ready to meet her."

"The next one is fifteen minutes late." Molly avoided looking at Drew, picked up his pen and made a deep *x* across the nanny's résumé.

The bells on the coffee shop chimed. Molly lifted her head to see Evie Davenport and Ella step inside. Evie waved and leaned down to speak to Ella. The young girl's smile brightened. The pair made their way over to the table.

Evie grinned. "You two look like you need some of my special blend Irish coffee, not the tame version you can get here."

"The nanny interviews aren't going as well as expected," Molly admitted.

"Do you want some help?" Ella asked.

"We're here on our weekly Friday afternoon coffee and sugar run for The Pampered Pooch staff." Evie checked her watch. "But we have a few minutes if you'd like another opinion."

"Please." Molly pulled out two empty chairs. Perhaps Evie would help convince Drew that some candidates deserved a second interview. Another chance to make a better impression.

Evie guided Ella into the chair beside Hazel's high chair and walked to the counter to place an order.

Drew deposited Hazel back into the high chair, putting her closer to Ella to the girl's obvious delight. Ella reached out until her hand touched the high-chair tray and Hazel immediately gripped Ella's fingers. Ella laughed. Hazel grinned. Then Ella launched into a childhood song about the wheels on a bus. Hazel babbled and hummed. The baby's gaze never left Ella as if the preteen transfixed her.

Molly set her palm over her chest. The girls' immediate bond hugged her heart. Had her considering more children once again.

That sibling factor. But a family of two was perfect.

Drew leaned closer and bumped her shoulder. "Hazel did not react like that to any of your nanny candidates."

"Do you want me to invite the nannies back for a second interview and a sing-along?" Molly couldn't quite stall the frustration from slipping into her voice. Why couldn't she see Drew as a peer who needed her help?

He pulled back. "I want Hazel to like the nanny the same way she likes Ella."

"That's not possible." Molly crushed an empty cupcake wrapper with her fork. "Ella and Hazel have a special bond."

One that she feared was unbreakable. Like her inappropriate thoughts about Drew, her client. Unlike the one supposedly around her heart. Brad had accused her of acting from her heart. Now her heart demanded a voice. Considered Drew as more than a friend and whispered about expanding her family. But Molly had promised never to open her heart again.

Evie slipped into a chair and touched Molly's arm. Evie's voice was gentle, her smile encouraging. "Don't worry. We'll find you a perfect nanny."

Molly handed over the résumés, including the discarded ones. But she really wanted to hand the kind older woman her heart for safe-keeping. Molly wasn't convinced she could quite protect herself.

Evie glanced through several sheets and shook her head. "Do they all lack experience with children under one?"

"Not all," Molly hedged. "But how is a nanny supposed to gain experience if some-one like me doesn't hire them?"

"You don't really want to be the family who the nanny learns from, do you?" Evie peered at Molly over the frames of her cat-eye-shaped glasses.

Drew gave a wry smile. "I told her the same thing an hour ago."

"This is a reputable company." Molly tapped on the top of a résumé where the agency's in-formation was printed. "I'm sure they only ac-cept quality candidates. And they have stellar reviews."

"Uncle Drew and Dad will tell you the agency bought those reviews to make their company look better," Ella chimed in before launching into another kid's song about a spi-der and a waterspout.

Molly arched her eyebrow at Drew.

Drew shrugged. "We're not wrong."

Evie covered her smile with her hand.

"What am I supposed to do?" Molly smashed her napkin on the table. "I have a court appointment Monday."

"I'll be there," Drew promised. "I can help."

"I can't ask *you*." Talk about those client–attorney boundaries. She'd be relying on Drew as if he were more than a client. She'd never asked a client or a colleague to babysit her own daughter. Molly shook her head. "It's not right."

"What time is your court appointment?" Ella asked.

"Eleven fifteen, Monday morning," Molly replied.

Ella frowned. "Too bad. I'm in English class, otherwise I could've helped you too. I could've joined Drew and Hazel."

"That's very kind." Molly reached across the table, grabbed Ella's hand and held on. "But you need to be in English class. Learning is important."

"That's what mom keeps telling me." Ella squeezed Molly's fingers. "But I wish I didn't need algebra."

Molly chuckled. "I think I once wished that too."

"I can help after twelve thirty on Monday." Evie set her phone down. "Unfortunately, I have an early morning doctor's appointment that cannot be rescheduled."

"You can't miss that." Ella sounded worried. "Remember when you fell and broke your arm in three places."

"That was almost two years ago," Evie said. "I'm sure I've healed."

"Still, you should see the doctor," Ella said.

"Hazel and I will be fine together," Drew said. "We've got this. I don't need help on Monday."

"If you do, you can text me," Evie offered. "I'll come right after my appointment."

"And you are on my approved list, to sign me out of school, Uncle Drew," Ella said. "So, if you need me, just go to the office and sign me out."

"Your parents will not like that," Drew warned.

"We don't need to tell them," Ella suggested, grinning.

"Okay." Drew held up his hands, as if asking for patience. "I'm not texting or signing anyone out of anything Monday morning. But I am watching Hazel and we will be fine."

Molly worked through all the reasons this was wrong. But what other choice did she have? A nanny she wasn't comfortable with, or Drew—a man she considered more than a friend. A man she was tempted to trust her heart with. Molly twisted her hands together underneath the table. She might be tempted, but that was all.

His perceptive gaze dropped on Molly and held. He arched one eyebrow. "Agreed?"

CHAPTER FIFTEEN

MOLLY CHECKED HER phone for the fifth time in five minutes and glanced up and down the empty hallway outside Judge Reilly's chambers.

Drew was late.

The same man who had dismissed two nannies last Friday for being late to their interviews was now imitating their bad behavior. Molly peered at Hazel in her stroller. Only a single green stain from breakfast discolored her daughter's short-sleeved cotton onesie with the clouds. Not exactly the look Molly would've chosen for Hazel to meet Judge Reilly, but she had no choice.

Molly produced a rainbow-print blanket from the diaper bag and covered Hazel from chin to feet. The stain hidden, Molly reached for the door of Judge Reilly's chambers.

"I'm here." Footsteps echoed on the marble floor. Drew waved at her and called out again, "I'm here."

Molly released the door handle and watched Drew skid to a halt in front of the stroller.

"Sorry," he wheezed and touched his chest. "Took longer to get the pennies than I thought."

"Pennies," Molly repeated.

Drew held up a plastic bag of pennies. "For the fountain in the park. We have wishes to make while you're in the judge's chambers."

Molly handed Drew the diaper bag and angled Hazel's stroller toward him. "Text me the address for the park. I'll meet you two there."

"It's a short walk." Drew stashed the penny bag inside the diaper bag and gripped the stroller handle. "Remember when you're in there, use honesty and candor dipped in sunshine."

"Professor Mason's favorite advice." The tension eased from Molly's shoulders. Their popular law professor had a creative spin on how to appeal to everyone from individual jurors, court reporters and judges to clients and their families.

"I prefer my honesty lightly dusted in powdered sugar." Drew lifted both eyebrows. "But whatever works for you."

What worked for Molly was Drew. In a suit or like now, in running shoes, athletic pants and a sweatshirt. What worked for Molly was Drew the friend who'd taken her to see Santa all those years ago. The friend who came to her rescue today as a babysitter. And the man who'd referred to her as special. But it wasn't the time or place to dissect her relationship with Drew.

She took a deep breath, let it go and flexed her toes in her heels. Walking through the same routine she did before every court appearance reminded her to stay grounded and confident. "I should not be long. I'm sure Judge Reilly has case hearings back-to-back today."

"Hazel and I are good." Drew pushed the stroller away.

Molly pushed open the door to Judge Reilly's office, greeted Daniel, the administrative assistant, and waited for him to escort her into the judge's chambers. She quickly ran through what she wanted to accomplish here. She wanted no hiccups with Hazel's custody. On the off chance something went awry, she wanted to be prepared.

And she was.

Twenty-eight minutes later, Molly shook Judge Reilly's hand and exited the judge's chambers.

When she'd first learned she was pregnant, Molly had envisioned debating wallpaper choices with Derrick or paint for the nursery. Deliberating over the most educational toys for the playroom and discussing whether a sandbox or swing set worked better in the backyard.

She'd never imagined the copious amounts of paperwork. Or Judge Reilly's lengthy explanation of parental rights, both maternal and paternal. Or the judge's mandate for a custody hearing in two weeks, ordering both parents to be present. Fortunately Judge Reilly had agreed to hold the hearing in San Francisco rather than Los Angeles.

Molly's filing for full legal custody of Hazel had become much more than notarized signatures on a stack of papers. But her daughter was her priority and the steps, although frustrating and tedious, were necessary. Molly texted Derrick the hearing details, explained it was a formality and set out her expectations that he would attend. Once custody was finalized, they could both move on. Derrick with his first wife and old ways, like he'd chosen. Without Hazel in his life, liked he'd wanted. Molly was determined to build a better future for Hazel and herself in the Bay Area.

Outside the courthouse, Molly opened her map app to locate the park where Drew and Hazel had ventured off to.

Drew had brought pennies to make wishes in a fountain. He hadn't hesitated in his offer to watch Hazel for Molly. He'd rescued puppies with confidence and ease. And recently he'd been rescuing Molly. First with an apartment. Then his case, giving her a client. And now babysitting Hazel.

Drew wouldn't walk away from his own child. Not like Derrick had. He would most likely barter for fun toys mixed in with the educational ones. And insist a backyard required both a sandbox and a swing set. After all, he still made wishes in fountains. But Drew's parenting skills were not involved here.

Molly would provide Hazel with the house, the playroom and the backyard. She wanted Hazel to know she could always count on Molly.

Suddenly she wanted to hold her daughter. Look into Hazel's deep blue eyes and remind herself Hazel was the reason. Her reason for everything.

The park took only minutes to find. Drew and Hazel only seconds to locate inside the lush greenery framed on all sides by towering high-rises. Drew held Hazel and pointed at the dozen fountains spurting water toward the sky and spraying metal fish, as well as frogs and turtles swimming in the extensive pool.

His head was tipped toward Hazel's as if, even in garbled babbles, Hazel shared the most important secret ever. As if Hazel mattered.

Molly wanted to run to the pair and step straight into Drew's embrace. To be held with the same protective tenderness. To believe she was wanted. That she made a difference in someone's life not because she could represent them successfully in a courtroom, but because she was valued as a person. As a partner in their life. She wanted to know she wasn't so easy to walk away from.

She forced herself to slow her steps. Center herself and her focus. Drew was not her partner in life. His arms were not the ones she wanted wrapped around her. Besides, her life was full. All she needed was her daughter. As for that loneliness, she'd always filled that with work. She just had to work harder now.

As for that pang inside her—the hollow,

empty one inside her chest—it would dull and fade in time.

Finally the fountain was in front of her. She reached for the bag of pennies resting on the river rock ledge rather than her daughter. Too afraid she'd reach for Drew, as well. She pressed a kiss on Hazel's sticky cheek.

"I lost the wipes somewhere between the ice-cream stand and First Street," Drew confessed. "I thought about dipping my fingers in the fountain water, then pictured Ella scolding me."

Molly noted a series of new dark stains on Hazel's onesie that turned the plump white clouds on her outfit into storm clouds. The triple stains were like a dotted line connecting Molly to Drew. Accidents happened. Her urge to hold his hand and strengthen their connection wouldn't be an accident. It'd be a mistake.

"Popsicles were a bad idea too." Drew wiped at Hazel's stomach, drawing out her quick giggle. "It broke right off the stick, rolled down Hazel's front and onto the cement before I could catch more than a spoonful of the fruity swirl."

"That's what the washing machine is for." Molly firmed her grip on the penny bag and lifted it into her sight line, forcing herself to redirect her focus away from Drew. "Looks like you two haven't made too many wishes."

"We detoured to touch the grass, the thick redwood tree trunks and sniff several flowers." Drew showed Hazel a penny and tossed it into the fountain. Hazel clapped wildly.

"Are you at least making a new wish every time you toss a penny into the water?" Molly opened the bag and scooped out a handful of pennies. She blocked her heart from stepping forward, using a hard hit of logic. Wishing wells were a distraction. The same as her attraction to Drew. Wishes were forgotten and readily replaced. As for her attraction, she simply had to replace that too.

"We're *supposed* to be making a new wish every time." Drew laughed and shook his head. "I just keep repeating the same one over and over again."

"I don't think that's how it's supposed to work." Molly launched a penny into the air. "It's one wish per penny. Otherwise you're buying your way to your wish coming true."

"How many pennies have you tossed into a wishing well?" Drew shifted Hazel to his other arm.

"The better question is how many of my

wishes have come true from the pennies I tossed into the fountains." Molly handed Hazel a penny. Let her look at it.

Drew's hand covered Hazel's palm and the penny. He captured Hazel's attention and lifted his voice in wonder. "Where did it go?"

Hazel peered at her now-empty palm. Her eyes round. Drew continued his show, finally revealing the penny in his pocket. He tossed it into the water and slanted his gaze at Molly. "After the first two pennies went straight for Hazel's mouth, I decided I needed to become a magician. She can touch, but not taste."

"Another lesson from Ella?" Molly smiled, picturing adorable and intelligent Ella tutoring Drew on everything baby.

"No." Drew tapped Hazel's nose. "Actually, the magic trick idea was all mine."

"It's a good one." Unlike Molly's idea to listen to her heart. To step closer to Drew and test whether her attraction to him was reciprocated. But what she felt was merely appreciation for Drew. And she couldn't fall for him because he treated her daughter well. Molly faced the fountain and rolled a penny between her fingers.

Drew stepped beside her and bumped his

shoulder against hers. "Well, are you going to tell me how many of your wishes came true?"

None. Was there harm in wishing again? Perhaps not. But trying again. Opening her heart again. Not a risk she could afford. "When I was a kid, I wished for a house."

"How come I don't know this? Where did you live growing up?" Drew reached up and patted Hazel's back. She rested her head on his shoulder and yawned several times, each one bigger than the previous.

"Apartments." Molly sealed the penny bag but failed to seal off her childhood memories. Or the words tumbling free. "More than two dozen different apartments before I was ten and then I stopped counting."

She reached for Hazel and settled her into the stroller. She covered Hazel from chin to feet with a blanket. If only covering her past made her feel as content as Hazel looked.

"Did you stop moving then?" Drew pushed the stroller toward a park bench behind the fountain, nestled in a copse of trees and shrubs.

"No. My dad left. Just walked out and never came back one night." And Molly never wished for a house again. Until Derrick. Then she began to hope. Hope for that house and family she'd always dreamed about growing up. Derrick hadn't shared her dream. Same as her own dad. And Molly had vowed not to let her dreams ever hurt her again. "I decided if I wanted a house, I was going to have to buy it for my mom and me."

Drew angled Hazel's stroller so he could push it back and forth with his foot.

He hadn't known Hazel long, but he already knew how to calm her. How to put her to sleep. How to make her laugh. Drew would make a good father. Molly flexed her fingers in her lap, expanded those boundaries and her detachment. She wasn't looking for a father for Hazel or a partner for herself.

Drew glanced at her. His gaze thoughtful. "Did you ever buy a house for you and your mom?"

"My mom passed away two years after we graduated from law school." Emotions swelled inside Molly, testing her distance. She'd wanted to give her mom what her mom had never had, and she'd failed her. Molly couldn't fail Hazel. Her throat felt scratchy. "I had student loans to pay off first, before I could afford a down payment on a house."

"I'm sorry." Drew reached over and linked his fingers around hers.

"I did rent a beach cottage for us." Molly dismissed those boundaries and pressed her palm against Drew's, seeking his warmth and his strength. "Wc spent her last few weeks gazing at the stars and listening to the waves roll onto the shore." And finally finding peace with the past. "Mom had always wanted to live at the beach."

"You granted her wish." Respect tinged his words.

"She would've granted all mine as a child if she could have." Molly tried to smile. That catch in her voice remained. "Mom always told me, *One day, there will be sand between our toes and sunshine in our hearts, Molly. But only if we believe and work hard.* The temporary bcach cottage hardly felt like enough."

"I'm sure it was everything to her." Confidence flowed from him.

"I hadn't realized until she was gone how much she meant to me. How much she'd been my everything growing up." Molly looked to Drew. "I want to be the same for Hazel."

"You already are." He lifted his other hand, brushed her hair off her cheek.

"That's kind." She could hear the doubt in her own words.

"You don't believe me, do you?" His earnest voice held Molly's attention. He added, "You are because you put Hazel first, always."

"But this is not exactly what I wanted for my daughter. What I wanted for us." One parent. No house. No other family.

"You have more than you think right here." He squeezed her hand. "And you're not alone. You know that, right?"

She nodded because he seemed to be waiting for her agreement. Her gaze dropped to their joined hands. Nothing forced or awkward about her hand in his. Only warmth and a steady reassurance. And if she wanted to look deep inside herself, she'd admit it felt right to hold his hand and confide in him. More than right. "Enough about me. Tell me what you've wished for." *Did you wish for me?*

"I used to wish for it to rain chicken nuggets and tacos," Drew admitted. A wry grin curved across his face.

Molly smiled. "What about now?"

"Now my wishes are a little more complicated." He leaned forward, brushed her hair off her cheek again.

Their gazes collided and held. She lost her

breath and her focus. And the best kind of chill—the kind that awakened anticipation, swept away her doubt. Her voice rasped, "So, are you going to tell me one of your wishes or not?" *Please let it be me.*

"I wished for this." His fingers slipped behind her neck. His head tipped toward hers. She leaned into the kiss.

One soft brush of their lips. One full surrender of her heart.

Her cell phone vibrated on the bench between them. Molly pulled away and picked up her phone. Pressing pause on her racing pulse wasn't quite as simple as answering her incoming call. "I need to take this. It's Lorrie Cote."

Drew blinked slowly. His gaze lifted from Molly's mouth, as if he'd been considering making another wish, and then his expression suddenly became serious and intent.

Molly answered her phone, kept her focus on Drew and her tone professional.

Lorrie Cote was nervous and hesitant. And not the Cote that Molly wanted to talk to. Still, she was grateful for Brad's quick work tracking down the family to let them know she had to speak with Reuben. Molly persuaded Reuben's daughter to listen to her side. Finally she put down the phone and touched Drew's arm as she would any anxious and worried client. One simple point of contact and it seemed so much more. She had work to sustain her, she told herself, and her love for Hazel to fulfill her. One kiss in the park would change nothing. "Lorrie agreed to meet tomorrow in Sacramento."

Drew exhaled, "Looks like we're taking a road trip."

And realigning my priorities. "We should head home. I need to get prepared for tomorrow."

Once inside Drew's truck, their kiss was like a fourth passenger, buckled in beside Hazel's car seat in the back row and looming like a holdout juror forcing a mistrial.

She'd built a career on never running from a confrontation. Yet there she sat in the passenger seat of Drew's truck and struggled to launch a talk about their kiss into the silence. Their kiss had been a major boundary violation.

When do you think we could try that kiss thing again? was what she wanted to say. Molly yanked her sunglasses from her face and cleaned the lenses. As if the smudged lenses were to blame for her lack of transparency. As if the lenses held her back from speaking her own truth. "What's the first thing you plan to do when the hearing is over, and your innocence is proven?"

"Set up my new office." He never hesitated.

Molly nodded and concentrated on cleaning her sunglasses. What had she been expecting? They'd shared one small kiss. Hardly anything to build a relationship on. She seriously had to impose a penalty for crossing her own boundaries again and again. Hadn't Derrick hurt her enough?

"What?" he asked. "You're scowling."

"I have a scratch on my sunglasses." Molly returned her sunglasses to her face and buried those soft treacherous emotions. The ones that led to bruised hearts and tears. "Won't you want to celebrate then with your family and friends?" *With me?*

"Sure, but that's what an hour or so one night." He shrugged. "My new office is where my future starts. Where I get to make a difference again."

He'd made a difference in Molly's life. "Your work completely fulfills you then."

"It's all that matters," he said. "I want my life back. There's still so much I want to prove. To accomplish."

Molly and Hazel were simply a diversion until his old life began again. The same as Molly had been for Derrick. Molly watched the city pass by outside her window. Caution tape and large orange cones surrounded an uncovered manhole in the street, warning drivers and pedestrians of the danger. Molly wrapped her arms around herself and tried to ignore the sign.

It was simple and straightforward really. Molly had to win Drew's case so that he could resume his life and his career. Just as he wanted. She'd add another checkmark in the win column and consider the case and their relationship closed.

She rubbed her chest and the twinge of an ache there. Nothing she couldn't backstop with more clients and more cases.

If they failed to secure Reuben's sworn testimony tomorrow, Molly would have regrets. She'd regret failing Drew. Even more, she'd regret that she had given Drew hope.

And if you're merely spending your time hoping, then you're not doing.

More of her mother's advice.

Molly wasn't hoping for love or a family. She was looking after her own family of two.

As for love, she could do without that.

CHAPTER SIXTEEN

DREW ANSWERED HIS phone, eager for the distraction from the heavy silence inside the truck. He'd upset Molly. That much he knew. He just wasn't certain how.

His brother offered a quick hello followed by, "Meet me at Dan and Brooke's house."

"Is this another dog rescue?" Drew asked.

"You were supposed to meet me in thirty minutes at my office," Brad said. "But I'm not there. I'm at the Sawyers' place looking after Nala. Brooke had to take the puppies to the vet and Dan has a shift."

Drew rubbed his forehead. He'd been distracted tossing pennies into the fountain and discussing wishes. He'd completely lost track of time. He could've easily lost more time kissing Molly. He concentrated on his phone call. "Right. I'm dropping Molly and Hazel off there now, so I'll head to the main house."

Drew disconnected and focused on the traffic, not reaching for Molly.

"You were supposed to meet your brother?" Molly asked.

"Brad and I scheduled a meeting this afternoon." Drew stepped on the gas pedal, eager to put more distance between himself and the park. He had to stop thinking about kissing Molly. She was his legal counsel, not his girlfriend. "Brad was just switching locations."

"I would offer to help with Nala, but Hazel needs a nap." Molly paused as if searching for something else to add to her excuse.

Drew nodded. He needed a moment to revise his strategy.

He hit every green light and reached Brooke and Dan's place in record time. Molly and Hazel went to their apartment and he escaped inside the main house.

He needed to take a step back. Yet he wanted to return to Molly's porch, apologize and kiss her. Kiss her longer, hold her tighter and lose himself completely. He shook his head and forced himself to repeat the reason he was there.

"Interesting place for a debrief." Drew walked into the laundry room and greeted his brother. Nala lifted her head and her tail swept rapidly back and forth across the tile floor.

"She didn't greet me with a tail wag." Brad sat between the floor-to-ceiling cabinets and Nala's makeshift bed.

Drew lowered himself to the floor and rested his back against the washing machine. Nala crawled toward him and laid her head on his leg. Her tail sweep continued.

"My wife and Brooke would say that you are Nala's person." Brad chuckled. "That she's claimed you."

Drew ran his hand over Nala's back. His fingers still sank between her ribs, but he couldn't deny the dog's spirit. Nala was a fighter like another mom he knew. "And if I'm not a dog person?"

"I don't think it matters much to Nala," Brad said. "She trusts you."

"Is that all it takes?" Drew asked. "Trust?" And one kiss—brief, but extraordinary. He couldn't recall the last time he'd kissed a woman and completely forgotten his surroundings. Like he had earlier with Molly.

Putting one memorable kiss aside, Drew knew it was all wrong between Molly and him. How could it be anything else? They were both at crossroads in their respective careers. She was a single mom, responsible for her daughter. He had his large group of friends and his family to focus on. And the kiss was a distraction neither he nor Molly could afford.

Brad stacked his hands behind his head, crossed his feet at his ankles and considered Drew. "Want to tell me about it before we debrief or after?"

"There's nothing to tell." Or discuss. One kiss was all they could share. Both Drew and Molly had to remain clearheaded and objective. And Drew couldn't afford to forget himself like that again. Not with his future on the line. And Molly's. And Hazel's. And Sophie's… "We're heading to Sacramento to meet with the Cote family tomorrow."

"That's a lot to tell." Brad set his phone facedown on the floor. His gaze never tracked from Drew. "Now tell me about Molly?"

"She's fierce as an attorney and a mom." He admired that and even more about her. That wasn't unusual. He admired all his friends. "She's also dedicated. Smart. And compassionate."

"But," Brad pressed.

"But I'm okay with my life." Drew smoothed his hand over Nala's back. "Or at least I am with the life I had. And I fully intend to get back my career."

"So then you plan to devote your life to your work once again," Brad said.

Drew nodded. "That's what I do. How I'm wired."

"Maybe." Brad shrugged. "Or maybe you just never had a reason to change directions."

Drew looked at Nala. She gazed up at him, one blue eye, one brown, watching him as if she understood his secrets. Understood him. He changed the direction of the conversation instead. "You think Nala is turning me into a dog person?"

"I think she already has." Brad chuckled. "Yes or no. You decided you'd do anything for that dog when you first saw her under that dumpster?"

"Yes." And he'd been determined to do whatever he could for Molly and Hazel. That hardly meant he'd be a good father or partner. "And it means I'm going to have to approve of the family who adopts Nala."

"Why can't you adopt her?" Brad asked. "Why can't you be her family?"

Those pesky wires tightened. He lived for his job. Always had. "I don't have the best home for a dog." Or a toddler.

"There's a park two blocks from your loft," Brad argued.

"Dogs are a big responsibility." As were relationships. Families. Careers. And failing at any of them had consequences. "The cats only want attention on their terms. But dogs are different."

"They require more of you," Brad said. "Same as a family."

"What if I don't have more to give?" Drew had worked over the years to disassociate from his emotions. Emotions never strengthened an oral argument or improved a cross-examination. Emotions only ever detracted. And he'd adopted the same philosophy in his personal life.

"You'd be surprised how much you have inside you." Brad opened a cabinet and took out a dog snack from a plastic container marked Treats. He gave the biscuit to Nala. "You just have to believe in the reason. In yourself."

Drew closed his eyes. "Well, maybe I'll start to believe once I get my old life back."

"Just be careful," Brad warned. "It might be too late then."

He disagreed with his brother. It was poor timing right now. His life wasn't settled.

Wasn't even in a place where he could consider a relationship with anyone, most especially Molly. She needed, no, deserved more than a part-time helper. But he wasn't ready or willing to be all in. That required a commitment he'd only ever given to his work. He understood the risks and rewards in his career. The same of upholding justice.

But the rewards of love were much more elusive. And the risks so high. Love offered too many hurtful scenarios and no guaranteed positive outcome. Molly and Hazel deserved a lot better than any chance it might work out. "That's all I have to share today. Tell me about this fraud group you and your team are investigating? The one you want me to help with."

Brad launched into his investigation, reconstructing the background and history of the fraud ring in detail. From its formation by two longtime friends to inclusions of family members to the corporate structure it now mimicked. Brad listed the crimes to date. They included counterfeiting, forgery and illegal loan schemes.

Drew settled in. He was at his best when it came to understanding and interpreting the law and how it related to suspected misdeeds. Love and relationships were not his strength. Or his specialty. Surely even Molly realized that.

It was past time to deal only in facts and undisputable truths.

Fact: Molly was his legal counsel.

Fact: Molly was the reason they'd discovered the evidence to exonerate him.

Fact: he was more than grateful.

Fact: gratitude was not love.

He had to plan his withdrawal. No more handholding. No more kisses. And definitely no more confessions.

As for those wishes he'd tossed into the water fountain, he'd keep those to himself.

CHAPTER SEVENTEEN

TEN MILES INTO their destination to Sacramento, Drew disconnected from his hands-free conference call with Brad and his brother's investigation team. The meeting had lasted for the whole hour and eaten up their entire drive from the Bay.

Now Drew was close. So very close to getting his life back.

Molly took out her earbuds and turned to glance at Hazel sleeping. He parked his truck outside the Cotes' home. A small but inviting bungalow. Drew exhaled. "You told Lorrie we wouldn't stress out her father, but I can convince her to allow us to speak to her dad frankly."

"That's my job." Molly put her legal pad away, gathered her briefcase and the diaper bag. "You have to let me do what you hired me to do."

"Sorry. I know that." Drew winced. "I've never been in the client's seat before."

Never had to cede control of his future to someone else.

He always led his cases. Always dictated the direction and managed the result. Now the outcome was entirely personal. And those emotions he'd cautioned his own clients to get in check stampeded through him. He needed to listen to his own advice. Especially since there were good, honest people caught up in this case. Though he was the client, he had to be mindful not to forget that.

"We're going to get you out of the client chair soon." Molly opened the truck door and stepped out to retrieve Hazel from her car seat.

He also had to be mindful that he wouldn't be standing outside Reuben Cote's home without Molly. He wanted to thank her. Wanted to kiss her. But he'd vowed to withdraw. After all, once he returned to his old life, his world would be in perfect balance again. And his focus would be on work, where it belonged.

He loved his work. Doing his best to uphold justice meant everything to him.

He accepted a smiling Hazel from Molly.

Hazel's big blue eyes locked on his. Her cheerful babbles joined the spring breeze. And her drool dripped onto his favorite courtroom shoes as if Hazel had just claimed him. As if he mattered very much to such a precious little girl.

Drew tucked Hazel against his chest and denied the surge of joy she infused him with every time he held her. As if she gave his life meaning. He liked kids just fine. Any kid really. Kids made him smile and laugh. Kids made him happy.

That hardly meant he wanted his own. Hardly proved Hazel was anymore special to him.

Besides, he was committed to his job. Ex-girlfriends had accused him of being emotionally unavailable. A workaholic and distant even when they were in the same room together. Not exactly glowing praise. Or high recommendation for him as a partner.

Clearly, he was better staying in his professional lane where he knew how to succeed. After all, failing Hazel and Molly wasn't acceptable.

Drew waited for Molly and together they walked up the driveway to the front porch. An ornate wreath of brightly colored ribbons and sunflowers adorned the door, welcoming spring and its visitors.

Lorrie Cote opened the door and introduced herself to Drew and Molly, then aimed her warm smile at Hazel. She blew Hazel air kisses. "It's been a few years since I've had a baby in the house. Do you think she'd mind if I held her?"

Hazel lifted her head off Drew's shoulder and patted her palm against her mouth. Lorrie's soft laughter carried across the pretty porch.

Molly handed Lorrie a llama-and-heart-print blanket. "It's her favorite."

Lorrie draped the blanket over her shoulder with the fast, precise movements of a seasoned mom and held out her arms to Hazel.

Hazel dropped into the woman's arms and continued trying to blow air kisses.

"The books all talked about babies at this age being wary of everyone but their mothers." Molly patted Hazel's back. "Yet this one doesn't seem to have much of a problem."

"Except with the nanny candidates," Drew corrected and glanced at Lorrie. "I think Hazel knew before we did that none of them were the right nanny for her."

Lorrie smiled and tapped her finger on Hazel's nose. "That's because she's smart and discerning. Babies have a good sense of things."

And Drew hoped Hazel sensed she had the task of distracting Lorrie. He wasn't there to pressure Reuben, but he wasn't prepared to leave without Cote's consent to testify either. If Hazel and her big blue eyes could inject her daily dose of adorable into the room, perhaps everyone would be in a more accommodating mindset. And the afternoon would remain stress-free for all the parties involved.

Lorrie carried Hazel inside the house. Drew and Molly followed the pair into a compact kitchen connected to a tidy family room. Lorrie transferred Hazel back to Molly. "My father's room is down the hall. Let me make sure he's feeling up to company."

Molly sat at the kitchen table, propped Hazel on her lap and pulled a fabric book about forest animals out of the diaper bag.

Drew paced in a small circle, his gaze skipping from the stained coffeepot to the dull counters to the hand-drawn crayon art of a happy stick-figure family taped on the refrigerator. "We have to come back if Reuben refuses to talk to us today."

"We will," Molly assured him.

Hazel scrunched a page of her book, babbled and kicked out her legs in joy. The tension inside Drew released. He moved to stand beside

Molly and glanced over her shoulder. Hazel tugged on a flap and cheered for the soft fox underneath. Again, the stress squeezing his spine eased. He wanted to believe it was only the Hazel effect. But he knew Hazel's mother played a part too. Having Molly beside him calmed him. Surely, because he knew her talent and skill as an attorney. She most likely calmed all her clients.

But was he just a client? Drew paced away from the truth. He'd already vowed to stay in his professional lane. That included with Molly. He glanced down the hallway. "I don't think Reuben is going to see us."

"Or he's getting ready to see us," Molly countered.

Drew pressed his palms over his eyes. "We have to convince him to testify."

"Drew, look at me." Molly's matter-of-fact voice ordered him to comply. "The man down the hallway is critically ill. He's also a decent man and a loving father and he will protect his family at all costs. He's already proven that by coming forward to exonerate Van."

Drew nodded and his gaze slid to Hazel. He wasn't Hazel's biological father or even her stepfather, yet he was beginning to understand a parent's protective instinct. The one that made someone want to move the universe to safeguard his or her own child.

Molly shifted and smiled when Lorrie reappeared in the kitchen. "Is your father up for a visit?"

"He is." Lorrie reached for the blanket Molly had draped over the empty kitchen chair. "And if you don't mind, I'd like to keep Hazel company while you three talk."

"Are you sure?" Molly stood and adjusted Hazel on her hip.

"If I'm honest, I'm being selfish." Lorrie's one-sided grin hinted at her playful, light-hearted side. "I'd like to hold this bundle of joy for a little while and remember what it was to be innocent and full of wonder."

Molly transferred Hazel into Lorrie's open arms.

"We won't take too much of your father's time," Drew said.

"I appreciate that," Lorrie said. "You should know my father leans toward a more outdated code. He still puts stock in firm handshakes and solid eye contact. And he distrusts cell phones and most technology and particularly when they're distractions."

Molly pulled her cell phone from her pants pocket and tucked it into the diaper bag she'd hung on the kitchen chair. "I find it's better not to be tempted when the notifications go off."

"Thanks for the advice." Drew turned his cell phone off and slid it back into his pocket.

"Dad's room is the last door on the left." Lorrie picked up the farm animal book and sat into the rocking chair near the front window. Drew smiled as Lorrie sang the first verse of a nursery rhyme. Her melodic voice added a comforting, welcome energy to the home.

At the end of the hallway, Drew opened the bedroom door and motioned Molly inside.

Reuben Cote sat in a rocking chair similar to the one in the family room. A patterned quilt draped across his lap. His grin pressed his wrinkled cheeks upward, closing off his eyes. "My daughter sings and her voice fills my tired old soul. I'm uplifted."

Drew left the door open to allow Lorrie's next song about sunshine to flow into the room.

Molly smiled. "Does she sing often?"

"Only when she feels safe." Reuben tugged the blanket around his waist and set his rocking chair into a slow sway.

Molly's gaze connected with Drew's. That,

he supposed, was at the core of every parent: wanting his or her child to feel safe. He'd want that for Hazel. And Molly. But would her heart be safe with him? Drew cleared his throat. "We will protect you and your family."

"I trust that you will try." Reuben paused. His chair creaked in the sudden silence. "Lorrie believes in you, as well. Otherwise she wouldn't have invited you here."

"Mr. Cote." Drew stepped forward, reached his hand out.

"Reuben, please. We spent too much time together working on that trial to be so formal now." The older gentleman shook Drew's hand, then patted the last few gray curls framing his otherwise bald head. "Besides, my wife, Trina, only called me Mr. Cote when I displeased her. I can tell you it wasn't often. And because of that we celebrated fifty-four years of marriage before she passed."

"We are sorry for your loss," Molly said.

Reuben nodded. But it was not sadness or despair that embraced him. More like love and gratitude for his wife and what they had shared. Drew glanced at Molly. What would it take for a marriage like that? Would Molly believe he could be a husband like Reuben? Did Drew believe?

"Trina told me she was leaving this life early to get things ready for us." A quiet wise smile dented Reuben's cheeks. "Promised she'd be waiting for me when I finished my work here."

"How do you know when you've finished your work?" Molly's arms were relaxed at her sides. Her voice was genuine. Her gaze sincere.

"My dear, I lived, loved and lied in this lifetime more than most." A wry gleam flashed in Reuben's deep brown eyes. "Married the love of my life and was blessed to raise a family. Tried to do right. Now, I can hear my Trina calling me."

Drew wanted Reuben to have peace. To be with his beloved Trina for all eternity. And, selfishly, Drew wanted very much to save himself too.

"But you both aren't here for life advice from me." Reuben's gaze settled on Drew as if the older man had been blessed with clairvoyance.

"We will welcome any advice you're willing to share." Drew meant that. He liked Reuben Cote very much. Would gladly return for a personal visit to learn more about his life. But to do that, business had to come first.

"But we've also recently discovered a recording of your first interview in the Van Solis murder trial."

Reuben rubbed his finger over his eyebrows. "I was told that recording had been destroyed. That's why I never mentioned it in my new statement to the boy's lawyer."

"Not exactly," Molly said. "Reuben, we need your sworn statement to verify the recording. To verify it is you and Cory Vinson in that video."

"I had to make a deal." Reuben's worry was palpable in the room. "I was told by Vinson that I was about to lose my home and everything I owned because of unpaid back taxes. I'd made a terrible mistake. The penalties and fines were more than I made my entire life as a mechanic. My daughter and grandkids would've been forced onto the streets. Lorrie had fallen on rough times. Vinson stressed I would spend years in prison. A man can't provide for his family in jail. I promised my wife I'd look after my family. Always."

Molly sat on the ottoman beside Reuben's rocking chair. "And you did that the best way you knew how."

"I took Vinson's deal, but I sentenced someone else's son to a life in jail." Reuben pinched his eyes closed. "Who was I to decide my life mattered more than that boy's?"

"I was the prosecutor," Drew confessed into the quiet. "I'm responsible for that outcome."

"You wouldn't have had that outcome without my testimony." Reuben peered at him. "No man should ever tamper with fate. I'll have to answer for that."

"We can correct things." Molly set her hand on the arm of the rocking chair. Her voice was earnest and forthright. "For the innocent and the guilty."

"I want things made right. I've waited far too long." Reuben's chin dipped. "Funny, the things I convinced myself of the past few years, since the trial ended, to lessen the guilt and the regret. But when your final days are staring right at you, it's only the truth that matters."

"Reuben," Molly said. "Your legacy will be all the stronger for owning the truth now."

"What happens now? I've recanted my testimony publicly and already gave a statement to Van's attorney for the boy's appeal trial." Reuben curled his fingers around the rocking chair armrests. "What charges will I face?"

"We aren't here to charge you." Drew

stepped forward, wanting to reassure the older man. "We'd like your testimony at my upcoming hearing to prove the witness-tampering charges against me are false."

"I gave my first interview to Vinson," Reuben said. "No one else."

It was Cory Vinson, the current DA, that should be accused of witness tampering and so much more. Drew said, "That's what we'd like you to say at my hearing."

"And if I don't agree to do that, what happens then?" Reuben asked.

"We'd like you to sign an official statement. An affidavit, like you did for Van," Molly explained. "Of course, we can't make you do anything. But you should know Drew's livelihood is at stake. He could lose everything at his hearing if he's declared guilty. I'm trying to ensure that doesn't happen."

Drew remained still and held the older gentleman's gaze. Reuben's eyes held wisdom and experience.

"Lorrie believes you're one of the good ones." Reuben rubbed his chin.

"Drew Harrington is one of the good ones." Molly set her hand on top of Reuben's arm. "Drew has built his career on trying to uphold justice. He's never faltered. Never deviated. Now he deserves justice too."

Molly's words gave him comfort. He added, "I want to keep doing my job."

"World needs more good ones," Reuben offered. "I want to help."

The tension in Drew disappeared. He smiled. "Thank you."

"I'll need to make arrangements. I want to do this in person." Reuben set his chair back to its slow rocking motion. "Though traveling is not like it used to be. Now I have doctors and a daughter who monitor every hour of every one of my days."

"We can arrange to return to video your witness statement," Drew suggested. "In case traveling is not approved."

"Don't you worry, son." Reuben shook his finger at Drew. "I'm going to be telling them where we're going, not asking."

"We appreciate this." Molly reached out and grasped Reuben's hand.

"I'm the grateful one." Reuben patted the top of her hand. "You're relieving an old man's weary, guilty soul. I haven't had a good night's rest in entirely too long. And my aching bones aren't to blame."

"Maybe tonight that will change," Molly said.

"That's the hope. Now my Trina isn't here, but that doesn't mean I've forgotten her ways." Reuben lifted his gaze to Drew and waved him closer. "Listen well, son. You'd best not let this lovely lady get away."

Molly jumped from the ottoman, her cheeks tinged an appealing shade of pink. Her words tumbled out. "Oh, we're just friends. Coworkers of sorts. Peers only."

Reuben chuckled and shifted his gaze back and forth between Molly and Drew. "Are you certain that's all there is between you two?"

Drew avoided looking at Molly and avoided answering Reuben's question. "We'll leave our contact information with your daughter. Call us if you need anything."

Molly retreated from the bedroom and offered a rushed parting statement. "I'll be in touch about the hearing date and arrangements for a notarized statement."

"And now you know my mailing address, don't forget to send me an invitation to the wedding when it's time." Reuben's laughter followed them down the hallway.

Business cards were handed out and goodbye hugs shared with Lorrie. Drew climbed into his truck and waited for Molly to buckle her seat belt. Hazel was fast asleep in her car seat—the same as she'd been in Lorrie's arms when they'd left Reuben's bedroom.

"That went well." Molly kept her voice on the low side to not disturb Hazel.

That was her habit. Once he started the truck and the engine became Hazel's white-noise machine, Molly's voice returned to normal.

Drew steered away from the curb of the Cote house. "This time I really want to celebrate."

Even more, he wanted to kiss Molly. And then celebrate. That was not the withdrawal he'd decided on. He wanted to blame Reuben for insinuating there was more between Molly and himself, but Reuben had only seen what Drew wanted to deny. What Drew would continue to deny. It was for everyone's own good. He spoke again, before Molly could respond and cancel his plans for celebration. "I know, I know. I can't get ahead of myself."

"But it's all coming together." Excitement came through in her voice.

"It is." He grinned and told himself he was still in his lane. He wanted to kiss Molly, but he hadn't acted on it. "We might need a *small* celebration. To take the edge off."

Molly reached into the diaper bag and

pulled out her phone. "What did you have in mind?"

A much longer kiss.

The silence vibrated around him. Drew gripped the steering wheel. Had he spoken that outrageous suggestion out loud? Slowly he asked, "Something wrong?"

More silence.

Worry was all he felt now. He stopped at a red light and touched Molly's arm. "Molly?"

She clutched her phone and stared at the screen. Her mouth open, her face ashen. Finally she pressed a button and slowly turned toward him. She slipped her earbuds from her ears. "A social worker is coming to the apartment for a site visit to make sure I'm providing a stable and safe environment for Hazel."

"Why?" Drew asked. She'd never mentioned a social worker visit at the park yesterday as part of the normal custody procedure.

"It seems my ex has sudden qualms about agreeing to give me full custody. Why would he do this?" Molly dropped her phone on her lap and scrubbed her palms over her face.

"When is this site visit?"

"Tomorrow." Molly spoke through her fingers. "Judge Reilly ordered an in-person hearing. She never mentioned a site visit. Derrick obviously pulled strings to make it happen."

And clearly her ex wanted to pull more than the rug out from under Molly. Drew frowned. "What happens now?" And how could Drew make it better for her?

"Well, the apartment isn't ready for a site visit." Molly rubbed her forehead. "I haven't done the laundry. Vacuumed. Gone to the grocery store."

"Grocery store?" Drew pulled onto the freeway on-ramp that would take them back to the city.

"I should have food in the cabinets and re-frigerator, right?" Molly drummed her fingers on her leg. "To show I'm providing adequate room and board for Hazel. What are the pa-rameters of adequate anyway?"

"I'm not sure, but you have help." Drew pressed the call button on the screen in his console and scrolled through his contact list.

Her ex, Derrick Donovan, might have a strong network of connections. But then so did Drew.

"Unbelievable." Molly dropped her head back on the seat. "The one time the courts decide to move at warp speed and it's for my custody hearing that wasn't supposed to be complicated at all."

Three calls later, his emergency crew was activated. Evie had promised to drop off cookie dough for Molly to put in the oven thirty minutes before the social worker arrived. Evie was convinced the decadent scent would put the person in a cooperative mood.

Brooke had volunteered to start the laundry and vacuum the rooms.

Nichole had offered to fill the refrigerator and pantry with wholesome foods, adding that she'd keep the wine at her house for after the site visit. Nichole had ended the phone call with a reminder for Molly to make her bed. Bed-making was the first positive task of the morning and that would start a string of positivity throughout the day. And if that failed, at least a prettily made bed gave the illusion that Molly had it all together.

Drew vowed to make his bed too and disconnected the phone call with Nichole.

"How did you do that?" Molly asked.

"What?"

"Rally your friends to help me get my place ready for the social worker." Molly checked on Hazel, who was sleeping peacefully in her car seat.

"They aren't rallying for me." Drew glanced at her and noted the confusion on her face. "They're doing it for you."

"Why?"

"Because they really like you and Hazel." He'd assumed she'd already known that. She had confessed he'd been her only friend several nights ago. He hadn't really believed her until now.

"Hazel is quite easy to like." Molly chewed on her lower lip. "It's very hard not to like a baby."

"Especially Hazel." Drew reached over and gripped Molly's hand. He'd get back in his own lane tomorrow. Tonight, he chose honesty. "It's also really, really hard not to like Hazel's mother."

CHAPTER EIGHTEEN

MOLLY RUSHED OUTSIDE and set Hazel on a blanket in the grass. Then she hurried over to Brooke and the two dogs, one a boxer and one a German shepherd that Brooke held in sitting positions.

The dogs had accepted Molly the first night she'd moved into the apartment and adored cleaning Hazel's face. Molly had quickly learned "gentle giants" was a real term and applied to the pair who'd been determined to assist her in getting over her childhood fear of dogs.

She tucked her phone with the SOS text from Brooke on it into the slim pocket on her yoga pants and looked at Brooke. "What exactly do you need me to do?"

"I need to get a tablespoon of hydrogen peroxide down their throats." Brooke scowled and pointed at a large brown bottle. "They ate both trays of brownies Evie had made for tomorrow's school bake sale."

"Chocolate is bad for dogs," Molly guessed.

"Especially, Evie's brownies. She uses the special baker's chocolate." Brooke handed the leashes to Molly. "You're going to have to tighten your grip."

"What are you doing?" Molly wrapped the leashes around her wrists and adjusted her hold. She peeked at Hazel, saw her daughter laughing and picking at the grass.

"I'm opening their mouths, pouring this in and waiting until they swallow." Brooke filled a syringe with the necessary amount of hydrogen peroxide.

"And then?" Molly patted the dogs' backs.

"You release them when I tell you to," Brooke ordered. "The hydrogen peroxide is meant to upset their stomachs and will remove the brownies rather quickly."

Rex, the boxer with a white muzzle and black fur framing his expressive eyes, accepted the syringe on the first try. Within moments, the dog was sprinting across the yard to heave his brownies onto the grass. Luna revealed her German shepherd intelligence and provided more of a challenge. It took three tries with the syringe before Brooke was successful, although she and Molly were splattered with peroxide in the process.

Brooke set her hands on her hips. "Luna, this is what happens when you are a bad girl. Remember this next time."

The dog's tongue lolled out and licked Brooke's arm. Molly wasn't certain but the dog appeared fine after getting rid of her forbidden brownies. Molly released Luna and the dogs seemed to console each other.

Brooke cleaned up her supplies and Molly turned around to see Cupid, Brooke's three-legged cat, circling around Hazel and covering her in gray fur. Hazel held a dandelion in her fist and giggled. Molly laughed.

A movement at the side gate ruined her humor. A stern-looking woman from her fixed bun on the back of her head to her staid suit jacket and skirt arched an eyebrow at Molly. "Are you Ms. Molly McKinney?"

Molly wiped her hands on her yoga pants and swept Hazel into her arms. "I am."

"I'm Gloria Serrano, from social services." The woman eyed Molly, flicked her gaze over Hazel, then shifted slightly to scowl at the recovering dogs lazing nearby. Her voice was deep, gravelly and intimidating. "I believe you were expecting me."

Not for another hour. Molly forced herself to smile and swallow the sudden worry coursing through her. "Yes. Let me give Hazel to my friend and I'll be right with you."

It was then Molly noticed Hazel chomping on the dandelion. Molly groaned and swiped the gnawed flower out of Hazel's mouth. She hurried over to Brooke, handed her Hazel and whispered, "She's here. Already."

Brooke smoothed her hand over Molly's hair. "It's going to be fine. Go. Go. We got this."

Molly wiped the grass off her yoga pants and twisted her hair into a loose bun. She'd planned to run the vacuum again and shower before Gloria Serrano's arrival. At least she'd remembered the cookies. Molly opened the door to her apartment and invited the social worker inside. She motioned to the counter. "Would you like a double-chunk chocolate chip cookie?"

Gloria shook her head. Her severe bun never wobbled, and her stern face only became more grim. "I'm afraid those won't be kind to my blood sugar levels."

Molly nudged the plate across the counter, away from the woman. Nothing dislodged the panic gripping Molly.

Gloria's glasses slipped down her nose, the attached silver chain catching the morning light and glinting. The woman counted the lightbulbs in the ceiling, then twisted away from Molly. "Do you always bring your work home with you?"

Molly squeezed her throat to stop her sudden gasp. She'd forgotten about the dry-erase board. The very one detailing the Van Solis murder trial. Molly forced her words around the knot in her throat. "I'm a criminal defense attorney."

Gloria offered her a one-sided flat smile, more grimace than grin.

Molly rushed on, "I will be moving into a suitable office space soon."

Gloria scrawled another note across her clipboard, then lifted her gaze over the rim of her glasses. "Do you have a date you'll be moving into your office space?"

Molly bit into a chocolate-chunk cookie to keep from lying to the woman.

Gloria pursed her lips, scratched her pen across her clipboard and headed toward Hazel's nook. She stopped once to press the toe of her serviceable black flats into a spot on the carpet. Then she studied Hazel's space and scratched more notes. Lifted her head, scrawled more notes. As if she were a renowned artist making a sketch for a commissioned piece.

Molly finished her cookie and reached for another one. Surely, the double-fudge goodness would calm the temporary distress she had.

"It's quite a quaint space for your daughter, isn't it?" Gloria wondered out loud.

Molly wasn't certain she meant *quaint* as in *cozy* and *cute*. More like *peculiar* and *bizarre*.

Molly finished two more cookies while Gloria surveyed her bedroom and bathroom. She wished she'd taken Dan's EMT lessons about how to properly make a bed with hospital corners. Gloria would've most likely appreciated the orderliness.

Gloria reappeared and fiddled with the lock on the bedroom door. She eyed Molly. "What are your childcare plans?"

Molly took a deep drink of her coffee. The coffee only clashed with the chocolate and swirled unpleasantly in her already upset stomach. "We had a not-so-positive experience at a local day care. I'm in the process of interviewing nannies."

Again, Gloria flipped to a new page on her clipboard and wrote a few lines.

"Ideally, I'd like to hire a live-in nanny," Molly added. Then pressed her lips together.

Was that good or bad? Was the woman writing that Molly intended to hire out her mother duties? That wasn't her plan. A live-in nanny simply offered more flexibility for those late nights when Molly was prepping for a trial. Or for unexpected client calls. "But I intend to be fully involved in my daughter's life."

Gloria offered only a drawn-out, "Hmm."

Molly wiped her damp palms on a kitchen towel and waited for Gloria to finish her seemingly endless notes. She'd seen court reporters with less paperwork from a year-long trial.

Finally Gloria lowered her clipboard to the counter. She took a napkin from the holder, placed three cookies in the center and neatly wrapped the stack. One wink at Molly and she said, "I believe I have everything I need."

"Are you sure I can't answer any other questions?" Molly reached for her smile, knew it was strained.

"I'll be in touch if I have any. Thank you for your time." Gloria stuck her cookie stash in her purse, picked up her clipboard and walked to the door. She looked back at Molly.

"This might be out of line, but I have a step-niece on my husband's side. Lovely child despite her no good parents."

Molly braced her hand on the counter and waited, unsure what to say or how to respond.

"She's putting herself through community college right now for her associate degree. She wants to eventually become a lawyer." Gloria paused and eyed Molly, a glint in her eye.

Molly nodded. "I would be happy to sit down with her and talk about law school and her career options."

Gloria's mouth shifted into the smallest of grins. Just a bare twitch. "My step-niece, Rebekah, that is, is also one of the best baby-sitters I've come across. She's good with children of all ages."

Molly discovered her first smile of the morning. "Do you think she might consider becoming a nanny?"

"If she could get out of her parents' house and keep going to college, she'd be wise to accept a position like that." Gloria stepped onto the porch. "And she's always been the smartest one in the family. Have a nice day, Ms. McKinney."

"You too, Mrs. Serrano." Molly walked to the front door.

Gloria stepped off the porch and glanced back. "And Ms. McKinney, that worry inside your chest about whether or not you're a good mom. Well, it means you already are one."

With that last sage comment, Gloria Serrano exited through the backyard, pausing to admire the puppies Brooke had corralled on the grass. Gloria lifted one from the blanket, accepted several puppy kisses on her nose before returning the dog to her siblings. Then she departed, a smile on her face.

Molly joined Brooke and Hazel in the backyard. The puppies played around Hazel on the large blanket. Nala watched Hazel and the puppies as if they were all hers to mother.

Molly sank onto the blanket and stretched out on her back.

Brooke picked up a bottle of bubbles. "How did it go?"

"You should've brought her a puppy sooner." Molly set her arm over her forehead, shielding her eyes from the sun.

"Was it that bad, really?" Brooke rose to sit up straighter.

"She never stopped taking notes." Molly picked up Wish and set the little puppy on her stomach. "Then she offered up her step-niece as a nanny."

"That's good, right?" Brooke blew bubbles with the wand for Hazel to catch.

Molly smoothed her fingers over Wish's head. The tiny puppy closed her eyes and sighed. "I have no idea. Was it a test? A bribe? Do I fail or pass if I hire her step-niece as my nanny?"

"What if her niece is qualified?" Brooke dipped the bubble wand in the solution. "What if it was a sincere suggestion?"

Molly glanced at her friend. "It doesn't really matter. I don't have the niece's contact information."

"You didn't ask for it?"

"Do you think that was a mistake?" Molly countered. Nala scooted over and stretched out against Molly's side.

Brooke launched another round of bubbles into the air. Hazel's laughter burst free and Brooke chuckled along with her. "I think we need a debrief."

"Isn't that what this is?" Molly captured a bubble on her fingertip.

"I mean a full debrief." Brooke laughed. "With everyone."

The bubble popped, leaving a residue on her fingers. "Who's everyone?"

"The usual people." Brooke set the wand into the bottle and sealed the lid. She picked up her phone and started typing. "Leave everything to me. We'll have it here in the backyard. Firepit turned on and the grill heated up."

Molly raised herself up onto her elbows. "This sounds more like a dinner gathering than a debriefing."

"S'mores," Brooke said, ignoring Molly's comment. "We need to make those. Everyone likes those."

"This sounds like a lot of trouble," Molly added.

"Trouble." Brooke looked up from her phone and grinned at Molly. "This isn't trouble. This is what we do."

"What is it we're doing exactly?"

"Eating good food with even better company." Brooke leaned over and touched Molly's arm. "And reminding ourselves that we're never alone. We always have each other."

CHAPTER NINETEEN

DREW WALKED THROUGH Brooke and Dan's house and stepped out onto the back patio. He scanned the yard until his gaze landed on his favorite redhead, then he spotted Hazel, secure in her swing. Ella and Wesley sat on either side of Hazel. Ben held a giant bubble wand and created a bubble large enough for the kids to slide through.

Satisfied that Molly and Hazel were good, he stepped over to the large table where his parents sat, immersed in what looked to be an intense card game. Evie, Dan's dad Rick, Brad and Sophie were their opponents and each one had a more serious game face than the next.

"Get a move on, Drew," Dan shouted from a corner of the backyard. The volleyball net had already been set up. "We've got a game to win."

"I thought this was a debriefing." Drew un-buttoned the collar on his dress shirt and directed his question to the card table. No one glanced up from their cards.

"It is." Brooke tapped Drew affectionately on the shoulder on her way to the stairs and the backyard volleyball game. "It's our kind of debriefing. De-stressing. And decompressing with each other."

Brooke had been the one to text Drew earlier. Her message had been short and to the point.

Dinner at our house tonight. Food is covered, just bring yourself.

Molly had offered fewer details and a dash of uncertainty in her text.

Social worker meeting was fine. I think? See you tonight?

Molly's text had prompted a quick phone call to her between his meetings about Brad's fraud case. Drew had wanted to hear her voice to know for sure she was fine. And he'd learned about Brooke's debriefing plans. He hadn't needed to promise Molly he'd be there. He'd been rearranging his last meeting to leave on time. As it was, he was the last one to arrive.

Sophie looked at him over her cards. "Can't be work all the time, Drew. There's no fun in that."

It hadn't been work exactly for the past several weeks. Not for Drew. He kept that response to himself. And consulting on his brother's case filled hours in the day, but not his entire day like his real job.

As for fun, he spotted Molly again and grinned. He supposed he had been having some of that and finally relaxing. He should thank Molly for the short respite. It would be over soon, and he'd return to work reenergized. He should be more pleased about that, shouldn't he?

He blamed the pang of disappointment on hunger and peeked inside the grill. "Tell me these are Rick's special recipe ribs wrapped in tinfoil and soaking in a dark ale?"

"Those are them." Rick's laugh boomed out across the porch. "But I don't think you'll be allowed to eat unless you join the volleyball game."

Drew glanced into the backyard. Molly went over to the women's side of the net. Her ponytail swung across her back. Her smile stretched across her face, up into her eyes. She looked happy and adorable. And Drew wanted to be beside her. Be near enough to hold her hand if he wanted. Make her laugh if he could. Just be with her. His fun hadn't ended yet. That was for next week after his hearing. Right now, he wanted to be in the moment.

He hurried inside the house, changed into his workout clothes and running shoes. Then sped into the backyard to join Chase and Dan, his teammates.

"Chase Jacobs, I don't care if you're an All-Pro quarterback and married to my best friend." Brooke stood in front of the volleyball net, her hands on her hips. "You're in my backyard now."

Chase grinned broadly and stretched his arms out to his sides. "Bring it, Dog Lady."

"Get it. Dog Lady. Since you like dogs so much." Drew high-fived Chase and restrained his laughter. "Should we play a different game like cornhole?"

"Not happening." Molly slipped her arm around Brooke. Chase's wife, Nichole, moved in on Brooke's other side.

Pride filled Drew. He liked how Molly quickly defended her friends—his friends and now hers. And that felt entirely right. As if Molly had always been a part of their family. As if she'd always belonged.

Molly tossed the volleyball from one hand to the other and stared at the men. There was a challenge in her voice. "Don't worry, height isn't needed when you have heart."

Molly had heart. Drew had seen it every time she interacted with Hazel. He'd witnessed it again when they spoke to Reuben Cote and his daughter. She possessed a gentle, kind and compassionate spirit behind her hard-edged attorney exterior. He'd been glimpsing her loyalty too. And realizing Molly had more layers he wanted to discover.

"That's how you plan to win?" Dan tied his running shoes and joined Drew and Chase for another round of high fives. "If heart is all you got, we'll be done before Dad's ribs finish cooking on the grill."

Nichole tightened her ponytail and rubbed her hands together. "I think we need to make this more interesting."

The men straightened and stepped up to the net.

Chase eyed his wife, amusement and speculation flowed through his question. "What do you ladies have in mind?"

"Ladies." Nichole motioned her teammates closer to her. The women gathered into a huddle to discuss their terms.

Drew watched Molly laugh and offer her own suggestions to her teammates, earning their approval. His grin grew every time she laughed. A punch landed on his shoulder, distracting him. He landed a return tap on Dan's shoulder.

"Harrington, you need to get your head in the game." Dan pointed at him. "We can't win with your puppy-dog eyes tracking Molly's every move."

"That's their strategy." Chase rubbed his hand over his mouth and considered the trio of women. "Distraction."

"We can't go down like that." Dan set a hand on Drew's shoulder, then his other on Chase's shoulder. "We need terms too."

The two teams reconvened and tossed out possible terms and started to negotiate. From the card game on the porch, Brad, their dad William and Dan's dad Rick shouted out their own suggestions. The kids—Wesley, Ben and Ella—paused long enough in their giant bubble making to suggest ice cream be included no matter what.

Finally the terms were set. If the men lost,

they had to plan a mystery date for their partner. Takeout and a movie at home were forbidden as a mystery date option. The women agreed to sing karaoke for at least an hour at The Shouting Fiddle Pub if they lost.

"Game on." Brooke tossed the ball in the air and caught it. "Best of three matches wins."

Drew stepped into position across from Molly. Dan shoved him aside, pointing to the other side of the court. "Over there, puppy-dog eyes."

Chase positioned himself behind Drew and Dan. He clapped his hands together. "Let's see what you got, Brooke."

Two games in with the last game determining the winner, Drew opened a water bottle and splashed his face. "The women have way more than heart, they've got game too."

"And luck." Dan grabbed Drew's water bottle and rinsed off his face.

Chase wiped his forehead with his T-shirt and glanced at Dan. "Your wife has skills, Dan. You didn't think to mention before now that Brooke can really play? Her short height is actually an advantage for her."

"Brooke keeps surprising me. Makes our

marriage more interesting and fun." Dan laughed and shook his head.

Marriage. Drew hadn't ever considered marriage, the dull or the good kind. Marriage required vows and a commitment. But he was dedicated to his work. That was enough, wasn't it?

He glanced across the backyard, watched Molly interact with the kids and Hazel. A warmth—a contentment—filled him. As if he'd suddenly found his place. The one that made life worthwhile. But he knew his place. His work fulfilled him. Sure, he was happy now playing and having fun, but this wasn't sustainable. His work would always be there. That had to mean something.

Drew tugged his thoughts away from the impossible and unwise, and focused on his two friends. "Nichole and Molly are also holding their own."

"My wife likes to pretend she's uncoordinated and too tall for things." Chase scratched his cheek. Admiration filled his voice. "But when Nichole steps up, she's all in."

Would Molly be all in for marriage? Did she want a wedding and a husband? He hadn't heard her complain about being a single parent. Not once. Could she want Drew as a husband?

Drew coughed and pounded on his chest to dislodge that absurd idea. Besides, he wasn't proposing to Molly, so marriage was not relevant. "We gave the women too much incentive to win. We gave them the edge with these mystery dates."

Dan nodded. "I haven't planned a date for Brooke and me in months."

Chase frowned. "Neither have I. I feel bad."

Drew splashed the last of the water over his face to clear his thoughts. Marriage was off the table, despite Reuben advising him not to let Molly go. As for a mystery date with Molly, well, that appealed. Appealed too much. That was bad. "We need to win and head to the karaoke bar."

"Or we could let the women win," Chase offered.

"You want to throw the game?" Drew challenged. "Let your wives win so you can plan mystery dates for them?" He'd have to plan one for Molly. His attorney. His friend. How was he supposed to stay in his professional lane on a mystery date? Did he even want to stay in his lane?

"Nichole deserves a night out." Chase raised his arms and lifted his shoulders. "She deserves way more than that."

Dan nodded. "Brooke too."

"Look, I get it." What Drew didn't get was why the idea of throwing the game enticed him so much. There could be no date with Molly. What if he wanted another one? Then one more. He would return to his sixty-hours-a-week job—when could he possibly go on a date? Molly deserved a real boyfriend—the kind that made her feel special and appreciated. She deserved to be put first. He ran a hand through his hair, already despising any man who wanted to date Molly. "But we don't play to lose. Ever. What does that teach your boys?"

"That their wives' happiness is important," Dan stated.

"Good point," Chase agreed.

"Okay, you can plan special date nights after we listen to the women sing karaoke at the pub. Got it?" Drew clapped his hands together as if pumping up his teammates.

"Wait." Dan wiped his forehead and eyed Drew. "You're not scared of taking Molly on a mystery date, are you?"

Chase moved beside Dan and eyed him from his head to his toes. "He could be. I've never seen Drew this head over heels for a woman."

Head over heels? Chase couldn't be serious. Drew was intrigued and interested in Molly. Not head over heels for her. "I'm definitely not that. I like her. I've liked women in the past. It's not shocking."

Chase and Dan shared a knowing look.

"What?" Drew asked. Now was the time to prove to his friends and himself that he had other priorities. "I like her, but work comes first for me. You guys know that."

"Until it doesn't," Chase mumbled. "But that's not our focus right now."

"Winning is our focus," Drew reminded them and turned toward the court.

Dan's words stopped him. "If we win, you have to still take Molly on a real date."

Drew closed his eyes, cursed his all-too-perceptive friends and counted to ten. One date. Surely, he could handle that. Not turn it into something more than it was. A night out with a friend. "Fine. Now can we finish this game? I'm hungry."

Chase and Dan ran back onto the court and began trash talking. Drew served the volleyball over the net, neatly and precisely. Too bad it wasn't as easy to launch his interest in Molly over the net too. As it was, he considered and discarded ideas for their one date with each point earned.

Nothing felt right. And if he was taking Molly on one date, it had to be perfect. After all, she deserved nothing less.

The women won in a tiebreaker and celebrated all the way through dinner and s'mores assembly. They were still high-fiving each other at the end of the evening during their goodbyes.

Drew couldn't quite locate his irritation that they'd lost. As for Chase and Dan, they were pleased with the outcome. They hadn't thrown the game—already a rematch had been scheduled. But they'd still won somehow. Over dinner, Dan had asked Drew for his baseball seats for an upcoming Friday night game, his mystery date plans for Brooke already set in motion.

Molly asked Drew to stop by her apartment before he headed home. She wanted to put Hazel to bed and discuss Reuben's upcoming appointment with the notary. Drew ignored Chase's raised eyebrows and Dan's jab in the ribs.

He made quick use of the shower in Dan and Brooke's guest bathroom and headed over to Molly's apartment. Telling himself on the short walk across the backyard that he'd stay in his lane. Keep it professional.

But telling himself and listening to himself proved to be two different things entirely. From the moment Molly opened the door, her cheeks scrubbed clean and her hair damp, Drew misplaced all thoughts of work and his case. He realized he only wanted to spend more time with Molly. Period. Molly, the woman. Not Molly his legal counsel.

"No work talk tonight. That's for tomorrow, in the daylight." Drew flipped over Molly's dry-erase board to reveal the blank side. He could learn more about Molly and not turn it into anything other than hanging out with a friend. He should know his friends. That was simply being a good friend in return. "Let's talk about vacation goals."

"Vacation goals?" Molly curled her bare feet under her on the couch and considered Drew. "I can't remember the last real vacation I took."

"Me either." Drew laughed. He hadn't taken a vacation in years. Never could find the time between cases. Yet now, looking at Molly, he considered it. But considering wasn't actually doing. All this fun was lifting his spirits, and he hoped Molly's. "But if you were going to take ten days off and go big, where are you going?"

"Easy." Molly grabbed a handful of chocolate candy from the dish she'd carried over to the coffee table and pointed at him. "A villa in Tuscany."

"I like it." *A lot.* Private villa set on the cliffs overlooking the ocean. . And with an extraordinary woman like Molly. He could book tickets tonight.

Drew uncapped a dry-erase pen, stoppered his own unusual impulsiveness and wrote vacation goals across the dry-erase board. This was only a silly game. "Can we stop in Venice too?"

"Absolutely." Molly leaned into the couch and popped a candy in her mouth. "As long as we take several gondola rides."

"That's a given." He'd seen pictures of the gondolas in Venice, couples cuddling as they passed under the historic bridges. He'd always believed he'd rather walk to get to his destination faster; but with Molly beside him, a slow gondola ride through the city tempted him more. Back to their conversation. "Next up. Weekend getaway."

"I have always wanted to stay at a bed-and-breakfast," Molly said. "On the coast."

"Or in wine country," Drew offered.

"Even better." Molly lifted her wine glass in a toast. "What's next? Staycation."

"Day ski trip," Drew tossed out.

"Too cold." Molly shook her head. "And a ski chalet sounds like it deserves a longer stay than a day."

"Agreed." Drew snapped his fingers. "Baseball game."

"Yes. Definitely. Seats behind the first baseline." Molly tapped her chin and grinned. "Ballpark hot dog and French fries with ranch dressing."

Drew stilled and considered her. "You're serious?"

She laughed. "I'm into most sports. Baseball, volleyball…"

He grinned. "Okay, champ." He had season tickets to the Bay Area Angel's baseball games. He'd been giving his seats away the past few years, citing work conflicts. The truth was he hadn't wanted to go alone, and he hadn't wanted to go with just anyone. "I've just never dated any women interested in baseball."

"You've been dating the wrong ones then." She popped another handful of candy in her mouth and smiled around her mouthful of chocolate.

He was definitely starting to see that he might've been dating the wrong women. The right woman sat on a couch in his friend's in-law unit, grinning at him. But if Molly was the right woman, then Drew had truly jumped out of his lane. And what was supposed to have been a fun get-to-know-you-better exercise had turned into something more serious.

As a last-ditch effort to keep himself fo cused on the fun, he searched for some uncommon ground. Anything to prove Molly wasn't the right woman. Not for him.

"Now I'm craving a ballpark hot dog." Molly touched her stomach. "Only place I eat a hot dog is at a baseball game."

"Do you eat out or cook more?" As a final attempt, it wasn't all that strong. Still, he ran with it. Desperate times. Finding the right woman hadn't been on his agenda. He was supposed to be getting his old life back.

"Unfortunately, a lot of takeout." Molly twisted her hair into a loose bun on top of her head. "I want to learn to cook more. Once I'm more settled, maybe I'll find a cooking class that specializes in quick meals. I should be making good choices as an example to Hazel."

"Cooking for one isn't the same." He sat on the couch beside her, purposely well out of accidental-touching distance. "What about when you were with your ex?"

"Derrick preferred to eat and be seen." She paused and frowned at him. "You're wondering why I was with him for so long."

Drew was curious. From the little he knew, her ex didn't seem to be a good fit for her. Already Drew was a better partner based on the similar likes and dislikes checklist. He was definitely more interested in seeing Molly for who she was than being seen with her. And if he were honest, he'd much prefer having her to himself—sharing more moments exactly like this one.

But all of that only mattered if Drew was interested in being her partner and if she was interested in him, neither of which was true.

"Derek and I worked together at Loft and Concord." Molly pulled the blanket off the back of the couch and covered her legs. "We made a good team and had great results. Everyone at the firm was thrilled."

"Naturally you should've been a good team

at home too." Drew set his arm on the back of the couch rather than take her hand.

"We should have been." She ran her fingers over the soft blanket. "It was nice for a while."

"What happened?" he asked.

"I got pregnant." She looked at him. The mix of emotions in her gaze swept into her hushed tone. "You really learn a person's core values in a life-changing event like that."

"What did you learn?" He edged toward her. Disliking her sudden sadness. Wanting only to see her joy return.

She considered him. "I learned good work isn't a good enough foundation for a relationship. I thought he loved me, would stand with me no matter what. Once I realized that wasn't the case, I left him and the firm."

"What is a good foundation?" What made him certain she was the right woman? What established a good foundation? What was it about her that pulled him to her? And made him want to seize Reuben's advice and not ever let her go.

"I'm not sure." She sat up. Strands of her hair slipped free, curved around her face. Her smile wavered. A trace of humor highlighted her words. "Maybe it's shared vacation goals, Santa pictures and mystery date bets."

"Maybe you're right." Drew couldn't push aside his feelings any longer. The pull toward Molly was too strong, too real. He leaned forward and twisted a strand of her hair around his fingers. He curved his other hand under her chin. "Or maybe it's something like this."

She met him halfway. And he lost himself again.

The kiss went on. Transitioned from learning to giving and receiving. To simply feeling.

And in that moment, he discovered a connection and the beginnings of the foundation he was looking for.

CHAPTER TWENTY

SEVERAL DAYS AND several good-night kisses on the front porch later, Drew carried an exhausted Hazel through the backyard to Molly's apartment. Their Sunday had been spent at the park. First, a soccer game with the Sawyer family. Then a walk around the pond to watch the ducks and swans. "I still can't believe Wesley made that goal against Dan to win the game."

"It was amazing." Molly grinned and pulled her keys from the diaper bag. "My teammates were the best."

"Next time, I'm picking the preteen soccer whizzes for my team," Drew said. He'd always picked Molly for his flag football team in college. "And you can have Brooke and Dan."

"I expected better after Brooke's volleyball play the other night." Molly shook her head.

"I should have known you had soccer skills." Drew nudged his shoulder against hers.

"I don't." Molly laughed and opened her apartment door. "Wesley and Ben made up for my lack of talent. And they might have shared a few insider secrets with me about Brooke and Dan."

"Totally not fair," Drew said. "But I like the boys' game play."

"Well, there's a rematch already scheduled for next Sunday," Molly said. "I suppose we'll have to revise our game plan now that I revealed our secret to winning."

Drew had a few secrets of his own too. Ones that included how much he liked Molly. How much he liked working with her. How much he liked being with her. "Hazel has a secret too."

"What's that?" Molly turned around.

Drew handed the baby to her. "In addition to needing a bath, she also needs a diaper change."

"So, you're handing her off," Molly teased. "Just like that."

"I need to clean up too. I plan to shower in the guest bathroom in the main house." Drew pulled several blades of grass from Hazel's hair. "You'd think Hazel had joined us for the soccer game."

"As soon as she's bigger, I don't think there

will be any way to keep her off the soccer field or the volleyball court." Molly laughed and brushed the dirt off Hazel's cheek. "As it was, Rick got more of a workout than we did following Hazel all around the park."

"She's a fast crawler and really starting to get her legs under her." Dan's father had walked Hazel around the perimeter of the soccer field, her tiny hands braced inside his. Drew had demonstrated how Hazel preferred to be assisted. Hazel and Drew had been perfecting the best place for him to stand to help her learn to walk the past few days. Not that he was bragging, but Hazel walked the best with him beside her.

"Then it's trouble ahead for sure." Molly moved toward the bedroom. "Showers and clean clothes, then we'll meet back here to discuss dinner."

"I could definitely use some food." Drew headed outside and crossed the backyard.

The last four days, they'd settled into a comfortable routine. Nap time and evenings when Hazel was asleep had been spent prepping for Drew's upcoming hearing. Drew would always return to his loft each night, alone, but no longer feeling lonely. Their afternoons had been spent walking around the park or playing in the backyard with Nala and her puppies. A volleyball rematch had occurred the prior evening. Once again, the women had won, so the tally for mystery dates organized by the men had now doubled.

Sophie had vowed to join the matches after the twins finally arrived, claiming she wanted a few mystery dates of her own.

The entire week had been fun-filled. And Drew had been upbeat. And happy. And every hour he spent with Molly and Hazel only made him want more time with them. He shook his head. He should be getting his head back into work mode. Instead he wanted to enjoy Molly and Hazel and the time they had together.

He supposed he should feel regret or guilt. Work came first. But no matter how deep he searched, he just kept discovering more layers of contentment.

Drew walked inside the Sawyers' kitchen and called out Brooke's name. Her reply came from the laundry room. He heard the showers on upstairs and assumed Dan and Wesley had already escaped to wash off the residual stains from their soccer game. "Okay if I use your guest bathroom?"

"Fine." Brooke kept her gaze fixed on Nala's puppies.

Brooke's distracted tone pulled Drew farther into the laundry room. Nala greeted him with her customary tail wag and welcoming whine. "Something wrong?"

"Wish won't eat her kibble." Brooke nudged a small bowl closer to the puppy. The tiny dog dropped back on wobbly legs. Her brother Milo waddled over and began eating the water-soaked dry food.

"What now?" Wish, the smallest and most fragile, teetered and lay down beside her brother. Nala licked Wish's face as if encouraging the puppy to eat, then shifted her all too expressive gaze to Drew as if requesting his help.

"A bottle in a quiet room for Wish." Brooke opened a cabinet and pulled out her supplies. "When she tries to nurse, her siblings push her out of the way."

"I can feed her at Molly's." Drew knelt, stroked his fingers over Wish's head, then reached over to stroke Nala's back for his regular rib-check. The mother dog had finally gained some much-needed weight. He'd been sneaking her extra treats whenever he visited. "It's quiet and no sibling distractions for her there."

"Would you mind?" Brooke asked. "I'll get everything prepared while you shower. It's family dinner night and Rick's choice. We're heading to Roadside Burgers soon."

Family dinner. Drew supposed he was having something like that with Molly. More of that contentment widened his grin. "Get the cookie dough and extra whipped cream milkshake. It's the best one there." Drew headed toward the guest room. "I'll be quick."

Ten minutes later, his hair still damp and wearing fresh clothes, Drew made his way back to Molly's apartment. A bottle of warm puppy formula in one hand, Wish cradled in the other. "We have company."

Molly smiled from her seat at the kitchen table. Hazel sat in her high chair and shoved a macaroni noodle into her mouth.

Drew sat beside Molly at the table. "Wish isn't taking to her kibble like everyone else. Brooke says she lost weight again."

"We'll get her eating." Molly opened a jar of applesauce. Hazel bounced in her high chair. The little girl tossed her arms over her head, sending bits of macaroni airborne.

"Maybe we need to find a kibble flavor that

Wish likes the same way Hazel loves applesauce." Drew laughed. Dinnertime had become more than a necessity for Drew. With Hazel and Molly, it was an experience. From the conversation to food trials, he couldn't remember when he'd looked forward to meals so much.

"That's not a bad idea," Molly dipped the silicone spoon into the jar. Hazel hummed. "But first, we need dinner ideas for ourselves. I'm starving."

"Delivery or takeout?" Drew stroked his finger down Wish's small head and made sure the puppy was still drinking.

"Delivery." Molly touched her leg and looked at him. "I'm not the slightest bit ashamed to admit this is the most exercise I've done in so many consecutive days. I'm sore."

"Understood." Drew stretched the sore muscles in his neck and adjusted his hold on Wish and the bottle. "No judgment from me. I'm feeling the same as you."

Molly flexed her legs. "Thank goodness I'm not the only one. I take it you weren't using the treadmill in the office workout room on your breaks either."

"I belong to the gym across the street from

the DA offices." Drew checked the amount of formula still left in the bottle. Wish was steadily and slowly drinking her dinner. Drew was steadily and slowly realizing he had to make his health another of his priorities. "I can tell you I walked by that gym almost every day, but going inside it did not happen as often as it should have."

"I told myself I was going to get more fit once Hazel and I got settled here." Molly scooped a spoonful of applesauce out of the jar and fed Hazel. "I think it's important to be a healthy mom."

Drew nodded. *A healthy dad.* He wanted to be that too. If and when he was a dad. "Maybe we should make an exercise deal." And he could have one more excuse to spend time with Molly.

"Become accountability workout partners for each other." Molly grinned.

Or just partners. That contentment leveled up. "Yeah, something like that."

Molly held out her hand.

He switched his grip on Wish and her bottle to slip his right hand into Molly's. And he stood and sealed their deal with a quick kiss. As if Molly, deals and kissing were a natural part of his day. "Now back to food. What's your craving?"

"I've chosen the last few nights." She stirred the applesauce around in the jar.

"And I've liked everything you've picked." Just as he liked her. Just as he liked being with her. "I know you have something specific in mind."

"You can say no," she said.

As if he wanted to. Molly had very specific food cravings. He found it adorable.

"Okay," she said. "I really want sushi."

"I know a place that delivers." He waited for Molly to wipe her hands on a towel and pick up her cell phone. "Look up Mission Sushi. They have an online menu."

Their dinner order placed and Wish's bottle almost empty, Drew settled a sleeping Wish onto the blanket bed he'd fluffed for the tiny puppy between himself and the armrest.

Molly curled beside him, picked up the remote for the TV and scrolled through the movie selection. Hazel babbled in her swing and chewed on a frozen teether. "I picked dinner. You pick the movie."

Her phone vibrated on the coffee table. Molly picked it up and said a quick greeting to Lorrie Cote. Drew assumed Lorrie was

confirming the details for the notary scheduled to take Reuben's official statement the
next morning.

But Molly dropped the TV remote on the
floor. Her gaze fastened on Drew's. Her face
paled. Nothing more than a whispered, "I'm
sorry," escaped between her lips into the cell
phone.

Drew placed his feet on the ground as if he
needed the stability. His heart raced. Dread
pooled in his stomach. And that contentment
dissolved like vapor.

Molly disconnected her call. Her phone
thumped against the coffee table, the sound
jarring the heavy silence. "That was Lorrie.
Reuben…he's…"

Drew scooted toward Molly and grabbed
her hand. Her very cold hand.

"Reuben is gone," Molly murmured. "He
passed earlier this evening."

Drew felt numb.

He'd spoken to Reuben only yesterday.
Reuben had been in good spirits. No pain.
He'd even asked Drew if he'd changed his
mind about letting Molly get away. Drew had
laughed and confessed, *I'm thinking about
keeping her.*

You think too long and you will lose her,

Reuben had replied. *Remember, there's a time to think and a time to risk. Could be it's the best risk you've ever taken.*

Now, Reuben was gone. Reunited with his Trina. And Drew was... "I'm going to be found guilty."

A man—a friend—had just passed and all Drew could consider was his own future. He scrubbed his palms over his face. *Selfish. One hundred percent selfish.* Yet, Drew couldn't stall his thoughts or the full impact of Reuben's death.

Molly shivered beside him and rose. "You haven't been proven guilty of anything.

"The video won't be admissible without Reuben's testimony," he argued. "Reuben was the one who could verify that it was him and Cory Vinson in that video. We both know the other person in the video could be anyone."

Molly wrapped her arms around herself as if holding herself together. Her palms ran up and down her arms.

He should be holding Molly. Except, he was falling apart himself. "That other person could even be me."

He pushed off the couch and stared blankly at the wall. He was lost all over again. Set up, with no way out.

"We need to pivot." Molly shook herself and pressed her hands against her temples. "Gina Hahn needs to testify on your behalf."

Drew shook his head. "We promised not to involve her any further."

"We can protect her." Resolve firmed Molly's voice.

"How are we supposed to do that?" Drew grabbed the bag of workout clothes he'd set on a kitchen stool and twisted the canvas in his hands. Frustration and disappointment, sadness and grief swallowed him whole. He headed for the door. The nearest exit. "I can't even protect myself."

"Where are you going?" She rushed after him.

"I need to go." He kept his gaze fixed on the door.

"We need to discuss our strategy." Molly jumped in front of him, blocking his path. "We need to talk this through."

"I can't right now. A friend just passed away." As had his freedom. All the while, he'd been having fun and pretending he had a new foundation. That he could have a different kind of future. The truth buckled his knees. "I need to be alone."

"Drew. Listen to me." Molly set her hands

on his shoulders and locked her gaze on his. "This isn't over. We haven't even really started the fight."

"That's what I always tell my clients after a setback." How hollow his words had been. How empty and insincere. "Then I tell my clients to check their emotions."

Molly's face closed down. No doubt she had told her clients the very same thing.

"Funny, I never understood exactly how hard that was until this case." He pulled her hands off his shoulders, released her grip on him. His grip on himself was harder to maintain. "I need a moment alone. I can't do this right now."

Molly opened and closed her mouth. He saw the desire to argue flitter through her gaze. Finally she stepped aside and let him leave.

Drew slipped out the side gate, ran into the delivery woman from Mission Sushi. He paid for the food and directed her to Molly's apartment. Then he climbed into his truck and let go of his emotions.

CHAPTER TWENTY-ONE

MOLLY PRESSED THE button for the twenty-fourth floor inside the elevator and watched the glass doors slide shut. She had no stroller this time. No Drew beside her. And Brad Harrington wasn't expecting her. But she doubted Brad would be surprised to see her in his office this early on a Monday morning.

Drew's truck had barely pulled out of the driveway last night when she'd picked up her phone to call Brad and fill him in. She'd wanted someone to talk to Drew and get him to listen. Even more, she hadn't wanted Drew to be alone.

Molly smoothed her palms down the front of her suit jacket and tugged on the sleeves. Her briefcase, not the diaper bag, hung from her shoulder. She wasn't the part-time mom, part-time attorney discussing strategy in her yoga pants.

Today, she was Molly McKinney, top-notch criminal defense attorney. From her favorite black heels and courtroom suit to her controlled composure. Today was about business and doing the best job for her client.

She offered a tight don't-question-me smile to the receptionist and pointed down the hall to Brad's office. "I'm here to see Mr. Harrington."

The receptionist opened her mouth and nodded.

Molly swept past the receptionist's desk. At the door to Brad's office, she knocked and said politely, "Sorry for the intrusion. Is this a bad time?"

"Molly. Come in. My meetings don't start for another hour." Brad motioned her inside and watched her closely. "Have you spoken to Drew?"

"Not since he left my apartment last evening." She had texted Drew. No response. She'd left a voice mail. Again, no response. Still, she had work to do. A case to conclude. "Have you seen him?"

"I saw him last night." Brad rolled his chair away from his desk.

An ache pulsed in her chest. Drew had shut her out, but not his brother. She was grateful Drew hadn't been alone, and yet she hurt. "I need that folder on Gina Hahn."

Brad twisted, picked up the purple folder from the shelf behind him. He stood and handed her the file. "How can I help?"

"You've done enough." Drew wasn't alone. He had his brother beside him, as it should be. Family came first for both Drew and Molly. What she accomplished over the next few days on Drew's case would benefit her small family of two. "I can handle things from here."

"What about Drew?" Brad's gaze tracked her with that same shrewd sharpness that Drew possessed.

Drew had walked away last night, refusing to talk. With everything at stake once again, she had to break a promise she'd given to Drew. How else would they prove it was Vinson, not Drew, in the video without Reuben on the stand to officially identify Cory Vinson in the recording? Vinson could just deny it all and push the claims of witness tampering back on Drew. There was no other way to win and thereby get Drew his old life back.

Her heart was always destined to lose. She'd known that all along and still let herself fall for him anyway. "I'm getting Drew exactly what he wants."

"And that is?" Brad leaned into the corner of his desk and crossed his arms over his chest, his posture casual as if he hadn't quite taken a firm position. As if he could be swayed. She recognized the stance.

But Molly had already defined hers. Already knew where she stood. "Drew wants his old life back."

Brad's eyebrows lowered. "He told you that?"

"Last week on our way to Sacramento." Okay, Drew hadn't said it since then, but Molly hadn't asked either. Afraid he hadn't expanded his wants to include both herself and Hazel.

Once she called in Gina to testify, and truly broke her promise to Drew, she knew she'd destroy any chance that he would want to be with her. Trust, once broken, was almost impossible to regain. She lifted her chin. "The right decision is to get Gina Hahn to testify."

"I agree," Brad said.

No challenge. No argument. Why couldn't Drew see it, as well?

But she already knew why. Drew protected everyone before himself. And he didn't want Gina Hahn in harm's way. He already carried so much regret and guilt for Van Solis's wrongful conviction. So that left Molly to watch out for Drew. And she would do it her way. "Can I call you if I need more information?"

"You can call me for anything," Brad said. "I mean that. Anything. You're not alone either."

"I appreciate that." Molly walked toward the door. "I'll be in touch if anything comes up."

She slipped out of Brad's office and headed for the elevators. The glass elevator descended to the lobby, and a different kind of loneliness draped over Molly. As if she'd already lost Drew and so much more. But she'd never allowed her emotions to interfere with her judgment or her decisions as an attorney and she refused to start now.

As soon as she stepped off the elevator, she pulled out the file folder on Gina Hahn, located the woman's current address and opened her ride share app to request a car. She detoured into Roasted Vibes Café, sent a text to Brooke to check on Hazel while in line, then placed a to-go order with Brandie.

The contents of Gina Hahn's file studied and absorbed during her ride-share trip, Molly stuck the folder back in her briefcase, gathered her to-go order and thanked her driver. She had the information she required to approach the woman for her testimony. She never reconsidered her plan. Simply descended the stairs that led to Gina's basement-level apartment and rang the bell.

The front door cracked open. Gina glared at her through the small gap. "I knew you would return."

"It wasn't planned or my first choice." Molly shifted to reveal the twin coffee cups she held. "Can we talk? I need five minutes of your time."

Gina opened the door wider, aimed her chin at the coffee. "What is it?"

"Double café macchiato. It was always a favorite at my old firm." Details mattered. Always. Drew had told Molly what he wanted, and her heart hadn't listened. Details she should've heeded.

Molly handed the woman one of the cups, hoping the caffeine might help whatever might be weighing on Gina's shoulders. "And strawberry lemon cream cheese scones."

Gina accepted the coffee, opened her door and padded barefoot across the nicked hardwood floors in the modest apartment.

"We received the flash drive." Molly noticed the stack of legal textbooks on a bookshelf next to an array of kid's books crammed in the corner. "Thank you."

"Then you have what you need." Gina stood in her kitchen and cradled her coffee in both hands. Her shoulders hunched as if she wanted to disappear.

"Not exactly." Molly faced her over the kitchen's breakfast bar. Clothes and towels were piled on the only two stools. "Reuben Cote, the key witness, in the Van Solis murder trial passed away yesterday."

Gina sipped her coffee. The edges of her eyes softened, but nothing else. "That's sad."

"And unfortunate." Molly pulled the bag of strawberry lemon scones from her purse and set them on the counter. "Reuben died before we gained his sworn statement regarding his first video testimony. And now he can't speak in person at Drew Harrington's hearing either."

Gina held her cup in front of her mouth and stared at Molly. Fear tinted the anger, turning her words into an accusation. "You want me to testify at Drew Harrington's hearing instead."

"We need someone who can authenticate the video and the identities of the two people in it." Molly kept her voice calm and her gaze on Gina. "That's you."

"You want me to come out and publicly accuse Cory Vinson of misconduct." More anger rushed into her voice. But the fear widened her dark eyes. "The current and very popular district attorney, who will be up for reelection this fall."

"I know what I'm asking," Molly said.

"Do you?" Gina flung her hand out. "You want me to challenge the district attorney. I have a daughter. My whole family's livelihood depends on that restaurant. I never came forward before in order to protect what little we have. Exposing my secrets exposes them too."

"I can help you." Molly indicated the stack of law books in the corner. "That was your dream, wasn't it?"

"Dreams die." Gina frowned at her coffee cup.

"No," Molly said. "You were forced to leave paralegal school because of one man. Blacklisted in the legal community because of that same man. I want to remove that stain you're carrying around."

"I don't care about the stain on me." Gina flung an arm out, pointing to Harper's toys.

"I left the DA's office to protect my daughter from her lying father. And that flash drive was my insurance that Cory stayed out of our lives for good."

Vinson was the father of Gina's child. Molly more than understood Gina's motives to protect her daughter. She smoothed her expression into neutral. "But you sent the flash drive to me."

"Because I trust you to make things right." Gina raised her chin. "Cory needs to be stopped. He's done enough damage."

"I will make things right. For you, too, if you let me help you."

"But you need my testimony." Gina tilted her head as if assessing Molly's sincerity.

"It's not complicated, Gina." Molly reached into the outside pocket of her briefcase.

"It comes down to your conscience. Pokes at your integrity." Integrity she knew Gina possessed. Molly set her business card on the edge of the counter. She walked to Gina's front door and turned back. "You need to decide if it's better to risk everything for someone who deserves it, or to remain silent for someone who doesn't."

CHAPTER TWENTY-TWO

JUST BEFORE DINNER that evening, Molly opened the door to her apartment and considered her client. No enthusiastic greeting slipped free. No welcome back.

"I tried calling you earlier." Drew rubbed the back of his neck.

"I had business to take care of." Molly leaned against the doorjamb and folded her arms across her chest rather than invite Drew inside. She had to restore those boundaries, starting now. "Then I spent the afternoon with the real-estate agent."

Drew nodded. "Did you find a suitable office space?"

"I have a few options." And no intention of elaborating further. She'd chosen to cross those boundary lines and she'd only hurt herself in the end. She had to stand firm now. "Why are you here? The hearing is tomorrow morning and you insinuated last night that we had discussed all we needed to."

"I'm sorry about last night." He winced, and the corners of his eyes flinched as if his apology jarred him too.

She pressed her lips together and nodded.

He cleared his throat. "I'd like to talk about the hearing. The video will be submitted to Judge Bartlett and the trial counsel at the opening of the hearing."

"A patient doesn't get to tell his cardiac surgeon how he wants his pacemaker put in." Molly narrowed her gaze on him and never budged from the doorway. "The surgeon is the expert. The surgeon knows how to proceed. It's why the patient chose the best cardiac surgeon in the state." It was why Drew had chosen Molly.

Drew tucked his hands in his dress pant pockets, rocked back on his heels, but never retreated. "I'm not just a client."

Nor was she just an attorney. "But you are my client. I'm still your attorney. And I need to advise against this course of action."

"We have to submit the evidence," Drew argued.

"And let Judge Bartlett and the trial counsel determine that you are the one in the video with Reuben Cote," Molly countered. "There's no one to deny it without Reuben."

Other than Gina, and as of five minutes ago, Molly hadn't heard from the woman. She believed Gina Hahn had a conscience; otherwise the woman would not have collected evidence on Cory Vinson over the years she had worked as his legal assistant. And if Gina had intended to use the information to blackmail Vinson, she would never have mailed the flash drive to Molly in the first place.

"What other choice do we have?" Drew tipped his head back and scowled at the porch overhang.

"We need to convince them that their evidence is compromised." With Gina Hahn's testimony, that would be a given. Molly wanted to pull out her phone and check to see if Gina had finally called. Molly had other arguments prepared just in case Gina decided to keep silent.

"This isn't a jury of citizens we handpicked," Drew said. "It's specially selected judges and trial counsel peers who are scholars more versed in the law and all its subtleties."

"I know who we are facing." The State Bar Association wasn't a trivial bunch. Judge Bartlett's decision tomorrow would be submitted to the State Supreme Court. The Court would have the power to take away Drew's legal career, past and future, in one final judgment.

"I should go alone to the hearing." Drew's voice turned somber, his gaze solemn.

"That's not how this works." Molly's fingers curled into her palms. Frustration swelled inside her. Stubborn man. Always protecting someone else.

His gaze narrowed on her. "Clients terminate their agreements with their attorneys all the time."

"Is that what you're doing?" Molly asked.

"Why put yourself in the line of fire?" He speared his hands out to either side, his own frustration clearly showing. "Why risk your reputation too?"

"Because I don't walk away from my clients or my cases. Because I don't give up." She wanted to risk so much more for Drew if only he'd let her. But he wanted to protect her—that was his way. She wanted to scream, be angry with him. She wanted to embrace him and admit she was touched by his worry. Instead she said, "Since when did you start giving up?"

"I'm not giving up." He shoved his hands

back inside his pockets, closed himself off again. "It's more about acceptance."

Could he have ever accepted what they shared? What they had together?

"You don't have to defend me tomorrow." His quiet words dropped into the evening air.

She didn't have to defend him, but she would protect him whether he wanted her to or not. "I'll see you at court tomorrow morning. Don't forget to polish your shoes and iron your suit."

As for Molly, she'd hide her heart and concentrate on the hearing in a place where she excelled: the courtroom.

"That's it?" he asked.

"We both need to get sleep, Drew. And it's past Hazel's bedtime." Molly reached for the apartment door. "We both need to be sharp tomorrow morning."

That lost look returned. The one she'd seen for the first time at the gala on the patio. She hadn't seen that look on Drew for a while. She wanted to believe she'd been the one to take away his loneliness. Still wanted to believe once they won that he'd admit how he felt. That he'd forgive her.

She had to face the truth.

He was and had only ever been her client.

"Good night, Drew." She shut the door, walked to Hazel's swing and picked up her daughter. The only family she needed.

CHAPTER TWENTY-THREE

DREW STOOD OUTSIDE the courtroom and patted his suit pant pockets. No stray coins. No pennies. No matter. The time for wishing had passed.

Soon Judge Bartlett would announce the start of Drew Harrington's disbarment hearing and invite counsel to proceed.

Clinton Curtis, the State Bar prosecutor, would set out to demonstrate Drew's misconduct in the Van Solis murder trial, leaning heavily on Reuben Cote's retraction of his eyewitness account of the murder. Reuben had lied under oath. On the witness stand. That was fact.

Also fact was that Reuben had lied to Drew during their days of pre-trial preparations. Reuben had lied every time he looked at Drew and stuck to his eyewitness account. Only Drew hadn't known Reuben had falsified that. And that was harder to verify. Not impossible, but not probable without Reuben's testimony now.

Drew buttoned his suit coat and tried to ignore the unrest deep inside him. He hurt for Reuben's family and their loss. Hurt for himself. Despised the defeat pulsing in his throat. Encouraged the defiance stiffening his shoulders. And welcomed the pride he couldn't suppress in his heart.

If he was going to lose his reputation and his career in the next few hours, he would not cower. He'd make his final courtroom appearance count.

He opened the door to the courtroom. His gaze scanned the twin tables at the front of the room, slowed and fixed on Molly. Her bold red suit radiated power and confidence. Her ponytail, sleek and fixed, sharpened her appearance and matched her shrewd gaze.

A different sort of pride roared through Drew for this amazing woman, who stood beside him now, and was prepared to defend him even as the odds of succeeding were against them.

He wanted to take her hand as if she anchored him. But that was wrong. What did he have to offer her? At worst, he had no career. At best, he returned to his former ways, immersed in his work. But his work mattered to people who'd been hurt or worse. He mattered at work. And dedicating his life to that hardly felt wrong.

Molly turned and noticed him. Her eyes barely softened. Her mouth didn't lift into a warm smile. And that felt entirely wrong.

He wanted her smile. Her laughter. Her affection. But only because he was greedy and selfish.

All that verified Molly McKinney deserved a better man than Drew.

A man that would commit completely to her. Put her first. Without hesitation. Without question.

Drew walked over to the table and set his briefcase on the floor. He faced Molly. "I know how to proceed. The video can be used as linkage evidence. It proves Reuben's retraction of his testimony is authentic. And the time-date stamp on the video strengthens the argument that I had no knowledge as I became lead prosecutor twelve days later."

"Drew. Sit." Molly motioned to the empty chair at the table. "I have this under control. I know what I'm doing."

But I don't. I don't want to lose. Not his career. Not Molly. Alarm and something eerily close to fear weakened his composure. He dropped into the chair. "What are you doing?"

Molly sat beside him and touched his arm. "You have to trust me."

Trust her with what? His career? His future? His heart?

Drew rose at the introduction of the Honorable Nora Bartlett. He pressed his fingertips into the tabletop as if he required the thick wood to remain standing. Judge Bartlett announced the case and invited the counsel to begin.

Everything proceeded as it should. Until Molly stood and called a witness not on the list.

Molly brought Gina Hahn to the stand. Then everything tilted and blurred as if Drew were watching the proceedings from a very far distance.

He watched Gina place her left hand on the New Testament and raise her right hand, swearing to tell the whole truth.

He listened to Molly question Gina, establishing her identity and connection to the district attorney's office and her personal, but former, relationship with the current district attorney, Cory Vinson. Then Molly submitted the video recording as evidence and attested to its validity.

Drew held his breath as Gina confirmed the recording was of Reuben Cote and Cory Vinson. She was positive as she had in fact recorded the video. Drew exhaled.

Gina continued, explaining that Drew could not have known about Mr. Cote's initial testimony or the recording at the time because she possessed the only copy. Cory Vinson had assumed Gina destroyed the recording when he'd asked her to. Molly submitted further evidence to corroborate the exact date Drew had stepped in as chief counsel on the Van Solis murder trial.

Molly returned to the chair beside Drew. Once again, he wanted to reach for her hand. But this wasn't a game. They weren't out to dinner, trying to keep a new relationship under wraps. They were in a courtroom, fighting for his innocence.

Worse, Molly had gone behind his back and brought Gina Hahn into the spotlight. How was he supposed to protect Gina now? He'd ruined Van Solis's life. He never wanted to repeat that mistake.

If he was cleared, and no one questioned Molly's decision, Gina could still be collateral damage. And every day Drew would question if there had been another way. A better way. One that hadn't included harming another life to save his own.

Molly ended her questioning. Judge Bartlett offered Clint, the trial counsel, his opportunity to cross-examine the witness. During the rapid questioning, Gina never stumbled. Never lost her composure.

But Drew cringed and wrestled his anger each time Clint insinuated Gina only wanted revenge on Vinson. Or maligned her character. Or questioned her credibility.

Clint, his voice mild and deceptive, asked her how she could be so certain the second man in the video was in fact Mr. Cory Vinson. Maybe she hadn't been the one to record the meeting.

Gina tucked her dark hair behind her ear and straightened. She offered that the man in the video wore an insignia ring on his finger that contained a family crest identical to that of Cory Vinson's. But it was the pencil thin scar that tracked from the man's ring finger toward his wrist that truly identified Vinson.

Cory Vinson had disarmed an intruder who had had a knife and obtained the scar on his hand. Or so Cory liked to tell the media during interviews. Gina confessed Cory had in reality given himself the wound when he'd incorrectly gutted a fish on a weekend cottage trip with friends.

Drew's mouth dropped open as if he'd been gutted. Even Clint stood still and silent as if frozen to the spot. Sitting at the table across the aisle from theirs, Clint's assistant counsel uttered a small gasp.

Beside him, Molly grinned. "And that's how it's done."

It was done.

Judge Bartlett called for counsel to approach the bench. Conversation ensued followed by Judge Bartlett's announcement that charges against Drew Harrington had been dismissed. Instructions were then issued to the trial counsel to open an investigation into Cory Vinson posthaste. Judge Bartlett exited into her chambers.

In a matter of minutes, Drew's world had righted. Justice had ruled.

Yet he was anything but content. The court clerk escorted Gina through a side door and the pair disappeared. Denying Drew the chance to thank her. Or to watch out for the woman.

"I've been called to Judge Bartlett's chambers." Molly returned to the table and quickly slid folders and her notepad into her briefcase. "But congratulations. You're free to go and celebrate."

Drew put a hand on Molly's arm, gaining her full attention. "We promised not to involve Gina."

"I had no choice." Molly closed her briefcase. Her face was set and her tone firm as if the discussion regarding Gina was closed too.

But Drew had questions. Wanted answers. He deserved those answers. After all, his hearing could ruin Gina's life. "How did you get Gina to testify?

"Excuse me." Molly dropped her briefcase strap on her shoulder and stared at him.

"Reuben's recanting had already helped Van overturn his conviction. Gina never had to come forward today. Now Gina's allegations open her to media scrutiny and possible legal trouble." Drew tugged on his ear as if reminding himself to slow down and listen. To let Molly explain. But his anger, mixed with his pent-up emotions, steamrolled over any caution. "Gina will be exposed. Every secret revealed, the good and the ugly. Her personal life and her relationship with Cory Vinson made fully public. And Cory Vinson won't go down without destroying her and her family in the process."

"Gina wouldn't have come forward to see justice served. She was too scared. But I got through to her, I had to. And she did the right thing finally." Molly eyed him. "For you. She's prepared to accept the consequences of her actions, but wants those genuinely guilty to be convicted."

"Not without incentive." Or persuasion. The risk to Gina was too big. But Molly was also too good. He appreciated her tenacity, if not her methods. "I don't blame you or her."

"That's very big of you." Molly crossed her arms over her chest. Her words dry like that quicksand Drew felt he was standing in. "After all, she's the reason you just got your life back."

"But at what cost to Gina?" Drew wiped his hand over his mouth. The guilt and regret remained like a bad aftertaste.

Molly studied him. Finally she straightened and pulled back. The motion almost imperceptible. Except to Drew.

To him, she'd recoiled as if she'd discovered he stood in a rattlesnake pit. Or worse, he was the snake.

"You don't trust me at all, do you?" Her

voice lowered into a cold whisper. But a sense of betrayal shone in her overly bright gaze.

Trust me. That's all she had asked of him earlier. And she had won. For him. But she'd broken her word and jeopardized Gina's world to ensure that victory. At the very least, he should have been included in the discussion. Then he might have trusted.

"You never did trust me." Molly nodded, the movement slow and drawn out.

"It's not…" His voice was weak. His defense inadequate.

"Just to be clear so we're on the same page." A quick slice of her hand out in front of her body cut him off. "You think I paid Gina off to testify. And now that I notched another win, Gina's future doesn't matter."

"Ms. McKinney." The prosecutor called Molly's name. He walked toward the same door Gina and the court clerk had used.

Molly signaled to the opposing counsel, holding up her finger to request one more minute. Then she swung back around to confront Drew. "Your silence is very telling."

"You gave me your word we wouldn't involve Gina further." And she'd broken her word. How could he overlook that?

"And I broke it to save your life and reputation," she charged. "But that's hardly relevant."

"I'm grateful." He spread his hands out. "Truly."

She curled her fingers around the strap of her briefcase. Her words were whispered through her clenched teeth "But I don't want your gratitude. I wanted your respect and I wanted your love. But you can't give me that, can you? You were never willing to give me that."

Love. Drew blinked and knocked aside his panic. The discussion was about Gina and the fallout the woman now faced. And how he could best help the former legal assistant. Not love. Love was never involved here. "This is not the time or place."

"There's never going to be a time or place."

"We need to talk about what happened here today. The ramifications, for everyone."

"You can't give me something you don't feel. Something you're incapable of feeling." She stepped backward. Once. Then again. "There's nothing more to say. Excuse me. I have a meeting."

She turned and walked off. Head held high, shoulders straight. Not one wobble on her heels. Not one small stumble. Not one misstep as if she struggled. Only Drew struggled. He should let her go. She was right about him, wasn't she? Drew called her name.

She turned, but before he could say anything, she spoke, "Let me know where I should send my invoice."

Then she disappeared through the side door.

Drew stood inside the courtroom. The court reporter finished her notes and slipped out, leaving him alone. He stepped outside and two of Judge Bartlett's assistants shook his hand. Another clerk offered a greeting as she passed. He was no longer the pariah in the legal community.

The charges against him had been dropped. But the loneliness remained.

Drew pulled his phone out of his pocket. His screen flashed, letting him know more than twenty unread texts and ten new voicemail messages awaited him. Drew clicked on the first text from Brad. Sophie had gone into labor at the same time Drew's hearing had started.

More texts included updates on Sophie's progress. And more demanded Drew fill the family in on the outcome of the hearing. Others were apologies from his mother, father and Evie for not being at court to support him. Throughout the texts and voice mails, he sensed their excitement for the twins' arrival and their concern for his future. And one thread was constant: their love for each other and for him.

Drew wanted to be only one place in that moment. With his family.

He turned around to look for Molly, to tell her the happy twin news. To take her with him to the hospital.

But she wasn't there.

He was on his own. Just as he'd always been. Just as he'd wanted. She'd given him exactly what he wanted. He should celebrate. He'd soon have new nieces or nephews to spoil. His old life was his to reclaim. Everything was as it should be.

Why then wasn't he celebrating?

CHAPTER TWENTY-FOUR

WITH MOLLY'S CARE package delivered and new mom Sophie ready for some well-earned rest, Molly slipped out of Sophie's hospital room. Sophie needed all the sleep she could capture before she and the twins were discharged in a few days.

Molly had stayed for only an hour. Long enough to hold one of the twins, while Sophie cradled the other. That had led the two women to search each newborn boy for a birthmark to distinguish the identical twins. Unfortunately they found nothing obvious to help tell the brothers apart. Molly had then switched to cuddling first Owen, then Evan while she guided Sophie through some breastfeeding basics, offering encouragement and reassurance, as well. Sophie had requested Molly's help, explaining she was less nervous with a friend beside her.

The visit had ended with Molly supplying answers to a few of Sophie's pressing questions. No, the baby weight Sophie had gained would not be gone in the morning. Yes, Owen's head would round out soon and they'd definitely need a different way to tell the twins apart before that happened. And finally, yes, Molly would bring Sophie whatever she craved for lunch tomorrow and the next day.

Molly was touched and delighted she could be there for Sophie as a friend. And as a mom to a mom. She hadn't realized how much she'd needed a friend until Brooke, Nichole and Sophie and their significant others had come into her life.

Her short time with Sophie and the twins had uplifted and restored her spirits. A reprieve she'd needed after Drew's hearing and their confrontation. She barely shut Sophie's hospital room door and her steps slowed. Her good mood dipped and dulled.

Drew stood no more than ten feet away, peering into the long wide window of the newborn nursery. And yet the distance seemed more like an uncrossable chasm. But she'd let the bridge burn after she'd turned her back on him in the courtroom. *You don't trust me, do you?*

He hadn't denied her claim. And she'd had to save her heart.

She'd purposely visited Sophie in the evening to avoid running into Drew. Her heart hadn't been prepared for another confrontation. Now the only way to the elevators and the exit was straight past Drew. She'd have to possess stealth talents she didn't have to get by him unnoticed.

Walking away in the courtroom that morning had been self-preservation. She'd discovered a vital piece of herself while facing off against Drew in the courtroom after the verdict. She supposed she should thank him.

Thanks to Drew, she'd realized how very tired, how exhausted she was from constantly defending herself. From continuously fighting to prove her worth and her value. To her ex and peers. And now to Drew.

She'd made the right decision at Drew's hearing. She refused to apologize. Or explain herself. It wasn't her responsibility to change his mind about her. Besides, changing his mind was only one piece. Changing his heart—well, he had to do that on his own too.

She tipped her chin up and gathered her broken heart. She'd deal with those jagged, uneven pieces later. When she was alone in the safety of her own home.

"Drew." She stopped far from hand-holding reach or accidental brushes of shoulders. "I thought you'd be out celebrating."

"I had other things to take care of." He ran a hand through his hair. Uncertainty shifted through his gaze.

Things like apology gifts? He'd given Molly those before. Hope flickered. The tiniest spark. "I'm sure you had a productive day."

"Quite. I'll be in my new office at Capstone Keyes tomorrow. They made an offer and I accepted." His voice was resigned, not excited.

That hope flared out. The spark faded. "That's fast. Everything is falling into place for you." *Without me.*

And those pieces of her heart shattered even more. The edges became even sharper.

"The partners at Capstone Keyes wanted me in my chair as soon as possible. They need me on several key cases." He shook his head, a tiny twitch as if he couldn't quite believe their invitation.

But Drew's skill and talent as a prosecutor had never been in question. The partners at

Capstone Keyes had hired him precisely for his legal mind. It was Molly who'd wanted something different from Drew. And it was Molly who was disappointed. It was Molly who hurt.

She searched his face. "You should be thrilled." *Do you miss us already too? Do you hurt too?*

"I am. Really." He shifted and touched the nursery window, but he didn't sound convinced. "Having identical twin boys in the family will be great."

Molly faced the window, sure that it was only her own wistfulness she saw reflected in the glass, not Drew's. She had to stop looking for things in Drew that weren't there. Yet she couldn't seem to stop herself. What did that say about how hard she'd fallen? And would the fall be over soon—she could only hope.

She kept her focus on the twins and away from her heartache. For reasons she refused to consider, she lingered. "I hear there is a new Harrington family contest going on. Have you submitted your idea for the best way to tell the twins apart?"

"I went one step further." He reached into his pocket and pulled out two bands. Colored paracord had been woven through black titanium links. One of the twin's names was engraved on each bracelet. "Owen's band is blue, silver and black. Evan's band is red, silver and black."

"Clever." *Thoughtful.* Molly refused to be affected. That was the problem. Drew was a good guy. Just not a good guy for her. That ache pulsed and throbbed, seizing her heart.

Drew grinned and held up the bands. "The bracelets expand as the boys grow."

Molly studied his face. He was the most animated she'd seen him all day. Even after his victory at his hearing, he hadn't looked quite so satisfied. He'd been too occupied questioning Molly and her integrity. Her smile wavered and she forced her stiff words out. "Sophie will appreciate those a lot."

The same as Molly would've appreciated his hug, not his accusations in the courtroom. *Why couldn't you trust me? Why couldn't I be enough?*

"Kyle Quinn is a good friend, and he wears one like this for a severe nut allergy." His words rushed out like a child retelling the best part of a playground adventure. "I called Kyle, and he put me in touch with the jewelry store owner."

"Friends like that are good to have." Molly

had friends now too. Ones she intended to keep in her life, despite her relationship with Drew. He could have his old life back. But she was going to treasure her new friends.

"Ava and Kyle return next week from England. Kyle's sister is graduating with her PhD from Oxford this weekend." Drew's smile reached into his eyes.

"That's impressive." Even more was his obvious affection for his friends. She wanted some of the same for herself. But he didn't trust her. It was hard, if not impossible, to build anything on that detail.

"Ava is expecting, but that's now our secret." He laughed and returned the bracelets to his pocket. "They're really excited about growing their family."

Family. That ache shook her knees. She'd considered making a family with Drew. Allowed her heart to imagine. But she'd known better than to trust her heart. She pressed her heels into the floor and braced herself. The fall was coming. Inside she fell apart, bit by bit. Piece by piece. How much more before she lost herself completely. She managed a small smile.

"Why am I telling you all this?" He paused

and considered her. "You haven't met Ava and Kyle yet."

Yet. Yet implied she would meet Ava and Kyle.

Yet implied Drew considered a future with Molly in it.

Clearly, she hadn't learned to set aside her hope yet. She stepped around Drew, forcing the quiver out of her voice. "It's late. I need to get home to Hazel. You should visit Sophie before she falls asleep."

"Good idea." Drew turned toward her. His earlier animation dissolved. His voice quieted. "Molly. Will I… We should…"

"Night, Drew." Molly cut him off. Unwilling to wait for his excuses. Unable to pretend any longer.

She rushed toward the elevators. Before that fall tripped her. Before the pain consumed her. Before she lost herself forever.

Inside the elevator, tears slipped free. Her breath caught and clogged her throat. Every part of her ached.

But she was more than a broken heart. She had to be more. Had to be better for her daughter.

She was a mom now. And moms raised strong children only by being strong.

CHAPTER TWENTY-FIVE

ONE WEEK AFTER his hearing, one week after he'd lost Molly and one week back in his old life, Drew stood at the wall of windows in his office at Capstone Keyes and watched the city wake up. Each bus that pulled to the nearby stop off-loaded more and more people, clutching briefcases, coffee tumblers and newspapers. The line at Roasted Vibes Café down the street started to extend onto the sidewalk. Lights turned on in the office high-rises surrounding the Capstone Keyes' top floor suite.

He'd arrived at work early, as was his long-standing habit. He was often the first one to his desk and the last one to leave. That routine had served him well for years. He'd thrived on work. Been content devoting his life to it. Until recently.

Staring out at the city wasn't productive. Drew turned his back on the view and he hoped on the discontent simmering beneath his skin. He had work to accomplish. Time to get to it.

He draped his suit jacket over one of the empty chairs at the small conference table and rolled the sleeves of his dress shirt to his elbows. As if his suit were responsible for his discontent. Once he dove into his research, he'd lose himself in the work again. Find his balance and his satisfaction.

"So, this is the view from the thirtieth floor." Brad walked into Drew's office and stood beside him at the windows. "Views all the way to the bay. Nice. I can see why you're distracted."

"I'm collecting my thoughts." Drew tugged on his sleeve, pulling the material into perfect folds. He recognized how irritable he sounded.

"Care to share any of your thoughts?" Meanwhile, his brother's voice sounded mild and compassionate.

Curiosity poked at Drew, turning him cranky. "Shouldn't you be at home with Sophie and the twins? And Ella."

"Ella had to be at school early for a student council meeting." Brad slapped Drew on the shoulder as if stamping his good humor onto

Drew. "The twins and Sophie are asleep. I'm all yours for the next two hours."

No. Drew wasn't entertaining company. He was working. Or he was supposed to be. "I have research to do. My first case for the firm."

Brad rubbed his hands together and sat down at the conference table. "I can help."

Drew set his hands on his hips. "You're here to escape crying babies, aren't you?" He should take pity on his brother, but he couldn't find any empathy.

"I'm here to check on my brother."

"Really?" Drew challenged. He didn't need anyone to check on him. He was back in his old life. Everything was perfect. The lie caught like an animal trapped in a snare. "Ella told me the boys are hearty criers."

"They are. In stereo." Brad laughed. "I wouldn't change it."

"You're lying." His brother wanted something to change. Everyone wanted change. "Ella asked if she could move in with me."

Brad sobered. "That's not happening."

Drew crossed his arms over his chest. His voice defensive. "I'd be happy to take great care of her. She's my niece."

"I know you would." Love and warmth

tracked across Brad's face and into his words. "But I'm her Dad. It's my job."

Dad. The word settled inside Drew's chest. Ella wasn't Brad's biological daughter. But he was her dad in every way that mattered. The same as Hazel wasn't Drew's. And yet he cared about the little girl like… He sideswiped that thought. "You're good at the whole family thing. The dad thing."

"You would be too if you let yourself," Brad offered.

Drew moved to the conference table, rolled out a chair and sat. "This is about you, not me."

"You shut Molly out, didn't you?" Brad braced his hands on the chair across the table and shook his head at Drew. "That's why you two aren't together."

"Molly was my legal counsel." His voice was monotone like a prerecorded message. No surprise. He'd been repeating those same words to himself for the past week. "The hearing is over." Now Molly and he were too.

"Your relationship was much more than professional." Brad stood and wandered around Drew's office, eventually stopping at the floor-to-ceiling built-in shelves covering the back wall.

Drew had unpacked his office boxes last week. Filled the shelves with his legal texts. The scales of justice paperweight waited on his desk. The executive pen set he'd placed in a desk drawer. The hourglass and antique mantel clock waited on another shelf. He hadn't even wound the clock or set it to the correct time. As for the coffee mug from Ella, that Drew had left at home. On his bedside table. But that wasn't anything he needed to share or explain.

Brad turned the hourglass over and set it on a different shelf.

Drew rose. "What are you doing?"

"It's all very impersonal in here." Brad waved his hand at the shelves and then moved the mantel clock.

"Moving it doesn't change things." No matter where Drew moved the picture of Molly and him with Santa, he still returned it to the coffee mug beside his bed. Preferring that picture to be the first thing he saw in the morning. Drew returned the clock to its original place. "I prefer it this way."

"You prefer things as they are?" Brad studied Drew. His gaze clear and entirely too perceptive. "Exactly like this?"

Drew held his brother's stare, refused to

blink and nodded. Although the doubt he ignored.

"Now who's lying?" Brad shoved him on the shoulder and dropped into one of the leather chairs reserved for clients as if he intended to spend the day in Drew's office.

"I got exactly what I wanted." Drew rose and sat in the chair across from his brother. "I'm good."

Perhaps not completely good. But he would be. In time. He had to settle into his office and his new cases. Meet his new clients. Learn the rhythm of his peers and the partners. It would be fine.

He'd been more than fine with Molly. More than happy to learn everything he could about her. More than willing to spend as much time with her and Hazel as he could. But that fun reprieve was over.

"Yes, brooding and gloomy are definitely a good look on you." Brad's stale tone dropped on the table like a brick.

"This is how I look at work." Drew straightened a stack of papers. "If it bothers you, you can always leave."

"You can't do it, can you?" Wonder entered Brad's gaze.

"What?" Drew knew he sounded defensive.

"Admit you miss Molly." Brad leaned forward. "Admit she was the best person in your life. Admit you want her back."

"Fine." Drew threw his hands up in the air. "I miss her. That work?"

Brad shook his head. "What's the but?"

"But we aren't good together." There he'd said it out loud.

"Because she challenged you. Showed you a world outside work." Brad motioned over his head. "Showed you a world outside this four-walled room. Helped you reconnect with friends and family."

"I don't need Molly to stay connected to my friends and family."

Brad's mouth twisted into a sneer. "When was the last time you saw the twins?"

He hadn't seen the twins since Sophie and the boys had returned home. "I was giving you guys time to adjust and get into a routine. Spend quality time together."

"Don't even." Brad frowned. "You're hiding again. In your work and your office. Behind your excuses, valid though they may be sometimes."

"This is who I am," Drew countered. Who he'd always been. His family, especially his own brother, knew that.

"But is it who you really want to be." Brad stacked his hands behind his head and considered Drew. "You were just looking for reasons not to trust Molly. It's what you always do."

"What I always do…" Drew folded his hands together and set them on the table, he was slightly interested, but more irritated by his brother's comment. His brother was supposed to be here for his own reasons; he wasn't supposed to be there to pick apart Drew's failings and toss them out like key evidence.

"You never trusted your exes. Not one of them," Brad continued, unaware or uncaring that his brother wasn't fully engaged in the assessment. "You only ever trust in your work."

Until his work had betrayed him. And Drew had needed Molly's help to exonerate him. "I trusted Molly with my case."

"But you didn't trust her with what really counted between the two of you," Brad said.

Drew rolled his chair away from the table as if that would help him avoid the truth. The one he knew was coming. "Like what exactly?"

Brad lowered his arms and leaned forward. "Like your heart."

Drew shoved out of his chair and paced his office. His gaze scanned the shelves, filled with legal texts. No inspirational quotes added dimension to the austere lineup. No artwork added any visual appeal or personal touches. No family photographs filled the space and hinted that Drew had more than his life at the office. He rubbed his forehead. "Why are we discussing this?"

"Because it's time for you to hear the truth," Brad said.

"What truth is that?" Drew rounded on his brother. "That I have trust issues. Or that I can't love."

Brad walked over to him and set his finger over Drew's heart. "The truth is that you can't give your heart to Molly because you'd have to accept hers in return."

Now they were discussing Molly's heart? He knocked his brother's arm away. But those fears resurfaced. Demanded to be heard. Demanded a voice. "You think I can't love her? That I'm incapable of loving Molly."

"I think you don't believe you can love her right." No judgment, only a bit of thoughtful wisdom.

Drew couldn't fight, didn't want to fight it any longer. He wanted Molly and Hazel in his life permanently. "What if I fail her? We're talking about love…"

"The most precious gift anyone can give or receive." Brad held his arms out. "It's utterly terrifying."

"And yet, you're in love," Drew said. "No qualms. No hesitation. No doubts."

"Because love, when it's right, is what makes life worthwhile." Brad touched Drew's shoulder, his grip and face earnest. "Love gives everything meaning."

"If my boys are going to talk about love, I'd like to be included." Nancy Harrington smiled from the doorway of Drew's office. "I feel as though I know something about the topic."

"Mom." Drew straightened and shot an accusing glance at Brad. "What brings you here?"

Brad laughed. "I didn't know she was coming here. Promise."

"Why can't I pay my son a visit in his new business environment?" His mother strolled into his office and set a gift bag on his desk. "I haven't seen you in days, not even at Sophie and Brad's house."

Her words carried a direct shot of guilt. Brad lifted his eyebrows in an I-told-you-so way. Drew cleared his throat. "I've been busy here."

"You should never be too busy for family." A warning recognized. "I'd hoped you'd realized that with Molly the past few weeks."

Brad quickly covered his grin with his hand.

"Are you here to tell me that Molly is the best person for me too?" Drew charged.

His mother eyed him, her mouth pursed. "I came to give you a gift and a reminder that family is the reason for everything."

"What are you saying?" Drew asked. "That you and Dad dedicated your lives to your careers for your family?"

"Your dad and I are dedicated to each other first," she said. "It's that love and devotion that gave us both the strength and courage to dedicate ourselves to our careers. We had a family at home to celebrate the ups and downs with. To have faith in us when we lost it in ourselves. And to always be our foundation."

"No matter what, your family is always there for you," Brad added. "Your family is your safe place if you let them be there for you."

Brad meant if Drew opened his heart and let them in. If Drew only trusted. In love and in himself. "I have you guys."

His mother walked over and grabbed his hand. "And you always will. But that doesn't mean there isn't room for more."

Molly and Hazel. Could he trust his heart? Could he risk? "Okay. I got it. Now I need to analyze some case files. Really."

"Then my purpose for being here is done." His mother kissed his cheek. "I'm off to pick up supplies at The Pampered Pooch and deliver more welcome gifts."

"Welcome gifts for who?" Brad asked.

"Molly found a new office space. Delightful historic spot a few blocks from the pet store. Lots of character. Good bones." His mother smiled. "She and Gina are moving in today."

"Gina Hahn?" Drew was confused.

"That's the only Gina I know." His mother waved from the doorway. "I know that young woman is going to be a terrific legal assistant for Molly."

With that final prediction, his mother disappeared down the hallway. Drew glanced at Brad.

His brother shrugged. "I've been busy with

the twins. They really do need me. I have to get home."

Brad slipped out of the office as silently as he'd arrived. Except his family had left behind more than a gift bag and a good-morning greeting.

Drew picked up the colorful bag from his mother and pulled out a tabletop fountain shaped like a wishing well. On a card attached to the box, she'd written, *Wishes are good. But the real joy and the true fun is in the wishing. In the living. Don't ever forget to live.*

The fun at the park, tossing pennies into the fountain with Hazel and Molly, hadn't come from the many wishes made that afternoon. The joy had been simply being there with them. Spending time, not on his phone and checking emails, but rather being fully present in the moment with Molly and Hazel. The fun had been the volleyball games, the s'mores eating and the laughter.

The living had been sharing time with Molly. Sharing pizza, sharing a bottle of wine and sharing secrets. The same as they'd done that Thanksgiving week so long ago. It had always been Molly.

His heart had always known. His past relationships hadn't worked out, not because he couldn't love but because he already loved. Loved Molly McKinney.

Always had. Always would.

And that fear—the one that urged him to hide in his work—shifted directions like a weather vane in a gust of wind. He'd spent years running, believing love was only a burden to bear. Now he wanted to run to Molly. And not spend another day without her beside him.

Because love…love was a gift. It needed to be treasured and valued…and celebrated.

Drew grabbed his suit coat and rushed from his office. His assistant stopped him on his way to the elevators. She smiled. "You're in a hurry. Late for an important meeting?"

"Yes." He was late getting his life started. Late embracing his feelings. But he hoped he wasn't too late to change Molly's mind. He grinned at his assistant. "I'm going to get my family back."

Her eyebrows pulled together, and confusion wavered across her smile. "I feel like I should wish you good luck then."

Drew and Molly had never wished each other good luck. Good luck implied there was something beyond hard work and diligence that controlled their achievements. They both believed in making their own luck through persistence, dedication and devotion.

Yet, Drew readily accepted his assistant's wish for good luck.

And then he gave a silent plea for every unseen force in the universe to be on his side. For the first time ever, Drew needed love to win.

CHAPTER TWENTY-SIX

LATE MONDAY MORNING and Molly sat on the stairs inside her new law office. Her laptop perched on her legs and her legal assistant bustling around her. Today was move-in day. Or more precisely, delivery day. A couch and carpet would arrive within the hour for the upstairs break room/playroom.

Molly had chosen the two-story office space for its versatility. There were two offices, a small conference room and reception space on the first floor. On the second, there was a large open space Gina and Molly had designated for personal use. Whether Hazel or Gina's daughter was there to play, or Gina wanted to practice yoga on her break, the room would be ready and available.

"You need to go home." Gina eased around her on the stairs.

"We have too much going on today." Furniture deliveries from four different retail stores. Internet and phone service installers, a plumber and an electrician had appointments scheduled too. If no unforeseen problems popped up, Molly's new office would be open and fully functional on Wednesday. State filings had already been processed and her new practice was registered with the State Bar. "I should be here to help."

"You should be at home preparing for your custody hearing tomorrow." Gina wrote *Molly's office supplies* in a black marker across the top of the box and reached for another. "I can handle this."

"What if you have questions?" Molly asked.

"I have a phone to call you." Gina tapped the marker against the box. "And we already mapped out where we want the furniture. Where we need more outlets and what we envision for the kitchenette upstairs."

Gina had recreated the entire office layout on paper and included room dimensions. Then she'd added cutout paper furniture with exact dimensions to create a full visual for Molly. It took the women less than half a day to arrange the paper cutouts to their satisfaction. "You're very good at design."

"My mother and my aunt studied the art of feng shui for the restaurant and their houses."

Gina shrugged. "I got to tag along on their shopping trips, and I paid attention."

"I can tell." Molly already felt the difference Gina made in her life and Gina had only been officially on Molly's payroll for less than a week. Not only had Gina *not* forgotten her legal background, she also brought an impressive level of customer service to the office. Her confidence and cool levelheadedness reminded Molly to remain the same, despite the onslaught of decisions and details coming at her.

Her eyes blurred. The document open on her laptop screen went completely out of focus. Molly snapped her laptop closed and rubbed her eyes. "I can't decide on a logo."

"We'll look over the options later on Thursday." Gina checked a calendar she'd tacked temporarily to the wall. "Narrow it down to your top three. Then make suggested changes to those and submit our feedback to the freelance designer."

"That works." Molly pressed her palms on the closed laptop. "He sent more than two dozen options and I want to change something on every single design."

Gina peeked out the floor-to-ceiling window in the reception area and grinned. "The furniture is here."

Molly had chosen to keep things minimal and only have a few vintage-inspired pieces for the office. Simple but elegant and, importantly, affordable. The coordinating file cabinets, bookcases and other accents continued the theme and brought a sense of charm to the historic space.

THE FURNITURE FINALLY in place, Molly sat in one of the twin ivory-and-gray-striped wingback armchairs reserved for clients. Molly's gaze skipped from the reception area to the round table in the small conference room. The glass walls dividing the rooms kept the entire first floor feeling open and airy. It was an office Molly wanted to return to. It was her office. Her practice to run.

Pride and pleasure washed through her, dousing any twinge of uncertainty or worry. "It's coming together rather well."

"It's a vision realized." Gina dropped into the armchair beside her.

"There's a certain satisfaction in that." Perhaps she wasn't completely satisfied with her life, but she was making strides in the right direction. That direction was forward. Not backward. She had a future to plan, not a past to miss.

"We should have an open house. Bring in a caterer. Welcome ourselves to the neighborhood." Gina drummed her fingers on the arms of her chair in an upbeat rhythm that matched the enthusiasm in her voice. "Invite local business owners and your peers."

But not Drew. The one peer Molly wanted there. The one man she wanted but couldn't have. "Maybe we should wait until later."

"You mean until after the Cory Vinson appeal hearing." Gina reached over and touched Molly's arm. "I'm not scared, Molly. For the first time in years, I'm not afraid and I have you to thank for it."

"Me?" Molly shook her head. "You were the one who testified. Shared your story and continue to share it."

"More people are coming forward with evidence against Cory." Gina tipped her head back and sighed. "I'm not alone."

No, Gina was not alone. Molly was not alone either. And yet there was a loneliness that twisted through her chest as if intent on revealing every empty space inside her.

Gina continued, "I didn't realize I wasn't

alone until you presented me with that choice and gave me the courage to speak out."

"I gave you a double macchiato and strawberry lemon scones." Molly lifted her voice into a tease, but then turned serious. "You always had the courage inside you, Gina, don't ever forget that."

"Well, you gave me a job that I am inspired to do. I can look forward again." Gina aimed a half smile at Molly. "I love my family's restaurant. But being a waitress wasn't my passion."

The buzzer chimed, announcing another arrival. Gina rose and hit the button to open the door on the street level. "That should be the electricians. I'm looking forward to the cameras, so we know who's really downstairs."

Brad and his team would be installing those later in the week. He wouldn't allow Molly to have anything other than the finest in security equipment installed at no charge. She would find a way to pay Brad back, even if it was in babysitting hours.

Molly stood. "Hazel's nanny has an early class this evening, so I'm heading home to relieve Rebekah. However, Hazel and I can come back here."

"I've got this. Stay at home with Hazel." Gina typed on her phone, then grinned at Molly. "Your ride will be here in eight minutes. A white mini-SUV."

Gina was turning out to be as strong-willed as Molly. Molly appreciated her even more. "You'll call me if anything comes up."

"If you promise to enjoy Hazel and not worry about anything here." Gina opened the office door for the electrician. He carried in a ladder and left to retrieve more tools.

"I'll try." Molly slipped her laptop into her briefcase.

"I'll call after the telecom technicians finish." Gina walked over to her desk and sat. "It'll be the first call from McKinney Legal Solutions."

Molly left Gina organizing her desk and the reception space, went outside and scanned the street for a white mini-SUV. Her ride-share car arrived exactly on time. Things were falling into place.

Molly knew where she belonged. Right in this community. On her own. Doing things her way for a change. She had Drew to thank for that really. He'd accepted her just as she was, and she'd discovered a power inside herself. A strength she hadn't known was there.

Molly, like Gina, had had a choice to make. She could own her decisions and her life as a mother and a lawyer. She knew now she possessed the courage to be the best in both roles. Not perfect, but the best she could be.

The car pulled to the curb outside Brooke and Dan's house. She thanked the driver and got out.

Rebekah and Hazel were in the backyard on a blanket, surrounded by Nala and her puppies. Wesley and Ben played basketball. Brooke waved and carried a snack tray for the boys to the table near the firepit. Rebekah greeted Molly with a warm hug, then the nanny blew a series of air kisses to Hazel, waved to the others and rushed out the side gate to get to her evening college class.

Molly kicked off her heels, dropped onto the blanket and kissed Hazel's cheek.

"I have serious nanny envy." Brooke sat down across from Molly, stretched out her legs and settled a sleeping puppy on her lap. "If I have a baby, I'm stealing Rebekah. You've been warned."

Molly laughed. "Are you having a baby?"

"Dan and I are talking." Brooke blushed and fiddled with the puppy's ear. "And I guess we're trying."

"It should be fun, right?" Molly teased. She waggled her eyebrows up and down, earning a giggle from both Hazel and Brooke. "The trying part that is."

Brooke pressed her fingers against her cheeks and her blush faded. "I'll be okay if it doesn't happen. I love my family as is."

Molly spotted the longing in Brooke's gaze. Brooke wanted a baby. Molly wanted that for her friend. "It's okay not to be okay too." Like Molly. She wasn't entirely okay still; she was slowly learning to accept that.

"I'll let you know when I'm not okay." Brooke set another puppy on her lap.

"And I'll be right here if you need me." Nala stretched out lazily against Molly's leg, but her gaze remained on her puppies and Hazel. Every giggle or squeal from Hazel and Nala lifted her head and ears to check on the little girl. Molly appreciated the support.

Brooke brushed her fingers over the solid black puppy. Only her ear and tail were white as if they'd been dipped in a paint can. "I'm here for you too. If you ever want to talk about things."

"You want to know about Drew and me." *Why I'm not okay.* Molly buried her hand in Nala's soft fur. But her feelings were harder to bury. Maybe it was Brooke and her quiet compassion that drew the feelings from Molly.

"I don't want to pry." Brooke looked at Molly, confusion and disappointment on her face. "It's just that you two were good together. Drew was happy like we haven't seen him in years. We were all talking about it."

Molly had been happy too. Really happy. For the first time in a long while. "I thought we were good together. I was wrong."

"Or Drew was scared." Brooke frowned.

"I gave him my word not to involve Gina in the trial. There was evidence enough for Van's conviction to be overturned. That left only Drew's situation and no other way to get the right outcome." Molly handed Hazel her teether. Hazel pressed her tiny toes into one of the puppies sleeping near her feet and grinned. One flex into the soft fur and a grin. Then she'd release and purse her mouth. Flex again. Smile again. Why weren't all relationships as simple as that? "Trust is nonnegotiable."

"Love is nonnegotiable," Brooke argued. "The rest can be worked out if the love is there."

Love. Molly considered Drew her best friend. Her confidant. She liked him. Admired him. And missed him with a depth that made her hurt all over. But love?

"You do love Drew." Brooke searched Molly's face. "I've seen you two together. It's obvious in the sideways glances. The casual touches. The way you turn to each other first. Dan and I are the same."

Was that love? Real, true love? Molly pressed her hands together. Her palms were damp. Her body was twitchy. "He's like my best friend."

"You can fall for your best friend." Brooke smiled as if she were ready and willing to step over any roadblock Molly put up.

"We're both lawyers." Molly tossed out another challenge. That twitchy sensation spread inside her. "Work relationships aren't wise."

"Tell me three things your ex and Drew have in common." Brooke arched an eyebrow as if she were about to knock over the next roadblock.

"They're both lawyers." Molly held up one finger and pictured both Derrick and Drew in her mind.

Derrick was an only child, profit-driven and shunned public affection to preserve his image. Drew was family-oriented, justice-driven and held Molly like he never wanted to let her go. That twitch softened into a shiver and a long sigh.

Molly put her hand down. "That's all I got. They're lawyers."

"Then that's it. You haven't fallen for another Derrick." Brooke nudged her tennis shoe against Molly's bare foot. "You fell for Drew. It can't be like last time. They aren't the same man."

Molly chewed on her lower lip. Hope swirled inside her. But logic overruled her heart. "But you risk losing your friendship."

"But if you risk and fail, will you be worse off than you are right now?" Brooke pressed.

Right now, Molly did not even have Drew as a friend. But that ache still throbbed inside her like a loss she might never recover from. She set her palm over her heart. "I have a broken heart."

Brooke grabbed Molly's other hand, understanding in her gaze. "You have to tell Drew how you really feel about him."

"I'm terrified," she whispered. Her pulse raced.

Brooke squeezed her fingers. "That's when you know it's real."

She shivered. Broke out in a sweat. Swallowed a shout. And her heart swelled, bumping aside her resistance and all her reasons not to fall in love. It was too late. She'd already fallen. So much joy. So much terror. Even more wonder.

She loved Drew. *Loved him*. It was more than real. It was everything.

Now she had another choice. Tell Drew she loved him or keep silent and lock her feelings away?

The choice was simple.

Finding the courage? Well, that was a different matter.

CHAPTER TWENTY-SEVEN

DREW SMOOTHED HIS hand over his tie and pressed his palm against his stomach. Beside him, Brad gave him two thumbs-up. Dan and Brooke offered the same silent encouragement.

His mother stepped forward and kissed his cheek. "You've rehearsed what you're going to say?"

Drew nodded. He'd been awake most of the night rewriting, revising and finally rehearsing every single word.

"Then it's time." His father opened the door to Judge Martina Reilly's courtroom and squeezed Drew's shoulder. "Good luck, son."

Drew accepted his dad's luck, his friends' support and entered the courtroom. It was smaller without a jury box and more informal than the trial courtrooms he earned his living in. The walls had the familiar wood paneling that carried over to Judge Reilly's bench and the witness stand. Twin tables waited in front of the bench. A remote video screen had been placed on one table.

Molly sat at the other table. Her eye-popping red power suit had been traded in for a calm, elegant dark blue one. She'd wrapped a silk green and blue scarf around her neck. The bold colors captured her courage and her confidence.

Drew went up to her and touched her shoulder. "Molly."

"Drew?" Molly rose from her chair and cast a sideways glance at Judge Reilly already seated at her bench and sorting through paperwork. "What are you doing here?"

Judge Reilly tapped her microphone. "I'd like to know who this is and his purpose for interrupting my time."

"Character witness, Your Honor," Drew said. "For Molly McKinney."

Judge Reilly shifted her gaze to Molly as if seeking her approval.

Molly cleared her throat. "Your Honor, this is Drew Harrington. I'd like to call him as a character witness."

"Very well." Judge Reilly waved her hand. "If you're ready, Mr. Harrington, the court will hear your statement."

"Your Honor, do you mind if I stand?"

Drew asked. "I'm used to doing that in the courtroom."

Judge Reilley lifted her eyebrows in a challenge. "Fine."

Drew clasped his hands behind his back and started to recite his statement. Then he realized one key point. This was the most important statement he'd ever give. He had one chance to get his words right. One chance to be perfect.

He paused and then spoke, not from a written statement full of cold logic and facts, but rather from his heart. "Your Honor, I can speak to Ms. McKinney's skill as a parent. Her mastery at scheduling feedings, naps and playtime into a full day as seamlessly as she balances work and life responsibilities from filing court documents to grocery shopping. And her strict adherence to a daily routine for her daughter's well-being. As well as her ability to successfully manage both her career and her role as a parent with grace, humility and humor. Her daughter, Hazel, should be the number one witness here. She's a happy, healthy baby being well cared for." Drew paced in front of Judge Reilly's bench, stopped and turned to set his focus on Molly. "But I'd rather talk about Ms. McKinney's devotion and loyalty to Hazel via another channel, through those she loves."

Molly straightened in her chair. Her gaze remained locked on Drew's.

His words came easy and freely. "Ms. McKinney is a woman who sets aside her own fears and her own desires to rescue others, whether it's a mother dog and her five puppies or a disillusioned lawyer with his career on the line. Ms. McKinney does what's right even if it costs her something in the end. There's no better testament that could be made for a person and a parent."

Molly's bottom lip quivered. Her chin tipped up.

"That's the hallmark of the best sort of person. Even more, it's the requirement for the best sort of parent. The parent who will put their child first. Be a great role model. Talk and listen. Establish a foundation on love and respect. A foundation that allows that child to become the best person he or she can be. Parenting is about raising good people."

Molly brushed at her eyes.

She'd made Drew a better person. Every day he'd been with her. And he wanted very much to be considered a good person. He continued, "Most of all, the best kind of parent builds a home for their child. A home like the one Ms. McKinney has built for her daughter. It's not about the size or the decor, it's about the strength and the love that fills a home. It's about heart and Ms. McKinney has that kind of heart."

Silence filled the courtroom. All he could do was stare at Molly and hope that she'd accepted his apology. He believed in her and trusted her. He moved to open his briefcase and from it pulled out several pieces of paper. "Your Honor, I also have a quality of character letter to submit, if I may approach the bench?"

Judge Reilly motioned him forward. Drew smiled at the older woman. "There are more character witnesses outside. Mayor Harrington is there, as are Brooke and Dan Sawyer, Ms. McKinney's landlords. Evelyn Davenport, a family friend. Brad Harrington. Chase and Nichole Jacobs. And—"

Judge Reilly held up her hand and looked over her glasses at Drew. "Chase Jacobs is outside my chambers?"

"Yes, Your Honor." Drew pointed to the back of the courtroom. "I can get him if you'd like to hear from him."

"No, no. Mr. Jacobs can please remain outside until this session has concluded. I happen to have a grandson though who is a very big Pioneers fan. And I may have to ask him for a favor." Judge Reilly accepted the paperwork from Drew and looked it over. "You've written quite a lengthy character letter, Mr. Harrington."

"Those are not all from me." Drew smiled and stepped away from the bench. "You'll find character references from the people I've mentioned and several others."

"Well done, Mr. Harrington." Judge Reilly slipped the paperwork into the folder and shifted her attention to the video screen. "Mr. Donovan, apart from the letters from a pediatrician and babysitter you intend to hire, do you have any character witnesses you wish to call on your behalf?"

"I do not, Your Honor," Derrick said.

Drew bent and picked up his briefcase from the floor near Molly's table. As he did so, he leaned in and kissed a surprised and stunned Molly. He hoped it said everything left unsaid inside of him.

He pulled away, tucked a stray piece of her hair behind her ear and whispered, "I'll be outside waiting for you. Let me know if you need me."

There was more to say. A lot more that belonged between Molly and him only. He'd just gotten started.

He joined his family and friends outside in the hallway and grinned. "I think love is going to win today."

THIRTY-FIVE MINUTES after Drew burst into Molly's custody hearing, Judge Reilly granted full legal and physical sole custody of Hazel McKinney to Molly.

She'd won. For her daughter. For her family. Molly sagged into her chair. Tears blurred her vision and dampened her cheeks. Her thank-you to Judge Reilly was waterlogged and sincere.

Judge Reilly slipped into her chambers and quickly returned without her customary black robes. She walked over to Molly's table and held out her hand. "I have another hearing in less than ten minutes in this room."

Molly set her hand in Judge Reilly's and let the woman help her stand. "I'm sorry. I just needed a moment."

Judge Reilly patted her hand. "My advice to you is to run out of this courtroom and into the arms of Mr. Harrington. And spend as many moments as you can capture with that man, who loves you very, very much."

Molly wiped a tissue across her face. "That is advice I'm more than willing to take."

"Good." Judge Reilly opened a courtroom door for Molly. "Now, I've got five minutes to meet Chase Jacobs and convince him to sign an autograph."

"He won't need to be convinced," Molly said. "He's good like that."

"You've surrounded yourself with fine people, Ms. McKinney." Judge Reilly released her. "Don't ever forget that."

Molly found herself surrounded and embraced by those fine people. Her friends. And even more, her family. Hugs and well wishes given, the group dispersed. Plans had already been set in motion to celebrate in Brooke and Dan's backyard. A volleyball rematch had also been agreed to and the menu determined.

Molly suddenly found herself in the hallway alone with Drew. "Why did you kiss me in there?"

"I wanted them to know." He stepped forward and took her hands in his. "I wanted you to know."

"Know what?" Molly tightened her hold on Drew.

"That I love you." He tugged her closer.

"Drew, I…"

"I know I have a lot to make up for." Drew squeezed her hands and locked his gaze on hers. "A lot more to apologize for. It wasn't you I didn't trust, Molly. It was me."

Molly searched his face. Her heart—the one with so much love for him—swelled.

"I know you need time to forgive me," he said. "I will wait. I'll be right here."

"I don't need time." She'd forgiven him the second he'd walked into the courtroom and announced he was her character reference. She'd fallen for him more with every impassioned word he spoke about her. "I love you, Drew. Always have. Always will."

"You're my home, Molly." Drew set his forehead against hers. "My everything."

"You're the family I always wished for." She leaned into him and kissed him like he'd kissed her in the courtroom. Heart-stopping. Breath-stealing. And with all the love inside her for Drew.

For the family of her own.

EPILOGUE

"I CAN'T BELIEVE you planned this." Drew sat in his seat behind first base at the Bay Area Angel's stadium, balancing his hot dog in one hand, his extra large French fries in the other.

Molly slid into her seat and kissed him. "I also have an engagement letter in my purse that I wrote up for us."

"An engagement letter?" Drew dunked one of his French fries into Molly's cup of ranch dressing. "Really?"

Molly laughed. "I figured it would be a good idea since our relationship started with an attorney–client engagement letter."

"And now?" Drew chewed on his French fry and considered her. She just kept surprising him. From arranging this baseball outing to her keeping him laughing and guessing.

"Well, it would seem we have another kind of arrangement." She bumped her shoulder into his. "I had planned to finish the custody hearing, track you down and state my case for us. I had worked out all the finer details."

"We have time before the first pitch." Drew waited for her to take a bite of her hot dog, then said, "You could state your case now."

Molly's cheeks deepened into an adorable shade of red. She chewed a couple of fries, swallowed and shook her head at him. "It was all part of my plan to win you back. But then you showed up at the custody hearing and beat me to it."

"And won you back first." He grinned and lifted his eyebrows up and down.

"Have I thanked you for that?" she asked.

"Every day for the past week." He kissed her cheek. "But I want to know more about this engagement letter."

"It was silly." Molly wiped a napkin over her mouth. "I turned it into a relationship engagement letter detailing the scope, expectations and responsibilities of us being together."

Drew finished his hot dog and wiped his hands on a napkin. "And this letter is in your purse right now?"

"The outside pocket." She motioned to the floor near her feet.

Drew pulled out the piece of paper in question. He scanned the document. "Do you have a pen?"

She reached into her purse, pulled the cap off the ballpoint pen and then handed the pen to him. He signed across the bottom of the paper, folded it and handed it and the pen back to her.

"Just like that." She eyed him. "No changes. No revisions. No edits."

"Yes. Just like that." He reached over and wiped the tiny spot of ketchup from her lip. "There's nothing I would change about you. Or about us."

"And you read the whole page," Molly clarified.

He worked to keep his smile contained. "Is there a section you think I missed?"

"Under scope, I listed vacations." Molly fiddled with the paper. "We have to take more than one every year. No excuses."

"And I have to plan at least one of those vacations." Drew nodded. "That's manageable. I have ideas."

"There was also a section about family." Molly tucked the pen and paper into her purse. "You read that one too?"

"Expanding our family. Subsection one,

possibilities." Drew rubbed his chin. "I saw it. The thing is, it's already happened."

"What do you mean?" Molly grabbed his hand.

"I spoke to Sophie the day before your custody hearing. Sophie explained she'd found homes for all the puppies, except Wish." Drew laced his fingers in Molly's. "I told her I wanted to adopt Nala and Wish. I even filled out the adoption paperwork to make it official."

"It's going to be a lot, you know? Two dogs, and Hazel isn't even walking on her own yet. We have work and—"

"And we have each other." Drew leaned over and kissed her. "We'll figure it all out. That's what families do."

"Family." Molly touched his cheek. "It's becoming my favorite word."

"Mine too." Smiling, Drew grabbed her hand and heard the crack of the bat. "Now, it's time for the fun to begin."

* * * * *

Get 4 FREE REWARDS!

We'll send you 2 FREE Books plus 2 FREE Mystery Gifts.

Love Inspired books feature uplifting stories where faith helps guide you through life's challenges and discover the promise of a new beginning.

FREE Value Over **$20**